Last to Love

Moonlight Rogues, Volume 4

Alexa Whitewolf

Published by Luna Imprints, 2019.

LAST TO LOVE

First edition. December 31, 2019.

ISBN: 978-1989384060

Written by Alexa Whitewolf.

"They think they can control me.
They think I give a shit.
I don't."
-Lucas Bianchi-

Author's Note & Acknowledgements

To my readers: This was a *hard* book to write. And I mean, wow, did Lucas make it extremely hard! You'll hear from writers how their characters take over the story and, well, normally I have a pretty good relationship with them and we get along. This time around, it was a bit like butting heads with a very angry, very hot-blooded Italian male. While that sounds fun and sexy, it was anything but haha! And yet... the end result is something I (and I'm sure, Lucas!) are extremely proud of. It wraps up the series nicely with the sense of family, and may still leave you wanting more towards the end – but that's ok!

One thing that was extremely hard was tying in Lucas' special gift to his Italian background. If you haven't before reading this, I highly, highly recommend you read Moonlight Rogues: Origins, at the very least Lucas' story in there (it's the first one!) as it'll give you a bit of context for his family. And, yes, it hints a little at his gift. Now you'll notice a mix of Etruscan, Greek and Roman myths in here, and that's on purpose and not because I was confusing my mythologies :P

I also want to give huge, huge thanks to my husband. His support during this journey, his shoulder to cry and vent on, has been instrumental to me finishing this series. Even more so since my concussion, and through the post-concussion syndrome recovering that's still ongoing. My furry brats,

Zeus and Achilles, as always provided the best therapy known to man – doggie cuddles!

Huge, HUGE thanks to my beta and critique partner, Candace Robinson, as well as the ladies who've supported the crap out of this series! Amber, Dianne, Donna, Siobhan – enjoy your boy Lucas! Your reviews and kind words have encouraged me time and time again and kept me going, and I appreciate the heck out of you ladies for doing what you do!

Y. Nikolova at Ammonia Book Covers[1] has delivered time and time again my vision for this series, and this last cover is no exception. A massive thank you there!

Everyone else who helped with the edits, proofreads, formatting – you guys rock!

And now... I leave you to the last Rogue ☺

Happy readings,

Alexa

---

1. http://www.ammoniabookcovers.com

∞ ∞ ∞

∞ Lupo ∞

"For the strength of the Pack is the <u>Wolf</u>, and the strength of the Wolf is the Pack."

-Rudyard Kipling-

Lucas

The sun isn't even up by the time I finish my workout routine. It's cold as hell outside, but sweat pours over me as I walk back to my house. I still haven't replaced the shit Dominic broke. Or, more to the point, the shit we both broke when we were too busy trying to kill each other.

Even as I shower, the tension in me won't let go. It hasn't since Lucrezia was killed, and came back to life. Like a switch has been turned in me, and the only way I can dim it is by killing off any light around me.

I step out of the hot steam and wrap a towel around my hips. If the bar in town was still open, I'd be heading there tonight for a stiff drink and a good fuck. Rather unfortunately for me, my usual methods of coping won't be satisfied.

After Tytus and his damned brother Declan had their showdown, my town was half-ruined by zmeu fire. If dragons are bad, there's something about Romanian zmei that's just ruthless on its own. Yet even on the sidelines, trying to help Finn's mate and my pack survive, I admired the raw power they dispersed. In another world, *forse* we would've been friends. *Maybe.*

And maybe I'll get lucky and Tytus will be out of the picture now. With Declan imprisoned by Ileana – Dominic's crazy Romanian fairy godmother – nothing should keep him here, leaving me alone with my wolves, their girls and the Reapers. This moment to regroup might make it easier for me to get my pack in hand.

My duty as their leader is to ensure my wolves can have a good life. And they will. Once we clear the rogue wolves that are out there turning humans and destroying what's left of this town... Soon as that's done, they'll have their happily ever afters. And I'll get my well-deserved *pace* and quiet. Since said peace has been lacking nowadays, one can say I'm looking forward to it.

As I roam around my house, my thoughts shift to Elisandra and Finn. Her newfound powers as the last female descendent of the zmeu race have been tough on her, going so far as to causing a split personality effect. Now that she's got that handled, all that's left is learning how to master the magic she was gifted with. If anything, my Irish pack member is well suited to tame her fire, given his faoladh blood and ability to sense everyone's emotions makes him the mediator in the pack.

Then I think back to Daniela and Tristan. I've admired her gutsiness since she walked into town demanding my protection, running from her crazy-ass brother and the witch who'd been turning all their lobisomem pack into hybrid wolves carrying *magia*. Daniela's still recovering from having to go against them and the extermination that then took place... But Tristan, with his own demons, understands it better than most. Their yin-yang duo sometimes adds more fire than it's worth to the pack, but they also bring strength with their particular gifts.

And then there's Lucrezia and Dominic... She used to be human. Now, thanks to Tytus and the protection he afforded her way before me, she's not. I'm not quite sure what she is, only that the newfound strength has made her more vocal, and less likely to back down. I miss the times she used to be shy around me, sometimes. But only sometimes. Dominic, on the other hand, constantly tries my patience, and it doesn't look like he'll stop anytime soon.

Ever since my mistake caused Lucrezia's death, he hasn't allowed me to get close to her. He's protective to the point of overwhelming, and I know Lucrezia humors him. She told me to cut him slack because he still wakes up in the middle of the night crying for her. She also said his outbursts are not intended to piss me off, but rather to ensure she never gets hurt again. It's a hard thing to remember when my wolves are supposed to listen to me...and do anything but.

While that's annoying, even I can't deny Ileana was right. Her presence here started all the romance in the air, despite her constant denials. And, well, it worked for Dominic, Tristan and Finn. I don't wish the same for me – none of that puppy love and protective shit, I've got enough to worry about. But my wolves, their mates are suited to them, and the new dynamic works.

At least if Dominic quits pushing the limits. Being headstrong is one thing, but calling the vrykolakas – his own pack of crazy hybrid wolves – on my territory was a reckless move. *Idiota.* One I've yet to punish him for...eventually.

I roll my shoulders, sipping some coffee while watching the sun peak over the horizon. That corded tension inside me is nagging, like it's waiting for the right catalyst to burst. I've never been out of control, and this makes me...uneasy.

We've just wrapped up another fight. I should be over the moon, yet I'm anything but. And this annoying pressure in my chest won't let up, even as I get dressed and leave the house, driving my pick-up out of the driveway.

My thoughts flit annoyingly back to Lucrezia. Perhaps because of her red hair, the hue so similar to Mamma's... I don't know why, but there was always a connection between us, maybe more nostalgia on my part.

I always admired her strength, even while keeping my distance. If I had bothered to look past my own arrogance, who knows? Perhaps it could've been more. But, I was late to the game and seeing her with Dominic makes it clear there was no one better suited. Still, when I thought she'd died, my world ended all over again.

And then she wasn't dead. Another reminder that life is too fleeting, too *corta*, and I shouldn't be getting attached.

Especially not to a female who's as fragile as they come.

Only, she's not anymore. Tytus had made it clear that Lucrezia is his to protect now more than mine. It won't stop me from watching over her, but realistically she and Dominic have nothing to stay here for. Other than cause *problemi*, that is.

My jaw throbs painfully as I grit my teeth a little too hard. I'm gunning the engine hard, the thought of my leadership being put into question enough to spark my fury. It rolls inside me, churning like an angry wave. My knuckles are white on the steering wheel, gripping it so tight I almost feel the cheap material give way. With a muttered curse, I pull over far enough from my shop and walk the rest of the way.

Anything to clear my head, though it doesn't work as well as I would like. Instead, my mind drifts off to my wolves again.

So that makes three. The Romanian witch warned me love was coming for all of us, but I didn't listen. I should have known better. After all, I grew up with the old learnings from my mama, Francesca. Italian by blood on my father's side, and Etruscan heritage via Francesca. The old gods, superstitions and all that shit was instilled in me since birth.

And despite it all, I still didn't listen. Fighting against Ileana and her machinations is impossible. Because there's no way I believe my wolves just conveniently started falling in love and rising up against me, one by one, all within months – or weeks – of each other.

Thoughts of Francesca still make me angry. Angry at my father, at Matteo... And so much more. Angry at myself for being unable to stop the events that took place.

Matteo's death. Mamma's death. A brother and mother, lost in the same night. If I let myself, those images will flash vividly in my mind again. His last breath in my arms. Me burying her body in the backyard of our mansion, on a frosty morning. Helpless to do anything.

Same as now.

I reach the run-down building where my shop used to exist, and cringe as I notice the back wall missing. This'll be fun to rebuild, but at least it'll give us a purpose until we find the rogue Reapers and get rid of them. Having blood-thirsty wolves in town that are turning every human to ravenous shifter is not a good thing. Especially when they don't have a leader.

I've fought it long enough, and the *lupo mannaro* in me is done playing nice. Despite the impact it'll have on my soul, despite the price I'll have to pay... It is time to get rid of them, period.

Stepping inside, I make my way to the back of the shop where my office is hidden. I stop half-way, sensing an odd scent in the air. Cinnamon.

With a growl, I storm the rest of the way, already breathing heavily. "Che cazzo are you doing here, Ileana? I am tired of your meddling ass."

She turns from staring at the mess inside and laughs. "Meddling ass? In all my millennia of existence, I have not heard the like."

When I don't answer, she floats towards me, her sun-filled eyes twinkling. I refuse to look away. "What do you want?"

"You are the last one standing, proud wolf. Are you not yet done with being alone?"

"I *like* being alone."

"Hmm. Not for long." She goes to leave, then turns my way, her tone pleading. "I know what you think about Dominic, and how he has reached the end of the road here. That is not the case. Do not make a decision you will regret."

She's gone before I can throw something after her, and I scream in frustration at the wall. Then I rip my sweater off, toss it in a corner, and start hoisting boulders out of my office. If I clean it up, then maybe I can rebuild the rest.

∞ ◆ ∞

Hours later, I hear a commotion at the front and head out. Dominic is opening the garage, as if getting ready to take customers. "What are you doing?"

He glances at me, then shrugs, indifferent – uncaring – of the warning in my voice. "Humans need their cars fixed. Most of them are trying to leave town, and considering it's our fault this shit has befallen them, the least we can do is help them leave. Right?"

The last is said almost as a side-thought, which alone spikes my blood pressure. "Are you trying to piss me off on purpose, amico?" I ask and stalk over to him, stopping only a few feet away.

Dominic drops one of the wrenches he'd picked up and straightens himself. "Not everything is about pissing you off, Lucas."

"Yeah? Then what do you call letting the vrykolakas on *my* territory?"

A flash of anger fills his eyes. "If you think I would've stood on the sidelines while we were clearly outnumbered and let Luz be in danger again, you're sorely mistaken."

I scowl at him. "I would have protected her."

"Like you did last time?"

It's a cheap shot, but it has the intended effect. My arm shoots out and I hit him square in the jaw, sending him tumbling back. It's odd, given his vârcolac strength overpowers mine, but I don't stop to question it.

Instead, I move closer, and Dominic drops the pretense of holding back. He shrugs off his jean jacket and lifts his fists. "Alright, I've been cool and collected long enough. Let's do this."

Before he can even approach me, someone calls out, "Stop!"

Our attention drifts to Lucrezia and Daniela, watching us from the reception area. Tytus is right behind them, the insufferable zmeu. Another problem. *Incredible* what luck I have.

I walk away from Dominic, and push past the girls without acknowledging them. Instead, I ask Tytus, "You here to say goodbye?"

His grey eyes narrow on me, then Dominic, then back to me again. "Yeah, I am."

"Good. Don't let the door hit you on the way out." Without looking back, I barge back into my office and the heavy manual labor awaiting me. Too bad there's no door left to keep everyone out.

Monica

They can't be serious. Alessandro and his crew told me to expect the worst, but this...

As I stare at what's left of the building, a shiver of something rakes up my spine. My nonna called it a gift, but it's practically a curse with the way I've used it. And for whom.

If she hadn't died of old age, she would have been disappointed in me. Even now, who's to say she's not rolling in her grave? After all, our *stregheria* kind are meant to be practicing white magic, herbs and the like, not...

Gritting my teeth, I pull the mirror down and reapply my lipstick, then fluff my hair and adjust my clothes. *Gotta look the part.*

According to Alessandro Conti, his son always had a weakness for the opposite sex. If I get him back to the family fold by any means necessary, I gain my freedom and can pursue life in another pack with Alessandro's blessing. Not easy to come by, given the man has no merciful bone in his body. I should know, I've worked for him since I was a young girl.

Some say the old man lost his marbles the night his wife and younger son died. Others say that's when he was reborn. I've only ever known the tyrant. So all the speculation, it's irrelevant. What is very much relevant is the freedom just out of reach, if only I perform this one last task. And, after all, that's what matters. No one's going to look after me, but me.

I'm my own damn white knight, period.

I straighten my off-the-shoulders grey velvet sweater, then open the door to the car and make my way inside. My boots' heavy heels sink into the grimy ground, not that it affects my balance.

Barely through the door of the dilapidated-looking auto shop, a group catches my eye around the reception area. Three girls – a redhead, a blonde and a brunette – and two guys – one blond and charming, the other with cropped hair, muscles abound and completely aloof.

The redhead talking stops when she sees me, her eyes narrowing slightly. "Sorry, we're closed for renovations."

I dismiss her perhaps too easily, focusing on the potential problems instead.

The two guys here are wolves. I'm used to dominating a room of them back home, having them all in various stages of arousal in seconds. These guys, however, don't spare me anything but curious glances.

On a second sweep around the room, I catch the feel of mates – they're all bonded, even the brown-haired Cinderella lookalike, though I don't see her mate anywhere. I keep these thoughts to myself.

Nonna did always say to keep my aces under my sleeves, and my heart tightly defended.

"I'm looking for the man in charge," I say instead, keeping my voice light, tinged just enough with worry. My performance wouldn't win me an Oscar, but it's enough to draw their full attention.

Even as they share a look, communicating in some unspoken undertones, I'm scanning the area. This place must have looked good before, but it's a serious dump now like a storm has just passed through. And something about this group...

Focus, Monica.

"He's busy," the reply comes from Blondie, quiet up until now. Something tells me not to provoke her, even as the amber in her eyes glows a bit.

"It's important." I soften my voice. Forcing my way through them would be stupid and raise unwanted attention. "Family related."

"Lucas has family?" The question comes from the muscular guy, and it's enough to stun all of them.

Their gazes betrays them, shifting around the corner, and I get my cue. Whoever this Lucas is, he better be the one I'm looking for because I'm not in the mood for games. My good intentions go out the shabby door and without pausing for permission, I stomp to the back.

Maybe I have the wrong spot – or so I think. But, nope. Karma would be too kind. As I turn the corner and waltz in what's left of an office, *he* grabs my attention.

Madre di Dio!

Lucas

"Need any help?"

Finn's walked in, but I'm in no mood to talk if he's here to smooth the waters. I focus on the boulders, and the strain of my muscles as I go about my task. It's almost cathartic. Almost.

"Lucas, you have to talk to someone."

I thrust another rock outside, the veins bulging in my biceps, and turn to him. "You want to talk? Bene. Dominic Konstantin – Kosta, or whatever the *fuck* he calls himself now – has disobeyed me for the last time. I made the mistake of not running it by you and Tristan the first time, but this time, I fully intend to go through with it. He will be gone from this pack before the sun sets tonight."

"You don't mean that," Finn says, trying to hide his panic. "Dom is as much part of this pack as everyone else. You've already thrown him out once."

"Sì, and took him back. Stupid me."

"If you throw him out, Lucrezia will go, too."

I shrug. "So? It's not like she needs our protection now."

"How can you say that, after she just died on our watch?" Finn seems taken aback by my callousness.

Guilt runs through me, but I push it away, stomping it way, way down inside me. My faoladh friend frowns at me as if

I'm a puzzle he can't figure out, then he says, "How are you doing that?"

"Doing what?"

"Controlling your emotions, hiding them from me."

I turn back to the rocks. "No idea what you're talking about."

Finn takes a few steps closer, grabbing my shoulder. I shrug him off, getting in his face, barely holding back a snarl. Not that it makes him back off.

"Something's wrong with you, mate. Ever since the fight, and now you want to go execute the last Reapers?"

The change of topic disarms me. I back off, shrugging and tossing another rock out the back. "And so?"

"It's not you." Finn pauses, as if struggling to find the right words. "You've spent all this time trying to keep peace in town, why go to the other extreme now?"

"Because morals are for weaklings," I hiss, grunting as I toss another rock. "And I am finally ready to live up to my name."

"What does that mean?"

I refuse to answer him. I've gone this long without telling them everything about me, there is no reason why I should reveal it all now.

Finn scowls. "Fine, don't answer me. But, Lucas, think this through, will you?"

I throw him a dark glare, but something else catches my attention. A smell of cherries, and the click of heels on stone.

In walks a leggy, raven-haired girl that could have easily stepped off a magazine cover. One perfect eyebrow arches over an icy blue eye as she takes in the mess in my office. "I'm looking for Luciano Conti."

Out of the corner of my eye, I see Finn turning to me, and I force my emotions down again. Only one person would call me by my real name, meaning she's sent here by the monster from my past. "You found him," I say evenly. "But I go by Lucas now."

Finn asks softly, "Lucas?" It's a question, a silent, *What's going on?*

I know my expression is blank, perhaps too much so, as I speak. "Leave us."

Finn hesitates, and I don't know how much my faoladh friend has sensed of my reaction. I can only hope he keeps whatever he did feel to himself.

My gaze narrows on the brunette the minute he's gone through the door. She opened a flood of emotions, things I never thought I'd think about ever again.

Matteo. Francesca – Mamma. A past as buried as it is painful...

All that flashes in my mind when the woman bursts into my office. I'm no fool, and her scent is too easy to determine

– she's a wolf, and she's got my father's stamp all over her perfect body. A splash of fear, like cold water, hits me, followed by a rage so deeply ingrained in me it's a wonder it doesn't consume me. And yet, despite my inner turmoil, I manage to keep my regular neutral expression.

"And who are you?" I finally ask.

"Monica Delucci," she says, swinging her hips as she walks to my desk, then takes a seat uninvited on what's left of a chair. "Your parents sent me."

Coldness sweeps through me at her admission, but I mask my emotions before they get the best of me. "Did they, now?"

Monica

Damn it, but they could have warned me what to expect!

Luciano Conti is nothing like I pictured. He's gorgeous and fine as a dark angel, sure. But he's also cold, and unsettling. And in control. I didn't miss the way his wolf responded, that flash of interest quickly squashed as soon as he realized who I am – nor did I miss the pack outside of here. Clearly, I've walked in the middle of a warzone.

The question is, how much more chaos can I cause before Luciano – or Lucas, as he calls himself now – throws me out of here? I bite my lower lip, noticing his gaze drop to it. My instructions were clear. Ruin the life he built here, and force him to come back home. If I do, I'd be free, and Alessandro Conti would ensure it.

Only problem is, as I'm standing opposite Luciano, it takes all my will to ignore the hum of electricity between us. I've always been the one in control – always. And yet his dark gaze does something to my insides that makes me feel almost...shy.

Basta! Don't be a fool.

In an effort to distract myself, I look around. "You've done well for yourself, Luciano. Your parents will be proud."

A noise escapes him, and I meet his unnerving gaze just in time to catch a glimpse of amusement. Then he schools his expression once more. I've known men who are good at that, but he makes it into an art. *He* is a piece of art.

Focus...

"What was so funny?" He clearly doesn't like my question. But it's his words that unsettle me more.

"What's *funny*, cara, is you keep mentioning parents as if I have two of them. My mother died years ago. Matter of fact, she committed suicide after my brother died in a failed deal – all thanks to my father. But surely Alessandro Conti told you all this, before sending you into the wolf's den?"

His grin is nothing short of predatory. And that dangerous glint in his onyx eyes causes a low tremor to start in me.

Merda! He doesn't know... And I've been had, that's for sure. Only question is, how the heck do I get out of this now?

∞ ∞ ∞

CHAPTER TWO

∞ Scintilla ∞

"From a little <u>spark</u> may burst a flame."

-Dante Alighieri-

Lucas

My fucking father. *Certo*. It took him the better part of two years, but he finally tracked me down at the most convenient time for him. Not that I plan to let any of this affect me. I've enough shit to handle here, without dealing with the past.

Time to squash this before it escalates, no matter how appealing this particular messenger looks.

"I guess he didn't," I mutter and contour the desk to stand in front of Monica. She's gorgeous, I'll give her that. Long legs I could see wrapped around me, a pouty mouth and eyes men have probably died for.

The grey sweater falls off her shoulders, exposing creamy skin, and the skirt she has on is just short enough to pull attention to those limbs. The way she's sitting, back straight, hair onto one shoulder, makes her look almost regal. And those shades of blue, those long lashes – another day, another place, I would've been interested.

Not now.

I know what she is – Alessandro's fixer. Even when I was there, my father had one under his wing to go and allure the men, have them entranced until he struck like the snake he is. More often than not, they were witches of some sort, which has me wonder if Monica has some hidden powers, too.

If she does, it makes her doubly dangerous. Not that I've ever run away from such a thing. Unfortunately for Alessandro, the young man I'd been is gone, and I'm not a scared child anymore.

"I..." Monica licks her lips, then starts again. Whether it was unconscious or meant to draw my attention, it works. "I did know about your mother, Francesca. Mi dispiace, Luciano, I owe you an apology."

A beat of silence drops between us. Her soft-spoken words unsettled the biting response I'd prepared. Instead, I hold her gaze and nod. "Continue."

"I shouldn't have said parents, but the fact of the matter is your father did, um, start a relationship with someone else. It was a slip of the tongue on my end. I...didn't realize you were unaware, and wasn't told."

"Hmm." Of course he did. Not that the bastard was ever faithful to Mamma to begin with. Annoyance runs through me, and I shake it off. "Hate to break it to you, but *unaware* is a way of life with Alessandro."

"Is it?" Her demeanor changes, and a slow smile spreads on her lips. "I find him to be quite accommodating."

Mm, I bet. I wonder if she's already part of his harem, or just on his radar. Even when my mother was alive, Alessandro did not lack for female attention.

Monica uncrosses and crosses her legs again, drawing my attention to her commando boots with spiked heels. Her manicured nails start tapping a beat on her knee. At first, the noise is nothing out of the ordinary, only background interference. But the more she does it, the more it drags my attention, until my entire focus is on the heady drum of her fingers, on the long expanse of skin turned rosy by the chilly air, and the rise and fall of her breasts under that sweater.

"He misses you," she says softly, as though not to break the trance. "He would like to see you."

My usual anger isn't as quick to snap to. *Che cazzo...* I was right, then. She's a witch, and definitely going to be a problem. Eyes narrowed on her, I manage to pull back from whatever it is she's doing, and level my stare on hers. "What are you really up to, cara?"

Monica's surprise is quickly hidden under indifference. "I haven't the faintest clue what you mean."

I can't resist it, that aloofness. After what she just tried to pull on me – *no one* pulls one on me. I lean over her then, my hands on either side of the armchair she's occupying. Her eyes widen and her breath catches in her throat, making the swell of her breasts all the more evident. Her pulse beats wilder, and I feel her rising emotion in the air.

Wait, what?

My eyes narrow further, and definitely – sì, the air is tinted with her perfume, but also her arousal and her excitement, fear, all warped into a mass of emotions. I've never sensed emotions before, but it's enough to make my wolf peak its head, nudging. Not like female wolves are in high quality around here. Reapers tend to turn only men, and don't associate with humans thanks to their racist tendencies.

And Monica... She's a delicacy, all right.

Ignoring my body's nudge, I grit my teeth. "You can tell my father I'm not interested in anything he has to offer. Least of all some pitiful excuse that he misses me."

We face off for a beat, and she doesn't move. What is it with people no longer cowering under my glare? Just as I taste her surrender, her retreat in the air, a soft rap on the edge of the door has me looking up.

"Everything okay?"

Lucrezia stares between me and Monica, and bites her lip as if holding back laughter. But underneath that, I also taste suspicion regarding the woman I've practically caged between my arms. *Sì, your instincts are correct, cara. Something's not quite right with this one.*

I pull back, releasing Monica. "Ms. Delucci was just leaving. Would you show her out?"

Lucrezia nods and waits. It takes a beat, then another, until Monica gets up from the chair. She flicks her hair backwards, and a hint of cherry hits my nose. I stop inhaling in an effort to ignore it, but my eyes won't leave her form as she walks away.

With one more questioning look my way, Lucrezia turns tail and follows her out the door. The minute they're gone, I grab another boulder off the ground and toss it through the open hole. The force used makes it crash and split against the cement in the back, not that I care.

Heart beating wildly with anger restrained, I walk to the one corner that hasn't been destroyed, and my decanter of whiskey hidden underneath. I pull out a cup since the glasses are broken and pour myself a triple.

"Who was she?"

I take my time turning around.

Dominic's my beta, and at times my friend, but he's also the reason we're in this mess. Our status quo seems to be fighting, especially given our history. And the fact we were at each others' throats just earlier this morning. Which explains why I'm not in the mood to see his face, let alone talk to him.

"No one of importance," I say and drop the whiskey cup on the desk.

"I wouldn't say that, given you've joined the rest of us into drinking because of a woman."

I whirl on him then, but realize a second later he's grinning to take the sting out of his words.

"I'm not."

"Whatever you say. May I?" Lucrezia must've talked his anger down – again. There is no other explanation for the sudden politeness. When I nod, Dominic moves closer and pours himself a cup. "Whatever you may tell yourself, you and I both know it's a lie."

And there goes the politeness. Snorting, I take another gulp of whiskey. "Monica's a pair of long legs and probably a good fuck. But there's none of what you and Lucrezia have."

"Did I even allude to that?" The amusement in his eyes shines brighter. "Mm." He takes a sip, then another. "That's good stuff."

I hold my cup in silent cheers, refusing to finish the conversation. Instead, I focus on something I can control, something my wolf has been aiming for. A *lupo mannaro* loves to fight, and asserting his control. It's probably what pushed me to the head of this pack, and I've been fighting against myself for long enough where the Reapers are concerned. *You win, lupo. Negotiations failed, so force it is.*

"Where is your pack?"

A wary look crosses his features, and he takes another sip. I don't blame him. It's no secret I'm no fan of his vrykolakas, and just this morning I accused him of bringing them back to piss me off.

Still, Dominic answers. "Around... Out of town. I don't want them tempted to take innocent lives."

"Bene," I mutter. "We have enough of that with the Reapers. Who knew Declan killing Cade would unleash their craziness even more?"

Dominic relaxes a tinge. It's what I need, so I let him lead the conversation. It's a game I've gotten very good at playing.

"Yeah, it's bad. At the rate we're finding bodies or missing people, and with the cops gone, it won't be long before this entire town is turned." He takes another sip. "I saw a couple cars leaving this morning. It seems only the old and tried humans have stayed behind... Maybe their age will protect them."

I snort into my cup. "Perhaps. And yet I find that when one thinks protection is in sight, is exactly when one is most vulnerable."

Dominic tenses again, reading between the lines. "The vrykolakas are only here to help, my friend. With Reapers turning humans every night, we need additional bodies for protection."

"I know," I say, and this time meet his gaze full-on. "Forget what I said this morning in anger. I want you to put them to use. Track every single one of those monsters and kill them."

Dominic seems stunned, silent for one beat, and another. Waiting for me to take it back, to plead for peace, for restraint. I don't do either.

"You're not serious?" he finally asks.

"I am."

"Finn was right, then. You've really lost it."

I drain my cup and smash it on the desk. The sound echoes in the room, but Dominic's gaze never wavers from mine. "Why? Because I want justice?"

"It's not justice, as much as an execution."

"And?" Straightening to my full height, I cross my arms over my chest and use my trump card. "Have you forgotten they're the ones who killed Lucrezia?"

The minute the words are out of my mouth, I realize they're the wrong ones. Dominic tosses his cup away and crosses to me in two strides, jabbing his index in my chest. "Luz was in danger because of *you* and your stupid ego."

"Nevertheless, it was the Reapers who did the kill."

"And I took revenge on that," Dominic mutters. "They have no leader now. It seems almost pointless to kill them."

"Not to me. And you forget, I call the shots in *this* pack."

Dominic's eyes flash with held back lightning. I'm surprised at his control, given he's the most hotheaded out of all of us. "Yeah, so I've been told multiple times."

My head throbs with something. I've never been prone to headaches, but today is just one of those days. Oddly, my lupo seems to waver, his strength waning and replaced by something more – something darker. The ache in my skull intensifies. "Dominic, I am in no mood to fight. Will you, or won't you, use the vrykolakas to properly protect us?"

He nods. "I will, but on one condition. We put it to a vote, let the whole pack have a say."

"Bene."

With a mock salute, he turns on his heels and leaves. I hear murmurs of voices at the front, but rather than go and talk to them, I turn back to the debris and my wasted efforts to clean my office. If nothing else, this work will keep me busy.

Monica

The redhead called Lucrezia follows me all the way out the door, and to my car. I finally turn to her, annoyed. "I didn't realize your receptionist job included these extra duties."

"It doesn't," she says smoothly.

"Then I guess you're only doing it for Luciano's sake? Unless there's more going on there, of course." I hate the words out of my mouth, but I can't hold them back. Bitch is my go-to mode when I'm cornered, and right now it feels like I've been blitzed.

I was meant to go in there with a surprise attack, appeal to Luciano's family side, and have him hooked by the end of the conversation. He wasn't supposed to destabilize me. He wasn't supposed to affect me. And he damn well wasn't supposed to make me wonder what it would be like to have his hands all over me.

With effort, I focus back on the redhead. Lucrezia's green eyes burn, and it must be a trick of the light because the gold seems to overwhelm the green. Similar to what happened with Blondie inside. A hum of energy fills the air, then she blinks and it's gone. Her smile is tight – she's a bigger person than me.

"Think what you will, I owe you no explanation. But since it seems your business in town may take longer than a day, you might want to check in at the local inn." She points down the street. "It's not much, but it's cozy and it'll be vacant, I guarantee it."

The fight leaves me as she walks away, and I begrudgingly whisper a small, "Thank you."

Lucrezia stops at the door and turns to me again. It's hard to read her expression when she says, "See you around."

∞ ◆ ∞

The inn is on the far side of town, and the old woman in charge gives me a suspicious look when I explain I was referred to her by a local.

"What brings ya here?"

"Car broke down," I lie smoothly. "I'll be out of your hair as soon as it gets fixed."

She doesn't seem too impressed, but the cash I hand her must be needed because she relents and ends up showing me upstairs. As we walk in the tight corridor, she mutters, "You picked a damned bad time to visit. After the gas explosion, most of the buildings here are in need of repairs. Folks are leavin', there ain't no point in sticking around and everyone knows it. Like the town is cursed."

Well, that explains that.

A shiver runs through me as she opens one door and waves me in. The room is tiny, but it has a bathroom and tea kettle, and that's what matters. I nod at the old lady and once she's gone, I reach into my worn Gucci handbag and pull out my phone. My hand brushes the bundle of leaves neatly wrapped in a Ziploc bag, and I pull it away like I've been bitten.

I'd only brought them as back-up, and hopefully they won't be needed. My nonna always told me using nature's gifts for coercion is the work of true evil, and the last thing I want to do is disappoint her. Well, disappoint her more than I already have. But if I don't do what I was sent here to, there's a strong chance I'll be losing my life in the process. And that, well, it's not going to happen.

If it's between me and everyone else, I'll always pick me.

I speed dial Alessandro, and he picks up immediately. "Sì?"

"I've made contact."

"Good." His praise makes me cringe. "Molto bene. Did he bite?"

I want to say Luciano almost bit *me*, but I swallow the words instead. "Not yet," I say, knowing he hates lies. "But he will."

"Bene, Monica. You please me. You have one week to bring him home, and you'll get what I promised you."

When I hang up, I try to get over the acidity in my mouth. There is no guilt here. No emotion. Just pure business. I have to keep that in mind.

And yet for long moments after the call is done, I simply sit on the bed and stare into nothing. I think back to Luciano's pack – it must be his, there's no other explanation for their deep connection – and the way they seemed to communicate so effortlessly.

With Alessandro, it's all fear and duty. There is no sense of family, of belonging. There's only our purpose as wolves, as witches, as humans – sì, he definitely doesn't discriminate when it comes to meeting his needs.

And really, is that a life? Of servitude, of isolation and abuse?

Despite whatever happened in this town – because it sure as hell wasn't a gas explosion – there is a sense of...peace, around. Or maybe I'm wrong. Maybe I'm simply so happy to be out of Alessandro's reach that I'm seeing fairytales and unicorns everywhere.

And what if you're not?

I could leave. It's not the first time I thought about it. On the long, long drive here, I realized for the first time I was stepping out of Alessandro's territory. It was a measure of his trust in me, but it was also a very, very loose leash. I wanted nothing more than to snap it, and run somewhere he could never find me.

Only, he would. If before he'd had a Mafia *familia*, the Conti name is now practically an empire. No matter where I run or hide, he will find me. And the punishment... I shudder. It wouldn't be worth it. Not when I can so easily buy my own way out.

Just be patient. Focus. No more thoughts of Luciano's hands.

Shaking my head, I peel off my clothes and step into the bathroom. The hot water runs out too quickly for my taste, but it's good enough to wipe off the grime of the drive and shut up my inner ramblings.

When I step out with just a towel around me, I feel calmer. More centered. I open the window and lean my head against it, taking a moment to close my eyes and inhale deeply. Pine, freshness and the smell of a small town filter through, filling my senses.

And then... I smell cinnamon. It's enough to put me on my guard, but a ripple in the air has me spinning around. The apparition in my room leaves me reeling. Long, flowing brown hair, a robe made of flowers and eyes that shine of the sun. She's not human, but she's no wolf either.

I glance around for something to use as a weapon, but have no time to pinpoint anything before she speaks.

"Welcome to Rockland Creek," she says in a smooth accent. "I am Ileana."

As usual, I cover my surprise with attitude. "Should I care?"

She smiles and floats a little closer. "You want Lucas, yes?"

Is she some ex-girlfriend? First Lucrezia, now this one. My eyes narrow on her, and something about her shimmering form and the power emanating from her tells me not to cross a line. "Luciano," I correct.

"Yes, yes." She waves at me impatiently. "You come from his father's side?"

"How the hell do you know all this?"

Ileana smiles. "It is my job to know things, just as it is yours to be a fixer. Tell me... Do you not wish more of your life?"

Her words echo my earlier thoughts too eerily, enough to stun me. Twice in one day, first with Luciano and now this one. What the heck is going on in this town?

Rather than answer, I cross my arms and tilt my chin up. "I'm not answering any more of your questions, so how about you get out of my room?"

She laughs then, as if I'm an amusing child. My temper snaps and without thinking I lift my hand, touching the pentagram necklace around my neck. Words form on my lips, but they die when Ileana turns the full brightness of those eyes on me.

"I would not do that if I were you, draga mea."

I'm immobilized. The bitch has frozen me without even lifting a finger, and the hum of power I felt before is now fully rattling the room, and me with it. My eyes go wide, then her expression eases into another smile.

"Now, can we talk civilly without you trying to hex me?"

I drop my hand to my side and nod, trying to hide the shaking of my fingers. It hadn't been a hex, per se. Stregheria uses ancient magic, old spells for protection, but the fact she even knew I was about to... Just who *is* this woman?

Ileana notices my trembling anyway and gestures to my unopened suitcase. "Get dressed, then we can speak."

If nothing else, I've been well trained not to go against more powerful people than me. So I dig in for a pair of sweatpants and a tank top, and pull them on fast. Nakedness around others has never bothered me, and it's not like she's watching me. More like she's staring out the window, her expression pensive.

When I'm done, she turns to me. "You have stregheria blood in you, do you not?"

I nod. "My nonna – my grandmother. Her side of the family, that's where it comes from."

"Hmm." Her gaze drops to my necklace. "And you practice magic, but in the form of herbs, and potions?"

Again, I nod, not daring to explain all the other ways I've had to use my gift – curse.

"La vecchia religione," Ileana whispers in Italian, and the surprise must show on my face. The *old religion* is what people call my form of magic, because we still honor the Mother Goddess.

"Who are you, really?" I ask her finally.

Ileana steps closer to me, almost near the bed. "No one you should fear, in so long as your intentions are pure."

I blanch. There is nothing pure in what I'm here to do. But can she see through me, know the reality of my purpose here?

"I like you." Ileana smirks. "Lucas has eluded what he needs for too long. You, my dear, will be perfect."

In a flash of flowers, she's gone before I can correct her. Or explain I'm not Luciano's mate, or anywhere close to it. Then the twinkle in her eye before she disappeared registers, and I rush to my bag. Only, when I look inside it, my leaves are gone, too.

"Merda!"

∞ ∞ ∞

CHAPTER THREE

∞ Istinto ∞

"There is no <u>instinct</u> like that of the heart."

-Lord Byron-

Monica

"I thought I made it clear you weren't welcome here."

I'd been having breakfast at a little diner still operating on the far side of town, but leave it to Luciano to ruin my mood. I look up from my coffee and arch an eyebrow his way. "I don't quite recall those being the words, Luciano."

He takes a seat in the booth opposite me, his onyx glare never once leaving me. What is it about this hot-blooded male that feels like he's constantly destabilizing me? I'm used to being a hell of a lot more in control of my hormones than this.

"The name is Lucas, not Luciano. Not anymore."

I sip more of my coffee, then set the cup on the table. "Hmm. Bene, Lucas. An odd choice of name."

He places his palms flat on the table. "Let's cut to the chase, shall we? How much is my father paying you, and how much do I have to increase it by to get you to leave?"

I lean over the table, knowing the way I'm perched is squeezing my breasts enticingly. Much to my dissatisfaction, Lucas doesn't even look, instead his gaze stays on mine. "You cannot afford me, pretty boy. I'm here to do a job, and I won't leave until it's done."

He keeps staring at me, then slowly gets up. His body looks too damned good in a white shirt and dark jeans, all muscled and tense. It's obvious my stubbornness is annoying to him. That clenched jaw – my fingers itch to trace it, and I grip my empty coffee cup harder.

Rather than leave, Lucas comes closer to me, and leans over my side of the booth. He's close, invading my personal space and not giving a damn. The smell of pine, fresh soap and man entices me a little too much.

Then I look into his eyes, and I swear they're a few hues darker. It does something to me, that intense stare, like he's reaching deep inside me and touching parts that have never been stirred by a man before.

Lucas smirks then, as if knowing exactly how he's affecting me. "We'll see about that. You're not the only one with tricks up your sleeve."

He's gone in the blink of an eye, and only then do I dare exhale. *Merda!*

Alessandro wants results, and the quicker I am about it, the better. Only, for the first time in my assignments, I'm unsure what the hell to do. No one in this dingy little town acts the way they should, and I miss....belonging. Even if I never truly did, it was nice to pretend.

With nothing else to do, and my body too worked up from Lucas' closeness, I roam the streets for a while until the damn boots I wear start hurting my feet. As I backtrack to the inn, I pass a bakery that's seen better days. I almost continue walking, but to my surprise it's open. And the smells wafting from inside are enough to make my gut churn.

Without thinking for once, I head straight in, letting my nose rule me. "Be with you in a sec!" Someone calls from the back.

I take my time looking around, noticing the freshly mopped floor, so at odds with the broken frames on the walls and one of the windows covered in cardboard. What the hell happened in this town, anyway?

My thoughts are interrupted again. "Hi, sorry about that. How can I–oh."

When I whirl around, I'm surprised to find little Miss Cinderella from the auto shop behind the counter. Her hair is in a messy bun, and there's flour on her cheek. Even her apron is dusted with it. And yet she still manages to look cute as a button. Hmm.

"I, um, how can I help you?" she asks.

"Could I grab one of everything you have? And any warm food you can scrounge." When she still stares at me, I pull out my wallet and wave it at her. "I can pay."

She flushes beet red, and ducks to find a box to put my stuff in. "It's not that, sorry. It's just, you were at Lucas' shop the other day."

"Sì, I was." I mull over my words, surprised at two things. First, that I actually want to talk to her about this. And second, that I'm not trying to see how to use her. It's been a long, long time since I talked to someone without trying to see how they would be best used. But this girl is so innocent, it makes me feel ugly even contemplating such a thing.

Shaking the thought off, I leave a couple bills on the counter that I'm pretty sure cover the amount due, and then some. The girl's eyes bulge out of her head when she sees the money. "That's way too much! I'll find you some change."

"Keep it," I shrug, and open the box of goodies she hands me, digging into a fresh croissant. A moan of delight escapes me at the buttery taste, and I devour it in a second. "Yum. So worth it!"

The girl stares at me, not disguising the questions in her eyes. It's also been a while since I've met someone so transparent. "What is it you want to ask me?"

Another delicate blush colors her cheeks. "You know Lucas?"

"Yeah," I say, this time digging into a fruit tart. The crust crumbles in my mouth, leaving decadent vanilla pudding and a mix of berries onto my tongue. I close my eyes at the blissful explosion of flavor. "What's your name?"

"Elisandra, but everyone calls me Elle."

"Well, Elle, these pastries are freaking *deliziosi*."

"Thank you, it's my grandmama's recipe," she beams. "Umm, so, how do you know Lucas?"

I take my time swallowing, then lick my lips before saying, "His father sent me to this town. He..." The slight pause to find my words doesn't make the lie taste any better. "He misses Lucas, and needs him home."

"Oh. We didn't even know he had family outside of here."

I glance around, not sure how to answer that. She sounds almost hurt. Has Luciano – Lucas – really been so secretive with them? And why? Alessandro never really said why he wants him back, only that it must happen. My guess is, if anything, Lucas has something his dad wants. Could it be there's so much more to the story, or is Lucas just the prodigal son too rebellious to step back into the fold?

The window covered with cardboard catches my eye again. "What happened here, anyway? Some kind of tornado?"

Elle winces, and busies herself rearranging an already perfect display of goodies. "Sort of."

I catch the hint, and am about to head out with my purchases when the bell of the door rings. The green-eyed guy from Lucas' office strides in. His smile falls when he notices me by the counter, and his gaze fills with suspicion.

"Finn!" Elle cries, and her delighted tone automatically takes over him. He dismisses me and contours the desk, before pulling Elle into his arms and kissing her neck. She melts into him, and something about the gesture seems too intimate to behold.

I turn away with my belongings, a flash of jealousy running through me. I've had great sex, and the occasional fling that lasted more than a night. But what they have, that tangible connection, is something as unknown and unattainable to me as a unicorn.

Before I can get away from their torturous sweetness, his voice stops me. "I reckoned it was only Lucas you were interested in."

Frowning, I face him once more. If I play nice, maybe I could find a way into Lucas' inner circle. "That's true."

"Then why are you here bothering my girl?" His Irish lilt is not soft, rather harsh and accusing.

"I wasn't." Holding up my bag, I smirk. "Was placing money into local business. Looks like you may need it."

Finn narrows his eyes on me. "You say Lucas' family needs him, but the air around you is wrong. You reek of lies, Monica. So what is it you're really after?"

How the hell did he know that? That gut intuition warns me again to thread carefully, that I'm not understanding the mess I really stepped into.

"Nothing except Luciano," I finally say.

Finn shakes his head. "I don't believe you."

Elle squeezes out from under his hold and mutters something about needing to empty the garbage. Leaving us alone, she heads to the back, and the full glare of his emerald eyes settles on me.

"If you bring havoc to Lucas, I don't really care. But don't feckin' drag my mate into this, you hear me?"

I mock-salute him. "Aye, sir."

Before he can respond, a cry from the back freezes us both. I drop my stuff on one of the tables and before I can even think it through, I'm following Finn out the door, and into the small enclosure. Elle is surrounded by four – no, six – wolves, all in various stages of disarray.

She glances behind at us, then her eyes flash golden. Just like Lucrezia and Blondie from yesterday... Then in front of my stunned gaze, she lifts her hand and draws something in the air – some kind of archaic symbol. It flashes golden-red, then bursts into a myriad of sparks that blind the wolf closest to her.

Elle expertly shifts to the side, avoiding his jaws, and Finn jumps into the fray without a second's hesitation, morphing into his wolf form. In moments, he's behind Elle in all his supple light grey form, covering her.

And once more, I'm utterly frozen. I've been in enough fights with wolves in Alessandro's territory, but nowhere have I seen anything like this. The way they move as one, watching each other's backs, is unreal. Mate connections are practically unheard of in my pack, so seeing one in action is...distracting, to say the least.

When I finally snap out of it, I take in my surroundings. Finn and Elle are both so busy with the attack, they don't notice the reason for the group of rogue wolves gathering.

Half-hidden under garbage bags is a young man, barely over sixteen. A large gash in his leg bleeds profusely, and his moans of pain grab my attention. With a quick check around, I head to him, all the while wondering what the hell I'm doing and why I'm getting involved.

There is no real answer. The kid is bitten, and he'll be turning soon. I've seen enough of those wounds to catch on pretty fast. He passes out in front of my eyes, then another wolf comes and drags him by the leg away. "No," I say softly. When he ignores me, I kick off my high heels and crouch on the ground, grabbing the boy's hand and ending in a veritable tug-of-war.

My eyes clash with the wolf's yellow ones. "I said *no*. Leave him be."

He growls and I smirk. When he lunges on me, I give in and let my girl take over. The transformation rolls over me like a wave, and I'm already smacking the other guy before he can realize what happened.

Destabilized, he loses his balance and I jump on him, pinning him to the ground with my paws. In Alessandro's pack, I quickly learned to defend myself as a single female, so this is no different. One bite into his throat, and his carcass stops moving as blood fills more and more of the area.

I stand to my full form, taking in a deep breath. I've just hunted outside my alpha's borders, on Lucas' territory no less, and without Alessandro's permission. All to save someone who obviously has her shit under control.

Merda! Something about this town is messing with my head.

Finn turns to me then, and I know what he sees. Black fur, blue eyes, and the mark imprinted on my chest. A thick C as large as a human fist, topped with a crown. Alessandro's brand. He says nothing, but even in wolf form, his expression is filled with questions.

Instead, he jumps on two other wolves, dragging them down with him. Elle, in the meantime, is busy drawing again in the air. I don't quite understand what she's doing until a gust of fire escapes the design, encompassing two more wolves.

Another goes to jump on her from behind, but I'm already lunging, taking the brunt of the attack as we both crash into metal bins. When I'm done with him, I turn to see Elle and Finn have taken care of the other wolf, and Finn's back to human form, fully clothed.

With an effort, I switch back to human, cringing at the thought of being naked. Yet when I check my body, I find my old clothes on, including my torn jeans and the fresh blood seeping through a laceration.

"Monica!" Elle rushes to me, gasping at the wound. "I'm *so* sorry you got dragged into this."

I shrug. "Not a big deal. Are you alright?"

She nods, apologetic. It makes me feel like shit – I'm here under false pretenses I don't even know, and now I'm doing crap I can't even comprehend the motivation for.

"How did you..." I wince and readjust my weight. "How am I clothed? What were those drawings back there?"

"Runes," Elle says. "I, um, the thing is I–"

Finn marches on us then, interrupting what she'd been about to say. "The kid's dead, and so are all the Reapers. Why did you get involved?"

Too tired to fight this, and with my injury hurting more and more, I settle on the truth. "I didn't realize Elle had...magic. I thought you'd need back up."

Finn's expression doesn't ease up, but Elle touches my shoulder softly. "I'm really sorry you got injured. The, um, wolves you saw, they're the bad ones here in town. Rogue ones. They're attacking humans and some days it gets out of control."

"Isn't your alpha doing anything about it?" I ask before I can stop myself.

"He's working on it," Finn says in a tone that broaches no counterargument.

I know when I'm not wanted, so with a mock-salute to them I wobble back inside the store. I pick up my pastries from the table, wincing at the sharp pain shooting up my leg. Just as I straighten up, luck would have the door swinging open and none other than Lucas strolls in.

"Ma che diavolo..." He stomps to me and grabs my elbow, yanking me to him. "Did I not say you're not welcome here?"

Nostrils flaring, eyes as dark as they'll get, his energy surrounds me. It's chaotic, and he means what he says. Yet I won't back down. But I can't help a wince, as the way he's gotten me off balance has weight bearing down on my injured leg.

Lucas frowns then and glances down. His jaw clenches when he sees the blood. "What happened? Why are you bleeding?"

I pull my elbow out of his grip, refusing to be intimidated. "Go ask your damn pack members. And I told you, your father sent me to do a job. I cannot leave until it's done."

Despite my best efforts to leave with my head held high, the moment I try to move I end up stumbling right back. Lucas draws me into him by the waist this time, practically gluing our bodies together. With his free hand, he lifts my chin up.

We're so close, it would take only one small move and I could kiss him. Finally get to know what those lips taste like, and if he's as good a kisser as I've imagined. His hands on me sure feel as good as my fantasy, even though it had involved way less clothes …

Lucas' gaze drops to my lips, and for a moment I think he'll kiss me. But then he lets me go abruptly, almost shoving me away. Luckily, the table behind gives me enough support so I don't fall on my ass.

His expression is cold, despite the electricity sizzling between us. "No amount of charm will have me in your bed."

The line stings, but I force myself to walk past him as calmly as I can. "We'll see about that."

Lucas

My wolf wants to go after Monica – fucking phenomenal. Like I really need another female to worry about. But she did get hurt on my territory, and enemy or not, I should check that she's alright.

Unless it's exactly what she wants you to do.

Those baby blue eyes of hers did seem rather interested – until they turned dark when our bodies were too damn close. I damn well almost gave in to the temptation to kiss her, but I'll be damned if I drop at her feet that easily.

Gritting my teeth, I stomp my way through Elisandra's shop and head to the back. The scent of iron hits me hard, and when I emerge into the small enclosure it's to see a bloody mess.

Wolves' bodies – Reapers. And one young kid. My eyes meet Finn's, just as Elisandra releases waves of fire to burn the evidence away. Not that there are any cops nearby to arrest anyone.

"What a mess," I mutter. "What happened here, amico?"

Finn runs an agitated hand through his hair, then shrugs. Despite his efforts to appear nonchalant, I read trepidation in his body language. "Elle got attacked. Six Reapers, trying to turn a human kid. She stumbled on it."

I inspect the carnage, frowning. "You think it was a coincidence it happened here?"

"No bloody way," he growls. "They can smell our scent here. And she's always alone, mate. From now on, I'm sticking here. You have enough bodies at the auto shop for protection there."

Rubbing my chin, I nod thoughtfully. "And Monica? Where did she come in?"

"You tell me. She was here when I arrived, asking questions."

"That's not true," Elisandra says and steps closer to him. She intertwines their fingers, leaning against his side and appearing exhausted from the magic use. "She was here to buy pastries. Then Finn came and rattled her up, and I left and walked in on these guys. Monica helped." Her eyes flicker between us, wide and pleading. "She could have run, but she stayed and *helped*, even getting hurt while having my back."

Something like a snarl escapes me, and Elisandra recoils against Finn. Even he seems taken aback by my reaction. "Alright there, mate?"

But I'm not. Nowhere close to it. Because it just dawned on me that my territory is under serious attack, and this needs to end. Now.

"Tonight," I manage to hiss through gritted teeth. "I spoke to Dominic about a vote to execute all Reapers, once and for all. I want the vote, *tonight*."

I turn to leave, not trusting myself when this rage inside me seems to get to a boiling point. Finn's voice comes from far away behind me. "Where are you going?"

"Away from here."

My feet can't walk fast enough, and it's only once I'm outside on the other end, far away from the blood and the death, that I gain some clarity. That was not a normal reaction. I've had anger blast through me before, but this...

Words from long ago echo in my head, said in anger to my mother. *It was my right to know I have a direct link to the Underworld. It was my right to decide whether taking lives was a stain I wanted on my soul, when each innocent death brought me that much closer to becoming the monster of legend. It was my choice, and you took it from me when you kept your silence.*

Is that what's going on?

When Lucrezia died, I was reminded starkly of my link. I could've helped her journey to the Underworld, if I'd known what to do. I lived in guilt for days on end, until I saw her alive and well again. But the thoughts never truly left me. All this time I've been hiding here, I've ignored the truth. I've wanted to keep peace, to stay away from getting my hands dirty.

My mother's Etruscan heritage didn't just stop at history and myths. Her blood was also filled with the chimera gene, enough of it that it passed down to me. And as far as she ever told me, the extent of its influence on me was that each time I take a life, I get closer and closer to the Underworld. Eventually, the link will be tangible enough and I'll be able to open the door to it, and probably get lost in its depths.

There's a reason I tried for peace and negotiation these last months, even when shit hit the fan so bad I wanted nothing more than to execute those standing against me. But it would have led to my ultimate downfall only faster.

And then Lucrezia died... And it didn't matter anymore. The deaths now affect me more, because of the many lives I'm responsible for extinguishing. And if that means I'll burn in Hell and become the monster of legend, then so be it. I'll make damn sure my pack is taken care of beforehand.

Pushing away from the wall, I head into my auto shop. Lucrezia is there, and knowing she walked Monica out the other day, I tap her desk.

She looks up at me, her green eyes tinged with gold and a knowing smirk on her lips. "She's staying at the inn on the other side of town. The only one still operating."

Without more than a nod, I walk back out. It's about time me and Alessandro's fixer have some one-on-one time. *Let the games truly begin, cara.*

∞ ∞ ∞

CHAPTER FOUR

∞ Seduzione ∞

"<u>Seduce</u> my mind and you can have my body. Find my soul and I'm yours forever."

-Anonymous-

Monica

I don't know why the end of that scene still bothers me hours later. What is it about Lucas' pack that's already gotten under my skin? And how did Finn know about my lies?

My cell rings just as I finish bandaging my wounds. Ileana might have taken the herbs I'd brought for Lucas, but my medicinal ones were in another bag. And thankfully, too. With the infusion I prepared and the clean towel wrapped around it, I'll be good. By morning, it'll be more healed, and I'll have full use of my leg by the day's end tomorrow.

The ring of my phone grows more incessant. I heave a sigh, reach out for it – and then there's a knock on my door.

Between that and the call, I choose the door. I'm wearing shorts with a heavy sweater over them, so hopefully whoever it is won't mind my atrocious sense of fashion.

And it better not be the old lady asking when I'm leaving again!

As it so happens, it's none other than Luciano there. Arm resting against the door frame and glaring at me darkly like I'm the cause to all his problems. "Why did you help out Finn?"

I roll my eyes and limp back in, leaving the door open. "You really need to work on communication with your wolves. I told Finn it's because I didn't realize Elle had magic. I... wanted to make sure she didn't get hurt."

His scowl deepens and he strides inside and shuts the door behind him like he owns the place. Maybe because of the infusion that's made me lightheaded, or maybe because of his own sex appeal – either way, it seems like he's taking over the room. And that damned scent of pine and fresh soap hits me again, causing me to stumble out of its reach.

When he only stands in the middle of the room and says nothing, I add, "Luciano –"

"Lucas."

"Fine, Lucas. I know you're making me into being the bad guy here, but what harm will it do to see your father? Just once. He's sick, he doesn't have long to live..."

He steps forward then, as if a decision has been made. "Non ti credo. Your words are lies, that's why he sent you" His expression is intense, focused on my every move in a way that makes my entire body tingle. "As his fixer, you really must be the best at evading answers, hmm? But that's not what *I* came here for." Another step, and his gaze heats in warning. That crackling electricity is back between us – and then he's dropping his mouth on mine.

I've been kissed before. Some, very skilled. But this is... possession. There is no other way to explain it. Lucas takes charge of my mouth and my body like he owns it, and in that moment, he does. The electricity that had been humming between us sizzles now, heating our bodies and driving me crazy.

My shirt itches against my skin – I want it gone, want to feel his heat permeate my own. This isn't about Alessandro, it's about nothing more than scratching an itch and winning this unspoken battle between us.

I break the kiss only for a second to toss my shirt over my head, leaving me clad in my black lace bra and panties. Lucas stares at me, letting loose a soft growl. A muscles ticks in his clenched jaw, and his fingers draw a pattern from my collarbone to my hip, then my injured leg.

"Does it hurt?" The question, much like his oddly tender touch, surprises me.

"Barely," I whisper. "Had some of nonna's natural salve with me and it should be healed by–" It seems Lucas didn't need that much information.

Hand on my neck, he yanks me to him, colliding our bodies as he once more takes ownership of my mouth. Then he picks me up and lays me on the bed, moving his mouth down my body, to my panties. His energy feeds into me, into this raw need between us.

A touch on my hip, then my thigh, and I'm spreading my legs unconsciously. He drops his mouth to my thighs, teasing with lingering caresses and light licks until my hands are fisted in his hair, pulling on it and begging.

Only then does he rip the panties away with one yank, and brings that gorgeous mouth where I need it. And that's when I really lose it.

I've had good oral sex, even great. But Lucas, holy madre di Dio –

It's like he knows exactly where to touch me, exactly where to apply pressure, because in less seconds than it takes me to breathe I'm coming fast, and hard.

Panting, I lift myself up on my elbows to look at him. He's already standing, shrugging off his t-shirt and tugging off his jeans, then pulling a condom on. My throat goes dry when I see him in all his glory, all hard abs, stone-like muscles and so, so ready for me.

Lucas glances down at me, licks his lips, and grins wickedly. "Let me know if your leg starts hurting."

And then he's spreading me wider, sliding inside me, and I forget my own name, let alone the number of times he makes me come that night. What I do remember is how he slows his thrusts, hovering just above me, his face taut with tension and restraint as he paces himself, driving us both to agony.

And then his gaze shifts, just a little, a flare of red coating the irises – just before he thrusts deep inside me, and I come apart under him.

Lucas

It doesn't take Monica long to leave the bed. She doesn't have to know the reason I came, the reason we had sex, is so her guard drops around me. Even if said-sex and the way she responds to me was fucking mind-blowing.

It's been a while since my one-night stands have been this... well, satisfying. My wolf is settled, like he's gotten hold of something unique. Which is ridiculous. *It's probably because she's a wolf.*

And yet I've been with women who were wolves, before. My father's pack had some unique specimens, after all. Of course, that all stopped when I got to Rockland Creek, but it's not like I'm a rookie in this. Quite the fucking opposite.

The thought nags at me, though. Why now? Why this weird fucking sensation? It's not just Monica's responsiveness, or the sense of forbidden fruit. After all, she's here on a job.

It's more than that. She drives my body to the brink of exaltation, and it's like a drug. A very physical, alluring drug. One I wouldn't mind sampling once more.

Not that she needs to know any of this.

So I keep the rise and fall of my chest slow and steady, but the moment I feel her get up from the bed I peek through my lashes. Her body drives me to distraction, especially the flush that's still on her skin, a clear reminder of the last hours. And then she bends over and picks out a phone from a small drawer, and my focus shifts.

Her demeanor changes as it vibrates and she answers after the first few buzzes in a whisper. "Sì?"

"Why were you not answering earlier?" I recognize his voice without fail. The same low baritone, demanding tone filters through the bad device. My ears focus on the sounds until I can discern the words. "Well?"

"I was busy."

"Too busy for your alpha?" When Monica says nothing, Alessandro laughs. "Ah, I see. It worked, then?"

Monica pauses, shifts the weight from foot to foot, and says, "Yeah. It's done."

My jaw tenses. For a moment there, even if it was under false pretenses, we had a good time. It was only the two of us, without his fucking machinations coming between us. But she's just confirmed this wasn't that, at least not for her.

And maybe it makes me a hypocrite given the reason behind me initiating the sex in the first place. Actually, it does make me an *ipocrita*. But I refuse to look deeper into why her easy admission annoys me so.

Instead, I focus back on the conversation. Alessandro's asking, "And?"

"It's too early to tell. I need more time."

"You have five more days, no more. Do not disappoint me."

He hangs up, and she stands there staring at the screen for long moments. I want to get inside her head, in that moment. Find out why she's doing this, what's in it for her. And what the five days deadline is for.

Another part of me, a stronger part, wants to kiss her senseless, toss her on this bed and make her remember who she belongs to.

The thought startles me. *Belong to? Definitely not me.*

I force the tension to leave my body as she turns my way. Her eyes peruse me, the intensity almost searing a brand in my skin. And then it's gone, and I hear the bathroom door close and the sound of the shower turn on.

A beat, then another. Once I'm sure she won't come out, I crawl out of bed and find the phone. Another ring startles me and I walk to my jeans, pulling out my own cellphone, while still holding hers.

"Sì?"

"It's me," Dominic says. "Where are you? I'm at your house."

I flick through Monica's phone, seeing only one number on repeat. To Dominic, I mutter, "Elsewhere, ovviamente. What is it?"

"You asked for the vote." A pause, filled with reproach. "We took it, after the attack at Elle's."

That draws my attention. How could I have gotten so wrapped up in Monica that I forgot where my priorities lie? Fucking hell. "And?"

"Luz and Elle don't agree, but everyone else is on board."

"And you?"

He pauses, and his tone is heavy with exhaustion when he says, "I cannot advocate for mercy. Not when they're obviously intent on attacking us. Finn told us in detail about the Reapers at Elle's shop."

I nod to the darkness, a weight settling on my shoulders. "Bene. Send your wolves to scout locations. Find out every spot the Reapers are hiding in. You and Daniela go with them. Her magic can help if needed."

Dominic sighs on the line. "Alright. I'll get on it before sunrise." He pauses again. "You sure you're good?"

"Excellent. Ciao, amico." *Che strano*. It feels weird having cordial conversations with him, but I won't complain when it meets my needs.

I toss my phone away and turn to Monica's. The number is easy enough to memorize, should I wish to call him. But I have no intention of doing so.

No, not yet. I need to see exactly what he plans before I show my cards. If my days are counted, if this Damocles sword is hanging over my head, then I need to move fast. Logic states I should be getting dressed and heading out, helping my pack to eradicate the Reapers. Logic also demands I leave Monica alone.

And yet before I know what I'm doing, I'm heading for the washroom. The knob turns, but what awaits me inside is not what I expected. Monica isn't relishing the hot water, basking in her victory. Rather, she's curled up in a corner of the bathroom, head on her knees.

The door creaks when I enter, and she lifts her head. Her eyes are wide and a sober blue, lashes wet with tears, yet there's no trace of them on her face. I frown at her, but say nothing. We stare at each other for the longest moment, then I hold out my hand.

Monica looks at it, then at me. When she doesn't reach for it, I bend over and pick her up in my arms. "What –" she starts, but stops as she realizes I'm moving us both into the tight shower.

As I let her find a grip on the tiled floor, mindful of her bandaged leg, she sways towards me, and our bodies touch. A gasp escapes her, followed by a moan as my hand drifts to her waist, then her lower back, to pull her closer.

She looks up at me again, her features a mask of confusion. My wolf nudges to the surface, insistent, desperate for another taste of her. I don't want to think about that call, or the reason she's doing this. What I know is she isn't faking it, and I'm going to damn well make sure I'm worth her time. And if it so happens I erase the memories of those tears, then a bonus to me.

Without a second thought, I drop my mouth and claim hers. Monica opens underneath me, then her hands tangle in my hair and she pulls herself closer, kissing me back just as ardently.

Her response nearly topples us sideways on the wet floor, but I steady her with one hand on her hip, and the other holding onto the wall. The sound of something breaking tears my mouth from Monica and I notice my grip on the wall has actually gone right through, causing pieces of tile to break apart.

"Is that normal?" Monica breathes, her mouth against my throat.

"No." I pull my hand back and tilt her chin up. "But you do things to me, tesoro, that I don't quite understand."

Her eyes darken at my words. Before she can come up with a smart reply, I claim her mouth again, this time pressing her against the opposite side for support. Then I pull back, flipping her over. "Hold onto the wall," I growl.

Once she's secure, I grab her hip again and spread her legs with my thigh. My free hand goes to her front, caressing one perky nipple and enticing a moan from her. "You good?" I ask, more mindful of her comfort than I'd care to admit.

She tosses her wet hair over one shoulder and groans, "Sì, please. Ti prego, Lucas...enough teasing."

"Con piacere, cara," I whisper softly. "It'll be my pleasure."

With one smooth thrust I'm inside her, and I forget everything but her moans and the tightness enveloping me.

When morning comes, I wake up to an empty bed and the sound of a shower running. After a stretch or two, I get up and put on my clothes, then exit Monica's room and head home. The walk home does nothing to clear my head.

Che diavolo was I thinking last night? I went there to tell her to stay away from my pack, and Elle who's still recovering from Declan's imprisonment and from nearly losing herself. And yet, one look at those big blue eyes and my basest of impulses took over.

And again after my father's call.

Annoyance flashes through me, and my steps become harsher on the ground. Without realizing it, I break into a jog and the morph takes over. A ripple of pain, then I'm on four paws, beating onto the pavement until I sneak into the woods, taking the longer way home.

My rusty fur stands out in the greens of the forest, not that it matters. After Declan's attack, humans have been sparse to find in Rockland Creek. It's fast becoming a ghost town, all the better for us to execute the Reapers.

And then what? The thought comes unbidden, and not for the first time. Once we clean town, do I move my wolves and their mates to another area, and start over? It would seem weird if we all pop up in the same place, but maybe there's not much of a choice.

Monica's words about going home ring in my ears. Home is here, not with my father. It never was. Finally, I get back to my house and toss my clothes off, then head into the shower. The water normally clears my mind, but not this morning.

By the time I get out, I'm still as annoyed.

Monica

Lucas is gone when I re-enter the bedroom. I can't feel sad, I mean after all it was a one-night stand. And an amazing one, at that. But what's confusing is the way he comforted me. He probably didn't mean it, but it sure came across that way.

Shaking the thought off, I look for my phone and find three missed calls from Alessandro. I dial him back, my stomach churning in anticipation.

"About time," he says by way of greeting. "I want an update, now. How did the morning after go?"

I gulp, loath to tell him about last night. But he's my alpha, and the only protection I have. *Think of what you'll get, once you do this one thing for him,* I tell myself.

"It worked," I say finally. "I mean, he spent the night. Your son doesn't get smitten, but he definitely didn't resist my charms."

A low rumble escapes him. "I knew he couldn't, not for long. And?"

"I'll keep pressing my luck."

"What about your magical teas?"

I bristle at the reminder. Those leaves were meant to entice Lucas' senses, act as an aphrodisiac if needed, and make him more susceptible...if it came to it. It's probably best Alessandro doesn't know they're with some immortal that smells like cinnamon.

"They're not necessary. But, if needed, I will make use of them."

In my mind, I can almost see Alessandro nodding, his cold, calculating gaze lost in thought. "Bene." He pauses, but just when I think he's about to hang up, he adds something else. "Is he alone?"

"He has a pack," I say. Each word feels like a betrayal, which is stupid because I don't owe these people anything.

"How many?"

"Three other males, and three females from what I could tell. All mated."

"Mated?" His tone changes, as though he's trying to hide his reaction. A hint of interest still trickles through, making me even more uneasy. "What are the females like?"

I frown at the odd question. "I haven't interacted long with them. The one I did speak with, she seems to have magic in her veins. Not sure about the others."

"Find out!"

There's more than a hint of eagerness now in his tone, and my gut tells me I've made a huge mistake opening my mouth. "But—"

"Do not dispute me, Monica. We wouldn't want to upset me enough to forget my promise, do we?"

I bow my head. "No, signore."

"Bene. Keep me updated, as soon as you know."

After I get dressed, I head to Claws Auto. Like before, Lucrezia is there, but alone. I glance around, noticing only

Tristan in the garage cleaning up a mess, but no trace of anyone else.

"Where's Blondie?" I ask.

She looks up from the computer as though only now seeing me. "Come again?"

"Blondie, the girl who was here with you earlier. I know Cinderella's name is Elle, and yours, but Blondie?"

"You mean Daniela."

"Yeah, her." I scan the reception area again. "So, they're not around?"

"Nope, out on pack business." Her eyes narrow on me, but there's a hint of amusement in them. "Are you here for Lucas again?"

"Maybe," I shrug and walk closer. My leg is still a bit stiff – also due to the night's activities – so I settled for regular boots, no heels, and jeans today. It feels weird compared to my usual designer clothes, but then again, I am running in different circles.

For now.

I cannot forget this is all temporary, and regardless of how easily these people are to talk to, I need to keep my defenses up and not get attached. After all, I'll be out of here by the week's end.

"Lucas is in a bad mood this morning," Lucrezia says, tapping her chin. "Would you have something to do with it?"

My eyes widen. "Not that I know of."

"Hmm." She leans back in her chair. "So... he *didn't* find you last night after asking me where you're staying? And he *wasn't* with you when my mate went to his house to talk to him, and found it conveniently empty?"

"I, uh..." I'm freaking blushing. What in the name of the Mother Goddess has gotten into me?

"That's what I thought," Lucrezia nods. "Finn says you're hiding things, but Elle seems to think you're okay."

"And you?"

"I haven't made up my mind yet."

Staring at her, I feel something weird. Almost a camaraderie blossoming. Another new thing – I never had girlfriends in Alessandro's pack.

"Well, I'm only here to try and get Lucas back to his family. His father wants to see him and..." I trail off. The acidity burns on my tongue this time.

Lucrezia nods again, softer. "Yeah, don't bother with lies around here. They get found out quicker than you'd think."

"Lucrezia, have you seen my spare –" Lucas comes around the corner looking scrumptious in jeans and not much else. A dirty shirt is in his hands, and he stops when he sees me. His eyes narrow, taking in my jeans and boots outfit. "I didn't know you could do casual."

I shrug, trying to pretend like his bare chest isn't affecting me. We both know that's not true. And judging by the way my lady parts tingle, I'm starting to realize he's got more the upper hand than I do.

Thankfully, Lucrezia digs under her desk and tosses him a spare shirt, which he pulls on immediately. It does nothing to hide the muscles underneath, and I find myself unable to remember the reason for my presence here.

"Did you need something?" Lucas asks, his tone indifferent.

I glance at Lucrezia, whose suspicious frown has been erased in favor of a commiserating expression.

Before I can even answer, Lucas steps closer, muddling my senses again. I blurt the first thing that comes to mind. "Can we talk in your office?"

He turns without a word and I follow. The minute we're in the enclosure, I try to gain upper ground. Swaying my hips, I move closer to him and wrap my hands around his neck. "You left early this morning."

Before Lucas can answer, I press my lips to his neck, and my tongue snakes out to taste his skin. He smells like man and fresh soap and wild, dark woods. I inhale it deep, and the scent does something to me. Soothes me, and my wolf, in a way I've never felt before. It makes me lightheaded enough that my grip on his neck tightens.

Lucas' pulse changes, the beat calling out to me. It's no longer slow and steady, but faster, harder, like he's not unaffected by my closeness and reaction to me. When I pull back a bit, I notice his eyes have a different kind of heat in them, and his nostrils are flaring like he's scenting me.

Then his expression changes, as though he's coming from a dream. He shakes his head and moves back from me, pushing me away.

"Aspetta." He holds up a hand, his features hardened by something way worse than anger. "What, exactly, do you think we're doing here?"

I look away, refusing to play into his game. I know he wants my answer to say we're involved, that I like him, so he can break it down to pieces. But I won't give him the satisfaction, because I'm not stupid enough to fall for a mark.

Not that any of this stops Lucas from driving his point home. His index lifts my face to his, and I notice his thin-pressed lips. "To be clear, we fucked, cara. Nothing else. I'm more than happy to continue to scratch that itch if you're game. But if you have a problem with that, the door's open."

I yank my chin out of his grip, and wrap my hand around his neck instead. Instead of the earlier sweet embrace, my nails now dig into his flesh and a soft hiss escapes him.

"Did I say the opposite?"

Then I pull his head down to mine, and our mouth mesh together. It's sloppy, and it would've extended into something else – but a knock sounds on what's left of the door frame. Someone clears their throat.

I move away from Lucas, keeping my back to them. Yet I sense his annoyance. At, what, being interrupted? Left with blue balls?

By the time I turn around, I'm in control – but he's not. His eyes are burning daggers at Tristan, who holds up his hands. "Don't rip my head off, meu amigo. Something's happened on the patrol. Dani and Dom need us."

∞ ∞ ∞

∞ Morte ∞

"Our life is made by the <u>death</u> of others."

-Leonardo da Vinci-

Lucas

The mood is broken, and grazie a Dio, as I just about lost my head. What is it with this woman? One minute I want to strangle her, the next her cherry fragrance is everywhere and my wolf wants her – and *I* want to kiss her. It's got to be more than her charms, unless she used some kind of spell on me.

It's just a good fuck. Great chemistry. That's all.

Keep telling yourself that, my wolf seems to nudge. His voice is fainter and fainter in my head these days. If I had the time, I'd bother to stop and try and figure it out. But I'm not an introspective guy, so I don't.

I follow Tristan out the door, but Monica's on my heels. "Let me help."

"Not likely," I toss over a shoulder. "Stay here until I come back, and we can finish this conversation before you're on your way back to Alessandro."

Monica scowls, and I sense her annoyance – sense? Again with these weird *feelings*. Next time I see Ileana, I'm going to strangle the immortal. Repercussions or not.

Our swift departure leaves Monica behind with Lucrezia. With a bit of luck, she'll be gone by the time we finish, and I won't have to worry about lack of control.

As we jump in my pickup, Tristan dials Finn and tells him to haul ass to the shop with Elle in case anything happens. That handled, we can focus on what's going on.

"They found all the Reaper hideouts, and weren't seen," Tristan briefs me. "But the last one, some scout was still awake. Raised the alarm, and a fight broke out."

My foot presses harder on the gas, wanting to get there faster. "Are they alright?"

"Dani and Dom, yeah. He has a few injured wolves, though."

I nod, and after ten minutes of quiet we finally arrive. I jump out of the car and head over. The land is deserted, with some kind of large industrial building in the distance. In the middle of the field, I can see ten or so Reaper bodies littering the ground. The stench of the vrykolakas also hits me hard, and I hold back a gag.

Dominic and Daniela are over on the side, crouched over one such wolf. Daniela's hands are glowing fire, as though she's trying to heal the creature, but then her shoulders slouch in defeat.

When he looks up at me, Dominic's expression is grim. "I'm sorry," I tell him. "Losing one of your own is not what I intended."

He shakes his head and stands, walking over to me. "Isn't it?" He glances around at the other vrykolakas. He has eight with him plus the one on the ground. Half of the others look like they're injured, too.

Dominic runs a hand over his face, exhaustion emanating from his ever pore. I head closer to Daniela, crouching low. The vrykolakas' yellow eyes meet mine.

These creatures are not like me. Half-strigoi, half-wolf, they're hybrid of the most unnatural kind – soulless. Yet Dominic sees something worth saving in them, and they listen to him. Time and time again, they've helped out with various battles, and I cannot deny the respect they have earned.

So when I reach a hand out, it's to silently tell the wolf about to cross over into the Underworld that I understand. I can read his pain, his ultimate demise. *And it's alright, amico. You will be fine.*

Before I can say any of that, something happens inside me. My wolf goes utterly quiet. Everything else fades into the background. And as I place my hands on his fur, a vibrating jolt runs from me, to him. The vrykolakas opens his eyes wide, and goes into a seizure.

I rip my hands from him with effort – they'd been stuck as though with a magnet – and scramble to get off the ground.

"What the fuck just happened?" Tristan asks as he helps Daniela up. Their eyes are wide on me, filled with concern.

"Non lo so – I don't know. Why are you looking at me like I've grown two heads?"

"Your hands," Dominic says as he inches closer. "Look down."

Thick, russet fur envelops my forearms. Out of all of us, Daniela alone can shift a particular part of her body, but I've never been able to. Now I'm in human from, yet my hands are furry with massive claws protruding from them.

"And your eyes," he adds. "They're red, Lucas."

That part, I cannot confirm. But I do feel that vibration in my body, the shake of it all. Something is happening. And whatever it is, it's not good.

Lordul morții.

The voice echoes in my head, and I look at the vrykolakas that had been dying. He's now standing, his head bowed as if in submission to his alpha – Dominic – as well as myself.

"What does that mean?" I ask my beta.

Dominic glances between us, his expression wary. "It means lord of death."

No... I take another step backwards, and another. Daniela says something, then Tristan, but I can't make it out. Everything is tuned out except my fast heartbeat, and the pulse in my ears. *I was right, then. It's happening, and sooner than I thought.*

Refusing to look at my pack, I turn around and run. My wolf takes over, I let it morph, and try to forget everything. Woods pass by, and roads, as I run for I don't know how long until the moon is high in the sky.

And when I'm done running, I find myself outside the inn where Monica is. I didn't want to end up here, but my wolf chose the destination. And now that we're so close by, I can smell her cherry fragrance wafting from the open window above.

Without thinking, without hesitating, I walk inside in wolf form, trot up the stairs, then morph back to human form at her door. The minute she opens it, looking half-asleep, I'm on her. Hands cupping her cheeks, kissing her, drowning myself in her.

She pulls back, frowning. "What happened to you? And why are you naked?"

"Nothing of importance."

"Lucas—"

I push her back in the room, and Monica's eyes darken to navy. She looks me up and down, licking her bottom lip.

"We laid out the terms earlier," I say, remembering how we left the conversation. "You want to talk now, or bed?"

She gulps, and I smell her arousal as well as hear her heartbeat. "Bed."

I move closer then, removing her sweater in one sweep and finding her naked underneath. A groan of pure, raw lust escapes me, and I grip her waist to toss her on the bed. Then I follow, stretching beside her.

I have enough sense left to ask, "How's your leg?"

"Never better," she whispers, then pulls me on top of her.

And once I'm inside her, I forget everything else. For a few moments, there is bliss. And then, there is darkness.

"Luciano.... Luciano, wake up!" I blink in the darkness of my bedroom, then rub a hand over my face.

After Monica fell asleep, I slunk outside and tried to calm my thoughts. When that didn't work, I walked back home and passed out.

It can't have been more than a few hours since, and surely I'm still dreaming. In the window is a translucent shape with flowing red hair and features I would recognize anywhere. I stand up in bed, jaw going slack.

"Mamma?"

She floats closer to me. "My beautiful boy."

"Ma che... What are you doing here?"

"Your father. You cannot go back to him." She flickers in and out, like a bad connection. "...knows about the gift."

"What gift?"

She comes even closer then, her expression full of pity. "I know you have tried to forget. But the chimera blood in you is not forgiving. Each battle fought, each soul taken has been a mark on you." She gulps, wringing her hands. "The Underworld will call soon."

I shake my head, recalling the vrykolakas' words – *lordul morții*. "Let it call, then. I've made my peace with it."

"Luciano..." She flickers again. "...wants it for himself."

"Who, Alessandro?" I snort. "If there is one thing he cannot take from me, it's this."

She shakes her head, as though knowing something I don't. And then she disappears, vanishing into thin air. "Mamma, wait!"

It's only once I get up from the bed, that I realize it wasn't a dream. She had been there. When I walk through the spot she stood in, the chilliness of the air sticks to my skin, refusing to let go.

For a moment, I'm frozen, stuck in time. It was so sudden, so brief, seeing her again. After she died, I had dreams of her. For months on end, all I could see was her pale face, crying for me, for Matteo. Then even those stopped, and I pushed all those memories again. Buried. Forgotten. And now... *Damn Monica for coming here, and bringing all this shit back to the forefront of my mind.*

Part of me knows if I talk to my pack, they can help. But I'm the one supposed to be leading them, not the other way around.

"Will you really be so stubborn?"

I whirl around to find yet another presence in my bedroom, this one not so welcome. "Ileana." Her name is more of a growl on my lips than anything else. "What do you want? I'm in no mood."

She looks past me to where my mother had stood, as though able to see something I don't. "Interesting. And here I thought you were just another stubborn wolf."

I really growl then, and move on her. "What do you want, Ileana? Don't make me ask again."

"You have denied love for so long. Isn't it about time you let it in?"

I snort. "What, with Monica? She's a good lay, that about sums it up."

Ileana shakes her head. "I have always known you were stubborn, but I never took you for being dumb."

I reach for her then, my hand going straight for her throat. Instead of going through like last time, I actually catch grip this time. Her eyes widen in tandem with mine, and I let go as if scorched. "What the fuck did you do to me now?"

Ileana is silent for a moment, a delicate hand going to her swanlike neck. Eyes narrowed, she circles me, not saying anything until she's facing me once more. "What are you? I should have seen it earlier, but you are no regular wolf."

I hesitate. I haven't told anyone of my mixed heritage. "What do you see?"

"I see a link to the Underworld, filled with rage under the surface. A rage that, if you let it, will consume you and your wolf whole, leaving behind only your other side."

Sighing, I run a hand over my face and reach for a shirt off the bed. Then I walk over to my destroyed living room. Over a shoulder, I add, "You coming? Or is it only in my bedroom you like to pay visits?"

Her presence follows me as I head to my whiskey decanter and pour myself a glass. Lifting it her way, I say, "I would offer you one, but..."

She arches an eyebrow my way. "Thank you. I take it neat."

Not bothering to hide my surprise, I pour her a drink and watch as she sips it delicately. For the first time, perhaps because of Mamma's apparition, I realize there is some truth to her words. I *have* been stubborn. Not least of all in cutting her off before I really heard her.

"I thought you were more similar to a ghost than, well, a human."

Ileana scoffs. "I choose to present myself in this form, but I am able to touch and feel like most immortals. Only, none have ever been able to touch *me*, at least not without my permission." She tilts her head to one side. "Will you tell me, then?"

I top off my drink, and halfway through it I finally admit, "I'm half-wolf, half-chimera. My mother was the last of her kind, and my father married her in order to procreate. She had two children, me and my younger brother Matteo. When he died, my gift was made known. And then Mamma died, so I left."

Ileana watches me carefully. "And?"

"And, the chimera blood if pure can open the Underworld, and link with Charon, the ferryman of souls. Our curse, as we're only part-chimera, is that with each soul taken, the link to the below is stronger, and eventually I won't be able to fight it. I'll be pulled under, become the monster of legend. Only, I'll be a slave to the Underworld, versus being a decisive part of it."

Ileana says nothing for the longest time. "And how far are you to that happening?"

"Too far," I say. "I haven't heard my wolf in ages, and after Lucrezia died..." I shrug, trailing off. There is no way to explain just how fucked I am.

The immortal takes another sip of her drink, mulling over my words. "You have to tell your pack. They need to be prepared, especially given you are being hunted by your father."

"How did you –"

"You are not alone in being conflicted. Give Monica a real chance, and she can help you."

"What does she have to do with it? Besides your matchmaking obsession, that is. We both know nothing can undo my dilemma."

Ileana laughs. "One of these days, you'll learn not to underestimate love." Then she's gone, leaving me to my thoughts and an empty glass.

Monica

I toss the phone onto the bed, annoyed. I've been trying to reach Lucas since waking up this morning alone, with no luck. It's like the man vanished. Something happened last night, something that bothered him enough to come running to me and not his pack.

But what?

With a sigh, I realize there's only one way I can find out – by talking to those closest to him. And out of all of them, there's one girl in particular who's more open to me. So I get dressed in black leggings, a short wool skirt, and another off-the-shoulders sweater. Zipping up my leather coat over it, I only grab my phone and head out.

Walking to the bakery, it sinks in for the first time how empty this town is. We're in the middle of the week, but there's no soul I can see. The old lady owning the inn mentioned most of the people are leaving – gas explosion. *Claro.* Because that would explain why only the backs of some buildings have fallen apart.

After a short walk, I reach the bakery and thankfully no one else is inside. Elle straightens up from behind the counter – which looks dejectedly empty. She smiles when she sees me. "Hey. Sorry, I didn't bother making much today, 'cause it's not like anyone's going to come around and buy, you know?"

"Not really." I keep my tone soft. "What *is* going on here, Elle? Lucas seems...bothered."

She bites her lip and looks away, then a heavy sigh escapes her. "I shouldn't really be telling you.... Finn still doesn't trust you."

The door opens behind me and I steel myself for Lucas' angry tone. Instead, Lucrezia says, "I see we're right on time."

I turn, surprised to find her all bundled up next to Blondie – Daniela. She nods at me, extending a hand while her amber eyes size me up. "I'm Daniela, but everyone calls me Dani."

When I shake her hand, a zing of electricity travels up my arm. Something about these women...

Lucrezia goes past me and helps Elle carry some croissants to a table, along with soft drinks. Then she sits and gestures to the seat opposite her. This practically puts me in a corner, surrounded by the other three.

"Are you Luna or something?" I mutter as I follow her unspoken order. In some packs, an alpha's female garners as much respect and weight as he does, especially among its female members. Given how Lucrezia has been acting, it's not such a jump to assume.

She laughs. "Only to Dom. But no, I've just been around these guys since before Dani and Elle got involved with them. One can say I'm a little.... Protective. And you've definitely caught Lucas' eye."

I tear apart the croissant, and busy myself with stuffing my mouth rather than answering.

"Did you see him last night?" Dani asks. Her concerned tone bothers me, and the pastry tastes bitter going down.

"Maybe."

They share a look, and I take it as my cue to ask questions. "What happened? He wouldn't talk about it."

Lucrezia snorts. "It's Lucas. He doesn't talk, period. He scowls and grunts and yells and acts all tough. But..." Her voice changes. "I think he's hurting. And I think you being here is making it worse." I open my mouth to say something, but she adds, "And better, in some ways."

That stops my raging venting. "How do you mean?"

"Just trust me on that," she says with a twinkle in her eyes. "Now, as for what happened last night... Well, it's a longer story that we're choosing to trust you with. It started with me and Dominic..."

As Lucrezia starts talking, Dani and Elle fill in the gaps when it comes to their own stories. And slowly, little by little, a picture emerges of a type of pack I've never known. Wolves and humans that are so tied to each other, they would give their lives to save one another. Women who stand by their men just as strongly, just as fiercely protective as they are. And men that respect them, even if they're overbearing in their own way.

It makes the bleakness of my own life pale in comparison. It makes my heart ache for something just as real, just as impossibly unattainable.

Needless to say, when Lucrezia reveals their powers and everything they have accomplished, I'm even more stunned. "So you... You used to be a human, but now you're a dragon-rider of sort that wields magic from the skies?" She shrugs. I look at Elle. "And you're the last female descendent of the Romanian dragons, called zmei, and you wield *their* magic." She nods, and I turn to Dani, gulping. "And you're a wolf shifter who can wield magic?"

"Yep," she says with a grin. "Among other things."

I shake my head, munching on the last of the croissant to get my bearings. Is Lucas doing this on purpose, having all these people with insane powers under him? Is this his way of getting back at Alessandro, of biding his way to a war?

"You also have something," Dani says. "I felt it when we touched earlier."

I gulp and look up. "Umm, yeah. My nonna – grandmother – was a human who practiced stregheria. It's an old type of magic, based in herbs and rituals and whatnot."

"I thought wolves couldn't hold magic?" Elle asks, glancing at Dani for confirmation.

She shrugs. "If my lobisomem pack was able to, there is no reason others couldn't, I suppose."

"There may be more to it than that," I whisper. "Alessandro – Lucas' father – he has a certain type of wolf under his command. Most of us are lupi mannari like himself, basically we're descended from the original Italian lupo mannaro."

"Like Remus and Romulus?" Lucrezia asks.

I nod. "Pretty much. So he, um, cultivates a certain kind of talent, which is why he insisted my nonna teach the girl wolves who showed promise."

"And you did?" Dani asks.

"Yeah, me and Ana." Thoughts of my blonde cousin swim in my head, but I push them away. She's not the same now, not by a long shot. "My cousin," I add to them. "We don't get along that much anymore."

When the silence lengthens to the point of becoming awkward, I break it again. "Why was Lucas so upset last night?"

"Dom and I ran into trouble when we went out with the vrykolakas," Dani says. At my confused frown, she adds, "They're Dominic's extended pack, basically hybrids without souls. Half-vampire, half-wolf, born and raised in the Carpathian Mountains."

"Dom's cousin brought them here," Lucrezia says, "and once Dominic killed him, he inherited the wolves. They're not the kindest, but they are extremely loyal to him."

"I... Okay. So, the reconnaissance mission with these...vrykolakas...went bad?"

Dani bites into half a croissant. "Mm, yeah. One of them was dying, and when Lucas came, he, um, pretty much resuscitated him. And then he freaked out and took off."

"He...what?"

Lucrezia reaches for a pastry. "He brought him back from the dead. Dominic says his wolf called him lord of death."

My head spins, and I stand from the table, barely holding on. Rumors from around the pack – Alessandro's pack – come back to me. That Alessandro's wife had been feared. That she could crack open the Underworld. That her sons had inherited her gift until the youngest one had died... I'd been afraid of Alessandro wanting Lucas for a reason, and now I know why.

"Monica?" Lucrezia asks, also standing now. "Are you okay?"

"I.... No." I shake my head, backing away from them. "Thank you...for what you told me. But I have to go find Lucas."

Dani stands, too. "We can drive you. I have Tristan's car."

The girls drop me off at Lucas' bungalow, then drive off. I stare at the laid-back brick building, lost in the middle of nowhere. For some reason, I thought he'd be living in a mansion, but I guess he's not like his father.

No. He's like his mamma. I'd heard different stories, some from my nonna, and more from Alessandro. According to him, it was Francesca's ambition that broke them apart. And if Lucas is anything like her, his entire pack is in danger.

Steeling myself against emotions, against feeling too much, I stomp to the dark wooden door and bang my palm on it.

Moments pass, and no one comes. I bang some more, then give up and walk around the property. At the back, there's a fenced-in backyard. I hear some grunts and when I turn around the corner, I stop dead in my tracks.

Lucas is doing chin ups. Half-naked.

A bar of steel is secured between two massive oak trees, and he's lifting himself up and down at a rhythm known only to him. Loose sweatpants hang off his lean hips, and his corded muscles ripple with every movement.

Beads of sweat drip down his back, but he doesn't seem cold. Not in the least. He looks *hot*. And I want to lick all over that body with an intensity that stuns me.

I take in a shaky breath, and he stops. Glances over his shoulder, his eyes burning through me. Then he lands on his feet quieter than a cat and turns to me. The sight of his naked chest completely evaporates what I was going to say, so I stand there staring at him instead, and holding back the urge to run into his arms.

"Come back for more?" he smirks.

CHAPTER SIX

∞ Combattere ∞

"The secret of change is to focus all your energy, not on <u>fighting</u> the old, but on building the new."

-Socrates-

Monica

Lucas' arrogance snaps me out of my daze, and I manage a shake of the head. With more firmness than I thought possible, I say, "No. I'm not here for *that*. This entire time I've been here, I thought you didn't know what you are. That you were oblivious, that the gift hadn't manifested in you. But you do know, don't you?"

His jaw clenches, and one of his hands flexes in a fist, before he forces himself to relax again. I know he doesn't mean the gesture for me, but he's definitely angry. Cornered. Like a lion caged.

Thread carefully, Monica.

"No idea what you mean," he says finally, and stalks past me.

His scent of man, musk and sandalwood hits me, and I sway on my feet again. Is this the chimera in him? Is it more? The energy in the air is unmistakably chaotic, though.

Focus!

I follow him through the French doors and inside the house. The kitchen is clean, but the living room I see past the open concept is a destroyed mess, drawing my attention. "What happened here?"

Lucas glances around as if completely disinterested and shrugs. "Dominic and I, we disagreed over a few things."

"Like Lucrezia dying?"

He freezes then and turns to me slowly. Coal eyes burn into mine, and I swear there's a hint of red there. "Come again, cara?"

"I know about your pack," I gulp when his expression becomes even stormier. "Their powers and...the mates."

"You've been snooping around, then?" He reaches for a glass of water and downs it in two gulps, his Adam's apple bobbing up and down.

"No," I whisper, unable to take my eyes off him. "I mean, yes. But not for Alessandro. After last night, you scared me."

An odd expression crosses his face, almost like regret. "Mi dispiace," he says softly, all anger gone out of him. "It wasn't my intention."

"I don't mean it like that!" As if to prove my point, I step closer to him, leaving only a foot of distance so I can keep some sanity. "The rawness of the sex was great, amazing even! I mean because of how much pain you were in, and your inner turmoil. I thought... I thought your pack should know. And today I ran into the girls, and we talked."

Lucas shakes his head. "Whatever they told you, it'll be their interpretation of something they know nothing about."

"Really?" I cross my arms over my chest. It's fine if he wants to lie to himself, but this is pushing it. "And what about the resurrection of the vrykolakas?"

Lucas' eyes burn dark fire again. "Do not put your nose where it doesn't belong, cara."

"And who are you to say where it does, and doesn't, belong?"

He takes a step closer, this time bringing us chest to chest. His nostrils flare, and his hand lifts up to grab my chin in a firm grip. "You are crossing a line, Monica. Trust me, Alessandro doesn't pay you enough for this."

"You ever thought I'm not doing any of this because of what your father wants?"

His expression shifts, and this time I can't read it. "Then it's even more dangerous. We aren't anything, tesoro. Three nights together don't make a relationship, not that I'd ever be interested in one."

He lets me go then and walks away into the living room. Not about to let this go, I follow him. "And why not?"

Instead of answering me, he pours himself a glass of whiskey, and stares at it. I smack it out of his hand, causing the glass to shatter against what's left of the fireplace.

"Answer me!"

"I can't love, alright?' He lifts his gaze to mine, eyes narrowed. He takes a deep breath and lets it out in a hiss. "Is that what you want to hear? That losing my mother so shortly after my young brother broke me? That I'll never get that attached to another female again? Well, there you go! You have your damned answer."

I shake my head, and try to touch him but instead he grabs my wrist and pulls me closer. "You're only going to get one thing from me, Monica – a good fuck. Nothing else."

And fool that I am, I lean closer, tilting my face up towards his. I don't have to speak. He reads me like an open book, even as my body hums in delight. And then Lucas drops his mouth to mine, and I forget everything else I'd come here to argue about.

We can be broken together. Surely that's better than a lifetime of loneliness?

Lucas

I wake up to Monica sprawled over me, and no real memory of how that happened. My body remembers, but it's harder for my mind to put things together. Then I realize what woke me, and glance at my phone.

A text from Lucrezia. *Come out for a sec? I just need a quick word.*

Gently, I push Monica off me and watch as she rolls over. Her long, raven hair is messy and spread over the pillows, and her body is practically begging for another round. She looks good in my bed – like she belongs.

Attenzione, Lucas... You're threading into the unknown. Yet not even my internal warning takes away from the satisfaction I – and my wolf – feel chest-deep.

Despite the tightness in my body, and Ileana's words ringing in my ears, I force myself to pull on pants and a shirt and head outside.

Lucrezia is shivering, pacing back and forth in my backyard. I don't see Dominic anywhere, which alone warns me what this is about. "Do you want to come inside?"

She looks up as I speak, and shakes her head. The tip of her nose is red from the cold, and her hands are buried in her parka for heat. "I'll be quick, I promise." A glance over my shoulder to the inside of the house, and she smiles. "I'm glad you two made up."

"Made up?" I realize she must've been who dropped Monica here. "It's not like that."

Lucrezia laughs, then her face sobers up. "Whatever you say. Anyway, umm, the reason I'm here." If there's one thing I always appreciated, it's her frankness. "I think you're not telling us something, and I think... It might've also had something to do with me coming back to life."

I step closer then, pulled in by her words. "What makes you say that?"

"What you did, with the vrykolakas... And what they called you. Lordul morţii. I asked Dominic, and he said it translates to lord of death."

"That doesn't mean anything, though."

"But it does." She jumps from foot to foot, shivering. "I worked it out, too. Tytus gave me the protection of my soul, but what truly stopped my soul from passing was the fact I also had your protection." She bites her lip when I don't say anything. "Can you deny it?"

I throw my head back and look at the night sky. Can I? "No. But I didn't do it on purpose, Lucrezia. What I am, what's in me, it's not... I can't control it."

"Then tell everyone. It's pointless hiding it, and there's obviously something else going on with you. We can help, Lucas."

I sigh. "Did Dominic tell his wolves to finish the job with the Reapers?"

She narrows her eyes on me. "Stop trying to change the subject. But no, he didn't. He's waiting to hear from you, and you've been...busy."

"That's new, him waiting."

Lucrezia clicks her tongue as if I'm a child in need of scolding. The funny thing is, it almost makes me sheepish. Almost. "Fine," I mutter. "I'll think about what you said, I promise. Just tell Dominic I'll see him in the morning, and to gather everyone."

"I will." She steps to hug me, and I watch as she leaves in the darkness.

Can I really tell them everything? And if I don't, how much danger am I putting them in by keeping silent?

Monica

I've never had a wolf leave my bed in the middle of the night to meet another woman. And yet, that's exactly what happens. When I feel Lucas get up, I wait for a beat before pulling on a robe and tip toeing to the living room.

Outside, I see a flash of red hair pacing, and in the faint light from the house I recognize Lucrezia. There must be a good reason for her presence here, but I can't see past my annoyance. Did Lucas have to go meet her, and right after blowing my mind in bed again?

A darker part of me whispers, *Or is this what he means by not being able to do a relationship?*

I lean against the wall, trying to make out what they're talking about, but it's a wasted cause. Lucas' house is sound proofed and I can't catch a single word. What I do see is Lucrezia's expression, and despite knowing she's mated, there's some other emotion in her features.

Gratitude? Do they have a history? And is it any of my business?

No, it's not. And yet that doesn't stop my annoyance from sky-rocketing. By the time Lucrezia goes in for a hug, I'm ready to go out there and rip out a few of those pretty strands.

Even after she's gone, Lucas waits for a few more moments as though dazed, before eventually coming back inside. He's so lost in his own thoughts he doesn't see me right as he walks in, not until I speak.

"What was that about?" I don't do jealous. Never in my life have I felt possessive over a guy. And yet, in that moment, my words are filled with the green little monster, and it pisses me off even more.

Lucas stops in his tracks and tilts his head my way. "What?"

"Why was Lucrezia here?"

His confused expression is replaced by indifference, and he shrugs. "Pack business."

"In the middle of the night?"

"Sì." Now he's frowning at me, and his clenching jaw should be warning enough I'm threading on thin ice. It's not.

"And you don't think that's messed up?"

At my words, Lucas runs a hand over his face and sighs heavily. "Che diavalo... I'm too tired for this shit. Say what you want to say, or drop this and let's go back to bed."

"Fine." I push off the wall and jab a finger in his chest. "You say you want no relationship, yet admit to being devastated when your beta's mate dies. Then that same woman comes to see you in the middle of the night, and you have no problem whatsoever going out there to see her, like a good little puppy. Right after a night of sex with me. Well, I *do* have a problem with it!"

His jaw grows tighter, and I swear his teeth are grinding. "Then it's a good thing I don't have to ask your permission, no?"

My index jabs harder. "You're a jackass, you know that?"

Lucas grabs my wrist, stepping closer to me. "I never promised you flowers and a picket fence, did I? Now either you come back to bed, or don't let the door hit you on the way out. I need sleep, Monica. There's some real shit going down and I'm going to need my wits about me."

No *tesoro,* no sign of regret in his voice. Whatever possessed me to think muddying the waters by sleeping with him was a good idea? *Ovviamente,* it isn't, since he messes with my head. Anyone else, I'd walk out on and not look back. But this guy....

We stare at each other for a long moment, the silence growing. Then Lucas drops his hands, and the fight seems to go out of him. "Come to bed, Monica." He turns and walks away, and despite feeling like he's got the weight of the world on his shoulders, I can't make myself follow.

Am I reading too much into this? Probably. But what does that say of me, other than I've completely lost track of my mission here, and have gone ahead and let this *lupo impossibile* get under my skin? Maybe even deeper than that.

Don't think that. This has nothing to do with your heart.

A ring by the couch draws my attention. My jacket is scattered there, along with Lucas' sweatpants. Our clothes were left in disarray all over from the chaotic sex we just had.

Heart in my throat, I tiptoe closer and pick up my cellphone. "Sì?"

A silence thicker than fog answers me. "I thought you were dead. I said to my men, there is no reason why she would not answer her phone after a few days there, unless she has been found out and she is dead."

"Alessandro –"

"Ana said you've always been reckless, but I told her I trained you well."

I grit my teeth. "You did."

"Then why is it you lean towards disappointing me?"

There is no easy answer, so I keep my silence. It doesn't take long for Alessandro to fill it in.

"Luciano got to you, didn't he?" When I still say nothing, he continues, "I underestimated him. For sure, I told myself, you will have the upper hand over him. I suppose, after all, you are only a woman."

He sighs, and the sound hurts my ears with its fakeness. "Did you find out anything about the girls and wolves in his pack?"

"Nothing interesting," I lie. "They're just mates, is all."

"Ah." He pauses again, and I hear something tinkling as if he dropped ice in a glass. "And I suppose they have no special powers, nothing that Luciano would be...*collecting*...do they?"

My heart drops in my stomach at his words. In the window, I see my reflection, and the paleness of my own skin. "*What*?"

"Monica, Monica, Monica. Bambina, did you really think he's untainted by corruption? Have you forgotten what I told you about his mother? Luciano has half her genes. The chimera in him, the beast he is striving to avoid becoming, it calls to him. And it demands that he creates his own harem of collectable pieces."

"No..." I think back to Dani, Lucrezia and Elle. "He's not like that."

Alessandro chuckles darkly. "That kind of ambition cannot be ignored, cara."

"I...No. That can't be true."

"Ask him, if you dare," he taunts me. "He will be unable to deny it."

I don't want to believe him. After all the crap Alessandro pulled on me, I shouldn't. But, earlier, when I tried to talk to Lucas, he changed the subject. He's not opening up, acting like he's got something to hide. "Why would he do that? What does he gain?"

"Besides power, cara?" He laughs. "Luciano also gains an arsenal of weapons. The chimera in him collects, because it can channel the various gifts and enhance his own power. It really is that simple. And in the end, regardless of what he does, he will put all their lives in danger. Unless...unless he already has."

My sharp intake confirms his fears, as he drops his tone and pretends to sound sad. "Sì, I thought as much. Did someone die?"

"I... No, she is alive. But only because she ended up under a zmeu's protection."

"A zmeu? The Romanian dragons?' The eagerness in his voice makes me realize I've said the wrong thing.

"I have to go before I get found out. I'll reach out later. Ciao."
Hanging up, I'm trembling. I glance towards where Lucas
disappeared, and the trembling increases.

I don't believe what Alessandro says... At least not his
version. But would Lucas even realize what he's doing, if he's
not aware of his full powers? Would he even be able to stop
himself?

Instead of joining him in the bedroom, I open the door to
the outside, shift to my wolf form, and leave in the middle of
the night. Wherever the truth lies, it's not in this house.

To say I feel like shit in the morning is an understatement.
There's no point hiding the dark circles under my eyes, not
even my best makeup can do that. So I pull on whatever I can
and head downstairs, only to run into the human running
the inn.

"Is your car fixed?" she asks me bluntly.

"Almost," I mutter and avoid her gaze, exiting the place in a
hurry. She really doesn't like strangers, I guess.

Rather than go into town, I make my way out towards the
woods. Restless energy fills me, and I know only one thing
will quiet it down. It's time I stop ignoring it and give in to
my blood, to the magic singing in my veins.

After about thirty minutes, I find a spot that'll do the trick. The sun shines through the trees, though they're close enough together to hide my presence from anyone in town.

One more sweep of the surroundings, and I start taking off my clothes one by one, until I'm naked in the forest with only my pentagram pendant. And then I do what I haven't done in forever – I tilt my head back, soaking in the sun's rays and breathing in the freshness of the forest.

My nonna used to take me and Ana to these rituals. Back then, of course, there was a lot more to it. But she always did say if ever I needed guidance, to return to nature like the day I was born and just soak it in. *Magic will do the rest, as will your innate connection to nature. Between the wolf and the stregheria, you are beyond gifted... And the answers you seek will come.*

She was right... Though they're not the ones I want.

Tears start streaming down my cheeks. I hate that I broke the pack's confidence and told Alessandro. I hate that he's not going to let it go. And most of all, I hate Lucas and his damn stupid rationale and closed heart.

And the only reason I'm feeling this much is because I'm freaking falling in love with him. *Merda!*

The snap of a twig in the distance catches my attention, and before anyone comes around I morph to my wolf form. The instinct serves me right, as it's two shaggy wolves that come out of nowhere.

Reapers. They must be, because they don't look anything like Dom's pack. Their growls echo as they advance on me.

Merda, am I on their territory? I didn't even stop to consider the implications before coming up here. But I won't back down, I was raised tougher than this.

Before they can make the first move, I lunge. Only, I'm not alone. A dark wolf joins me, covering my back and attacking the second wolf. By the time we've dealt with both of them and their lifeless bodies and cooling off, I'm staring into blue eyes.

Dominic?

He tilts his head. *What are you playing at, all alone in the woods?*

Forget that! How is it I can connect with you? It shouldn't be possible, I'm not part of your pack.

He shrugs. *Aren't you? Lucas sure spends a lot of time with you since you waltzed in.*

Lucas can go to hell.

I try to move past him, but he blocks my way. *What's going on?*

I don't mean for all of it to come out, but it does, and in the worst way possible. *He's playing all of us, is what! You think everything that's happened is coincidence? It's not! His damn chimera blood is at fault, and the longer you leave him in power, the worse off you'll be.*

Lucas

Annoyed is an understatement for my frame of mind. After Monica's outburst last night, and her disappearance, I didn't sleep much. When I enter Claws Auto – or what's left of it – I'm immediately aware of not being alone.

Tristan's tapping Luz's desk out of sheer boredom, but no one else is around. *Did my message for a pack gathering not get through?* I wait for him to say something, he's ovviamente bursting with it.

"So.... Rumor is it you and Monica are getting it on?"

I scowl at him. "How is that your business, amico?"

Tristan grins. "Are you kidding me? After everything you put us through with your sanctimonious bullshit, it's about time you bite the dust. We all know Ileana meant for us to fall in love, and neither of us is complaining."

"Not me, amico." I move past him, but Tristan follows me all the way to the back.

"Where's your girl?"

"She's not mine." Whispers of *harder*, echoes of her moans in my ear, say the exact contrary. As does my body, tightening at the thought of her.

"You went after her, time and time again. You've been distracted, no longer intent on exterminating the Reapers."

I whirl on him, baring my teeth. "I only went to interrogate her. Away from all of you."

My shout seems to draw in my other wolf, as Finn steps in. His emerald gaze settles on us, and he arches an eyebrow. "What's going on here?"

"Nothing," I mutter and try to walk off. But they're too intent on getting answers, and it's my own stupid fault for being so careless. I grip the edge of my desk, tightening my fingers until it feels like the wood's about to give.

"It's something," Finn says. "First Dominic calls us in the middle of the night, saying to meet here first thing. And now, this. Why are you shutting us out, Lucas?"

"Yeah, why don't you tell them?"

My grip slackens on the desk. *Dominic.* I turn to him, taking in his stormy expression and feeling like real shit is about to go down now. "Tell them what, *amico?*"

"I figured it out, you know." There's a new steely quality to his gaze. Is everyone around me losing their minds? Before I can say anything, Dominic scowls. "You've been doing this on purpose. All this shit about being a pack, protecting us... When in fact, you're collecting us."

A beat of silence follows his revelation.

"Scusi, but what?" I glance at my other two wolves, each with mirrored expressions of confusion. At least until Dominic starts explaining.

"You're half-wolf, half-chimera. A chimera is able to soak in the gifts of those reporting to it, of channeling them. That is why their packs were sought in the past, and that's exactly why you went to build your own."

"How did you find out?"

"You don't deny it, then?" Dominic takes another stop. "So that's what you do. Running away from your daddy, only so you can find another way to fight him through others. Same as you've been using *my* wolves to fight *your* battle with the Reapers." He clenches his fists, looking like he's about to lose it. "I don't know if you ever planned to use us and the girls against your father, but you can forget that shit."

"I have no clue what you're talking about."

Dominic crosses his arms over his chest. "Really? Monica told me everything. Including that your father kicked you out of your old pack because you killed your brother."

A haze of red descends on me at that. My body starts trembling with it, despite all my efforts to contain it. "*What* did you just say?"

"There's no point in lying, Lucas."

I'm on him in the next breath, my fist colliding with his jaw with enough force to reverberate in my arm. Dominic stumbles back, then catches himself. "That's what I thought. Come at me with brutal force to shut me up, yeah? Same as you used my vrykolakas to clean up town."

"You've fucking lost it!" Then we're grappling, fighting, tossing each other into shit and trying to inflict as much pain as possible. What's left of my office goes to pieces, and still it doesn't satisfy our desire for mutual destruction.

Finn and Tristan jump in the fray, both to restrain me. They have a hard time, on account of the red haze pushing me, dictating what I'm doing. My body shakes, my torso enlarges, and my hands get covered in coarser, red hair.

I shake them off easily, and they slam into a wall. My promise to Finn, my good intent of pack consensus – it's all forgotten in my rage.

In a deeper voice than before, I grip Dominic by his throat. "You've crossed me for the last time. You are hereby banned from this pack, Dominic Kosta, and exiled from this town. You have twenty-four hours to get out, otherwise I will hunt you down and kill you."

Then I toss him to the ground. Holding onto his throat, Dominic looks past me to Finn and Tristan. "Watch your backs, and your mates. Lucas will bring down the entire wrath of the lupi mannari on you, and nothing will protect you while you're bound to him."

Angrily, he gets up and stalks out. After a few deep breaths, I calm down enough to revert the change – whatever the fuck that was. Once I see my hands are normal, I turn to my two other wolves.

Finn's green gaze is filled with worry, even as Tristan asks, "You alright, chefe?"

"Yeah." I go to move past them, but Finn stops me.

"You promised this time, it would be a unanimous decision."

I stare him down, and whatever he sees in my expression it's enough to make him drop his hand, and bow his head. "Alright, mate, have it your way. One more question, though. Is any of what Dominic said true?"

Part of me wants to deny it, but something about Dominic's certainty and rage makes me believe there is a grain of truth in there. Only, I'm not the one collecting. It's my father. And if Monica told him...

"I don't know," I say instead. "I don't fucking know anymore."

Then I head to the back, though I don't plan to stick around. The minute I'm sure they're not following me, I head out to find the cunning minx. She's got some answering to do.

∞ ∞ ∞

CHAPTER SEVEN

∞ Testardo ∞

"Stubborn and ardent clinging to one's opinion is the best proof of stupidity."

-Michel de Montaigne-

Monica

After Dominic leaves, I curse my impulsive side. Something tells me this'll come back and bite me in the culo, but it's not until a few hours later that I realize just how badly I screwed up.

By that point, I'm in a dingy bar on the far side of town, luckily with scarce customers around. The club sandwich in front of me remains untouched, and the coffee has long since gone cold.

It starts with my cell ringing, and Alessandro's voice sounding way too satisfied for my liking. "I wanted to praise you on a job well done, cara." Unlike when Lucas says it, the word makes me nauseous.

"Which part, exactly?"

"Why, the information you provided. Your hunch was right, and Rockland Creek is a pool of specimens I simply need to see up close. I will send a team shortly, have no fear. Your work there is done."

Panic seizes me. "Wait, I –"

"You have done well, but let the professionals take over now."

"But why, Alessandro? And what about Luciano?"

"They can pick him up while they're there, too."

My pulse races. I know that tone, that determination to get his way. "Luciano won't go down easily."

"He is no match for my men."

I think back to the previous nights, to what I've seen. "You don't know that."

"Do not fret. You can return home, and I will release you properly from your bonds to me." He pauses. "Unless there is something else holding you there?"

I don't answer, and the silence lengthens.

"I did not think so. Bene." He hangs up before I can further protest, and I gape at my phone. My breathing increases to the point of hyperventilating as the full impact of what I've done descends on me.

Shit. Shit. Shit.

"Merda!"

As if that's not enough, Lucas strides in at that moment, all dark features and blazing eyes. He grabs me by the arm and yanks me away, stumbling on my heels, until we're in a corner of the bar.

After he places himself in front of me to shield us from anyone watching, he scowls. The fierceness in that gaze has me shiver even more. If he finds out what else I did...

"What the fuck did you tell Dominic? What's this about chimeras and collecting?" His grip on me tightens. "And why the fuck would you believe I killed my own brother?"

Out of everything he says, that last part gets to me. "Because... Didn't you?"

Lucas slams his palm on the wall, and I jump. It wasn't meant to intimidate me, it's almost like he's filled with an energy he can barely control. As I watch him, his biceps tense, the veins almost popping out, and he focuses on a point above my head, swallowing convulsively.

Then his grip on my elbow relaxes, and he sticks to caging me in. "No," he finally says. "I didn't."

"I don't... What happened, then? Alessandro says –"

One hand drops to my mouth, touching my lips with his index. Lucas' gaze lingers there for a moment, before meeting mine. "Don't. Say. His. Name. Not right now, when I'm having a hard enough time to holding myself together."

He drops his hand, resuming caging me in. "As for what happened, it's simple. My father dragged Matteo to a deal that went south. He was young, impressionable, wanted to please him. Despite my better efforts, he was shot that night, and didn't survive."

His tone is cold, emotionless, as if he's relating the story of someone else's life. I can't help myself, and I reach out for his cheek. He jumps as if not expecting the movement, and I whisper, "I'm sorry. I should've known Alessandro lied about that."

"And I wish you'd have asked me before spreading false information to my pack, but it's too late. I cannot undo what I did."

"What..." Panic seizes me. "And what is that, Lucas?"

His eyes narrow on me. "I kicked Dominic out of the pack. He was out of control after what you told me, and so was I. Things escalated...fast."

I look down, unable to hold his gaze anymore. "Is he okay?"

Lucas snorts. "Now you care about him, after last night you accused me of getting it on with Lucrezia?"

There's nothing I can say to that, so I don't. The silence lengthens. Someone leaves the bar. I have a feeling besides the bartender who's in the kitchen, we're all alone now. The awareness raises tingles up my spine, and not in a scary way.

"Monica..." Lucas groans. In a gesture completely unlike himself, he drops his head next to mine, letting our foreheads touch for the barest of moments. Then he straightens up, determination in every hard angle of his features. "Stop side-tracking me. Why did you tell Dominic I'm collecting them? What's all this about the chimera?"

The confusion under the anger is what gets me. "Did your father never tell you?"

"Tell me what, cara? I'm running out of patience with your riddles and games."

"It's not a damn game!"

He leans closer to me then. "Then fucking tell me."

I take in a large gulp of air, and try to explain what I've already told Dominic. "Your mother, Francesca..."

He lifts a hand, and I flinch. The gesture has him pause, eyes narrowed. "What else have you suffered at my father's hands?"

I look away, unwilling to tell him of the punishments I've faced. Or those I'll face if I come clean with him. But Lucas doesn't let go. He touches my chin to raise it, and the blaze is gone out of his eyes, replaced by something almost...tender.

"Monica, I would never hit you. If nothing else, you must know I'm not my father." And just like that, his previous annoyance with me is gone. Frozen, fighting wave after wave of emotions, I try to hold myself together. Lucas makes it even harder. "Tesoro... Why are you trembling?"

That does it, and the waterworks begin. Out of all his mercurial moods, it had to be him crossing into tenderness that breaks the dam and causes me to lose it. Guilt chokes me up over what I did, over everything I've ruined since coming here – and everything that *will* be ruined once Alessandro's soldiers come running.

Lucas holds me while I dirty his shirt, then I pull back and try to clean the mess of mascara, tears and snot on my face. He gives no indication that I'm hideous, instead only watching me with a pensive look.

When I've finally calmed enough, I say, "Okay, here's the deal. Your dad married Francesca not for love, but because he bought her. I know all this because my grandmother was in your pack at the time... She sent me away once my parents died to protect me, but I've never known another family. So when Alessandro's men came to recruit for stregheria learning, I volunteered and ended up under Alessandro's thumb anyway."

Another gulp of air, then I continue. "Luckily, only his thumb, and not his bed. My cousin Ana was less lucky. But he's a demanding master, and he loves special shifters. Like your mom, like you...like me."

Lucas' eyes narrow on my pentagram necklace, then his expression clears. "Your magic, you mean?"

I shouldn't be surprised how much he picked up on. If not him, his wolves probably filled him in from what I told the girls.

"And a bit more... I sense things. Like how I sensed your pack was mated, and how I knew you were more than just, well, you. Anyway. Point is, Alessandro loves collecting. That is what he was building with your mother. A chimera in a pack acts like a conduit. If used properly, it can be the most powerful tool. But it needs nourishment, and that's where the special shifters come in. Your father sought far and wide, but by the time he gathered them Francesca saw past his crap, and wasn't willing to put her soul in jeopardy to open the Underworld. Because once a chimera accumulates all the gifts, takes enough souls..."

"The conduit of them all will open the Underworld, and thus a path to the river of eternal life." Lucas finishes the sentence for me. "I've known since before she died, it was why I was careful until recently with the lives I took. Now, it doesn't matter." His gaze narrows on me again. "Why did you not tell me all this upfront? Why go behind my back, to Dominic of all people?"

Tears fill my eyes again. "It wasn't on purpose. He caught me when some Reapers were coming by to attack me, and I was mad at you."

He looks me up and down. "Were you hurt?"

"No," I whisper.

"I still don't understand how you thought I, of all people, was collecting those around me."

I look up at him then. "You really can't see it from where I'm standing?"

Lucas shakes his head, and lifts a hand to pinch the bridge of his nose. "I am tired, Monica. So fucking tired of all these games. Is anything real anymore?"

I scoff. "You ask me that? You, who runs away from everything?"

His eyes blaze. "Careful, tesoro. You don't want to cross me when I'm barely holding on." His threat is pretty much negated by his earlier words and the promise he'd never hurt me.

As if realizing as much, he sighs and tries another tactic. "How did my father get into this? How did he even know…?"

I shrug. "Best I can guess, is greed. He doesn't want to die and face what's waiting for him."

"I always used to think he wanted a quick out, something over his enemies. A chimera would be useful in keeping their souls and getting rid of the bodies easily. But you're saying my father was doing all this because of his stupid fear of death?"

"Sì, he was." I chew on my bottom lip for a moment, two, then add, "That's also why he wants you, I'm pretty sure. He knows you've killed, he knows your link to death is strong being only half-blooded. You wouldn't be able to morph into the full monster, at least not according to the legends, but Alessandro wants whatever you can give him."

Lucas shakes his head, then runs a hand over his features. "Madre di Dio! He has lost his damned mind."

I nod, taking an interest in the floor again.

"Thank you," Lucas adds. 'You didn't have to tell Dominic all this and make my life worse, but I can understand why you believed what you did. However, I am not my father."

"I know." And then the tears come again.

Lucas inches closer, wiping them away with one callused thumb. "Shh, don't cry, tesoro. I'm not mad anymore."

"But you will be when I tell you this..." I take a deep breath, look him in the eyes, and say, "Your father knows about your pack, and their gifts, from me. I didn't realize... It doesn't matter. There is no excuse. Bottom line is, you're all in danger because of me."

His hand freezes midair, then drops. "How long do I have?"

"I... I'm not sure."

Rage flashes in those onyx eyes again, followed by betrayal and cold indifference. "I see," he says. After one last look at me, he takes off.

Lucas

For the first time, real fear freezes my heart. I never intended for my wolves to suffer, for their mates to suffer. But if what Monica told me is true, if my powers extend that much, this is going to be hell. And my father will not let go, not until he has his collection.

I have to stop him.

I can't get to the shop fast enough, and at first I'm completely in my own mind, missing the obvious. Then I notice Dominic's truck out front, and the fear in me morphs to something else. Something darker.

Especially when I realize he's not alone, but he's there with Finn and Tristan, and the girls. Even when I made it clear he's banned, and meant to be exiled, he still goes behind my back.

Whatever the fuck they think they're doing, it's not going to work. Not with this wolf. I burst into the shop, letting the door slam hard enough behind me that the windows rattle.

Lucrezia looks up from the receptionist spot and her eyes widen. "Lucas! You're not supposed to—"

A growl tears from my throat as I jab a finger her way. "Not another fucking word, cara. Where are they?"

She bites her lip, then her eyes slide to the corridor leading to my office. Another blaze of red descends on me as I push past her. "If you know what's good for you, you'll stay back. Your sweet talking won't save him now."

I'm already halfway to my office by then, but her boots behind me warn she followed. No matter. Voices escape the small room, Tristan first.

"Maybe it's some kind of post-traumatic stress disorder. When I get in my moods, nothing can get through to me."

"It's not PTSD," Dominic contradicts, and my anger spikes up a notch.

Nostrils flaring, I burst in. "What the fuck do you think you're doing, amico?"

Unlike what I pictured, he's not sitting in my chair or near my desk. Not trying to take over my pack and oust me. On the contrary, he's the closest to the door. It should make me think twice, but it doesn't.

"Did I not kick you out of this pack?"

Dominic only stares me down. "You did. And yet I'm still here, because they called me."

I glance at Tristan and Finn for confirmation, and their shrugs tell me everything I need to know. One step, two, then I'm shoving him.

Dominic stumbles, but catches himself and glares at me. "What's your problem?"

"My problem is that you're meddling – again. And I warned you last time what would happen."

Finn moves from the back, hands held up. "It's not what you think, mate. We're worried about you. This isn't some kind of feckin' conspiracy!"

"Claro," I mutter. "Because it's all so simple."

"It is," Tristan says softly. "I know better than most what hallucinations are like, chefe. But we swore allegiance to you. What reason do we have to break it?"

"There is always a reason," I growl. I've known these men for ages, but it's like I can't see straight anymore. My wolf, so connected to them before, is drowned under this rage that's boiling inside me.

Nostrils flaring, it's all I can do to hold it in.

"It's happening again," Dominic says as if I'm not there. "The eyes."

"Maybe it's some kind of berserker rage?" Finn asks.

"*Basta!* Stop talking as if I'm not here!" I punctuate my shouts with another shove, which this time slams Dominic into the wall. He seems shocked at my strength – and for good reason. Normally his vârcolac is stronger, even as a human.

"Lucas–" Lucrezia starts behind me. It's a soft whisper, but my ears perk nonetheless.

I don't know why her voice always makes me listen. Maybe because she's the first female I cared for after Mamma.

Regardless, this time it's barely enough to pull me from the brink.

"Tristan is right. Please."

My gaze locks with each of my wolves. Blue, brown and green, they stare at me without blinking, not hiding anything. Are they really that concerned? Is that all that's going on here?

Finn moves closer and touches my shoulder. Just like that, my anger abates, enough that I can breathe deeply. "Now will you listen?" he asks.

"You shouldn't be using your powers on me," I say, but follow it with a nod, and a deep breath. Then I run a hand over my face and stumble to my desk, dropping heavily into my chair.

"Can we please talk like adults?" Lucrezia asks, glaring at everyone in turn. "I've known you guys for long enough to realize this isn't normal. And I don't care how much the dynamic here has changed, or the fact you kicked Dominic out of the pack again." She takes a step forward. "We're still family."

I can't look at them, not now that my rage is gone. Everything feels so far, so...*bizarro*. Why have I been acting like this? Did Monica get into my head this much? Is it Ileana's games?

Someone clears their throat, and I look up. It's then I realize we're missing a few members. "Where are your mates?" I ask Finn and Tristan.

"Out," Tristan says.

Finn's answer is different. "They're together," he says slowly, weighing his answer as if catching the undertone of my quesiton. "What is it you're afraid of?"

I roll my eyes at that. "I'd really love it if you learned to keep your sniffing to yourself, Irish." His shrug doesn't help, but I add, "Just call them. Tell them to get here instead."

As Tristan makes the call, Dominic paces the room from wall to wall. He knows something's up. Despite being kicked out – twice – and being a pain in my ass, something tells me he knows more than he's letting on.

"Can we start with some basics, at least? It feels like it's been go, go, go since Monica came into town. What should we even call you?" Lucrezia asks. "Monica said your real name is Luciano Conti."

"My old name." I nod. "Lucas is what I go by now."

"Why?" I really do miss the days she was shy around me.

"My old life... it's complicated."

"So why don't you tell us?" Dani walks in then, Elle on her heels.

I turn to Finn and he shrugs. "They were getting bored and wanted some action. Dani's teaching Elle what she can about zmeu magic."

Another thing that escaped me. I really should be paying more attention. Finally, I sigh and for the first time in my life, don't hold back and tell them everything. "I was born into a hybrid family, one could say. My father is a lupo mannaro, and my mother was the last of her kind – a chimera."

"Like in Greek mythology?" Elisandra asks.

"Yeah, what gives?" Tristan adds. "I thought you were Italian."

A deeper sigh escapes me. "I guess I'll have to go back even deeper, then. My mother's family comes from an Italian region known as Tuscany. That's where, ages ago, the Etruscans lived. You wouldn't know much about them unless you're a scholar, but they were a people who didn't leave behind a lot. A lot of their culture was later assimilated into Rome and Greece itself."

Noticing I have a rapt attention before me, I lean my head back against my chair and lose myself in the story. "Some people say the first account of a chimera was among the Etruscans. Maybe, maybe not. Either way, their culture worshipped many gods, and my mother, Francesca, grew up with those teachings. She then passed them to me. It was always about what the gods want, what's expected, how life was out of our control. Needless to say, I didn't particularly buy into the whole thing."

Memories of those lessons with her run through my mind. She loved to make me draw, because I was horrible at it.

Alessandro hated hearing our laughter in the nursery, it always sent him in a rage.

"History lesson aside, I took after my father. Or so I thought, at first, until I learned differently. I also had a younger brother, Matteo, who didn't buy into the whole Etruscan way of life, either." My throat clogs at the memory of him, but I force myself to continue. "Probably because of our wolf's innate capacity for fights, for control. See, a lupo mannaro is prone to violence. Battles, turf wars, they egg our wolf on and we live off that. It makes us perfect for less savory occupations like drugs, cartels...the Mafia."

"Your family," Dominic says, finally moving closer. "They're Mafia?"

"Sì," I nod. "My father, anyway. My mother hated the life, and my brother...he's no more."

Everyone falls silent, until Finn breaks it. "I'm struggling to understand, mate. You say turf wars get your blood boiling, yet you've always avoided them with the Reapers."

"I did. Because I found out about my mother's lineage, and the price associated with it. I said before how I thought I took after my father... And for a few years, I did. My wolf relished the violence, to some extent. But then, I started having nightmares. With each death I helped him, I dreamt of the Underworld. Of being chained there. And one day, I accidentally stumbled onto my mother confessing to a local priest."

The memory of that day hits me with a bittersweet pang. Everything changed, after that. "She was worried about me, about what I was doing, the road I was heading on. That's when I learned the full extent of it... That's when nightmares became reality for me – the day everything fully sank in."

"But you had already killed," Lucrezia says softly.

"Sì." A scornful laugh escapes me. "And the funny part? My father knew all about it. See, there is not really such a thing as a half-chimera in a male heir. The male pretty much inherits the whole trait, but doesn't grow into it until his twenty-fifth birthday. He can't morph fully, as I learned recently from Monica, but he does develop other abilities."

"Like collecting special shifters?" Tristan asks.

"Not on purpose," I mutter. "I had no idea it was happening when you all showed up here, one by one. All I knew was the need to dominate, then I had a pack. Something to call my own, and that really felt like family."

They stare at me, and no one says anything. Then Lucrezia asks, "What happens if the chimera doesn't, umm, grow into it? Say, he was suppressing it."

I throw her a look. "Molto perceptiva, cara. Yes, I have been suppressing everything because I don't want to be some legendary monster." Glancing at my fists, I clench and unclench them a few times. "I only want my wolf, nothing else. But if the male represses his chimera side, yet still allows himself to be exposed to a lot of violence, and death... With each soul taken, the chimera's link to the Underworld grows stronger. Then it gets greedy, overpowers the wolf, and demands to take over."

It's harder than I thought, this sharing thing, but I owe it to them. After all this time, I owe the full truth. The only thing is, how much longer do I have left to put everything right?

"Eventually, the theory goes that with enough killing, the male loses himself to the chimera and becomes a slave to the Underworld. Opens the door to it, is able to get souls in and out, the like."

"For the sake of clarifying... We're talking Hades' Underworld, here?" Lucrezia asks.

"The one and only." When that sinks in, I add, "I tried to fight it. To hold off. My father kept pushing me into a life I didn't want, and started dragging Matteo into it. One night...everything went desperately wrong. I was too late, Matteo died in my arms, and I felt for the first time the chimera's pull. That same night, my mother committed suicide and I buried her...before leaving forever. I thought I was done with all that...until my father sent Monica after me."

When I'm done, the tension is tangible. A humorless chuckle escapes me. "Now do you see why I said it's complicated?"

Lucrezia mutters something about stubborn wolves her breath, then comes to my side and hugs me. It takes me by surprise, and I return it while checking on Dominic over her shoulder. I half expect him to snap again, but he makes no move to stop her. Instead, he catches my eye and I read the sympathy he's wordlessly communicating.

"And what is Monica to your father?" he asks. "How does she know so much, and what the hell is it with the collecting part?"

"She's his fixer," I say. "I thought I could turn her to our side, but as I found out today, I've only delayed the inevitable. Mi dispiace, but I owe a big apology to all of you. For being a fool and putting you all in danger. But now my father knows you are my pack, and he will not stop until he finds and captures us all."

A noise at the front startles us. Slipping from Lucrezia's arms, I give chase only to see a fleeting glimpse of dark hair exit the door. Without pausing, I burst into the garage and exit through the half-open door, catching Monica at the next corner.

"What were you doing here?"

Her features are expressionless, but for a brief moment I notice a flash of fear. My grip on her tightens. Finally, she gulps and says, "Looking for you. I didn't like the way we left things, and I really want to fix–"

"Yeah? Sure you weren't spying for my father?" Her eyes widen, panic now clearly evident.

"I... You...?"

I scoff, trying to push aside my own feelings. There is no room for emotions in this mess. "You're wasting your time if you think your good girl act is going to fool me. The only reason I fucked you was to get in on what you're telling dear old papà. Now that I know, I have no further use of you."

Sharp pain flashes across her features, followed by a hurt too real to fake. A pang of something – guilt – crosses through me, but I shove it down.

Instead, I let go of her and place my hands on either side of her head. She looks away, but my face inches closer. "You can't really believe any of that was real. But, you can go back to Alessandro and tell him all about it."

She scowls then and her eyes shift behind me. "Tell him yourself."

∞ ∞ ∞

CHAPTER EIGHT

∞ Sopravvivere ∞

"To <u>survive</u> it is often necessary to fight and to fight you have to dirty yourself."

-George Orwell-

Lucas

I turn away from Monica and the temptation to strangle her. A black SUV with tinted windows is pulling up near my shop, followed by another one. Understanding rushes through me when I catch sight of the eight bulky men who exit. Hair cropped, black outfits, massive guns strapped to their backs, they scream military but I know they're also something else – wolves.

"Merda, he wasn't kidding!" Monica mutters under her breath.

I catch her wrist in mine without taking my eyes off the men. There's no point asking who the *he* is. "Kidding about what, cara?"

"Sending a squad for you, and your pack."

That does it. As quietly as I can, I push us fully around the corner and flatten her against the cold brick. My hold on her wrist tightens in tune with my fury. "Thanks to the information you gave him."

Monica stares back at me, a fire in her eyes. "Sì, I guess so. But at least I never pretended to be someone I'm not."

"Didn't you? What about all this bullshit of a relationship, and caring about me? What about getting involved with my pack, when all he really sent you here for is to attract my eye?"

She inhales sharply, but the movement only makes her breasts push up against my chest. Distraction is the mother of all stupidities, and because I'm a fool, I only lean closer until our lips almost brush.

"You could have walked away. Left me to deal with all this shit. So why the fuck are you still here, Monica?"

Her lips part, blue eyes wide and vulnerable. The noise of feet on the ground – more wolves – should worry me. Should draw my wolf out. Yet he's too entranced by the woman in my arms, almost stupidly so. Whatever spell she cast on me, it must've been a fucking good one if I can't think straight.

With an annoyed growl, I stop resisting the pull and crush my mouth to hers, stealing a kiss she has no intention of surrendering – yet I do it anyway. Monica pushes against me feebly with her other hand for the barest of seconds. Then she gives in, grabbing a handful of my shirt and pulling me closer.

Moments pass and I could've owned her mouth – and her body – right then and there. But the Italian commands I hear whispered are enough to finally make me snap out of it.

"See what I mean?" she mutters and looks away. Her lips are swollen, her eyes glassy, and there's a blush in her cheeks hinting at other activities. Something in me wants – needs – to give in to that.

What the fuck, Lucas? I mentally smack myself.

I have no time to argue with her, not when the wolves are taking stock of the situation, and already heading to surround the place. Pulling my cell out of my back pocket, I dial Finn. "Get everyone out of there. My father's goons came for us."

He shouts in the background, then he's back on, panicked. "I need to get Elle."

"What do you mean, get Elle? She was right there!" Monica makes a move as if to head to the bakery, and I grab her wrist again, pulling her against me. "Don't move."

"She forgot something at the bakery and went to get it," Finn hisses in my other ear.

I check around the corner, noticing the men spreading out. "Fine. Where's Dominic?"

"Went to pull his vrykolakas back from the Reapers' execution."

There's no time to get annoyed over that. "Amico, listen to me. There is no time. Go get your girl. Leave Tristan and Daniela to protect Lucrezia. And, Finn?"

"Yeah?"

I scowl when one of the wolves meets my gaze. "Call Dominic. Tell him to bring reinforcements."

A stunned silence answers me, then Finn says, "You got it, mate. What about you?"

"I'll be fine." Hanging up, I don't let go of Monica. Instead, I lean over her again. "Now, you've got a choice. Either you fight with me, or go join them and head back under Alessandro's thumb. What will it be?"

She peers around the corner, before her gaze slowly drags to mine. "I'm with you. I never meant to drag Elle and the rest of them into this."

"I believe you." And for that part, I do. The rest of the betrayal? I don't have time to process it.

The wolves are heading towards us, and I step back from Monica. "Let's split. Run them amuck to give everyone a chance to escape, then meet back here."

She nods, and turns away to morph. My intention to walk away is shattered by the beauty of her transformation. A ripple runs through her, then her entire being is enveloped in a faint light, and her human form bends, contorts, until it's replaced by the primitive one.

Monica's wolf is as sexy as she is, lean and with the same blue eyes staring back at me. What stuns me is the C with a crown burned into her chest. My father's mark, one I've seen on his wolves before. On her, it stirs my dark side again. I thought I'd felt rage before – but the utter red haze that descends on me in that moment consumes me.

I don't even realize I'm shifting, my wolf's transformation triggered by her own. Within moments, I'm on four paws instead of two feet. I feel clumsier – bigger – and a swift check down to my paws confirms they're twice my regular size. Has my wolf automatically enhanced itself, in an effort to protect her?

Are you okay?

My eyes find Monica's in surprise. *How can you link with me?*

I'm not sure. The same happened with Dominic earlier.

Lupi mannari cannot do so unless it's with their alpha.

She tosses her head back and snorts in a very Monica-like movement. *You wish.*

Before I can argue more, a piece of brick bursts right next to my muzzle and I jump to the side. Turns out I'd narrowly avoided a very badly aimed gunshot. I scan the surroundings, noticing I stupidly gave these bozos enough time to fan out and set the stage.

The only lucky bit? No humans around. That, and the fact I know these grounds like the back of my hand. *Andiamo!*

When arrows of tranquilizers start shooting around me, I move. Bulk or no bulk, I need to give my pack time to escape. And since I was their original prize, chances are these *cretini* will make me a priority.

Two of the wolves rush after me, and the rest head for the shop. Monica disappears around the corner, and when they don't follow her I'm left wondering if she played me – again. Just as I'm about to head back and pull the others' attention, a howl resounds from above. My gaze moves there, to find Monica perched atop. When she has the men's attention, she strikes the already precarious roof and a bunch of damaged bricks fall. Enough to cause some injuries, if the cries I hear are anything to go by.

The last I see of her, she jumps on top of them, her lean form intertwined with their black getup. That need to turn back and help her runs through me again. It's an impulse I haven't felt in a while, one of protection – of family.

My wolf.

All he's ever craved is blood, power and violence. Then the need inside me grew louder than his own voice, and he was shackled by my own inaction. Now, no longer shuttered by the anger inside me, and this otherness that's been growing and developing, he bares his canines and demands I return to Monica.

It takes everything in me to fight him off. *Later.*

It's like arguing with a strong wind. Each step forward, he tries to drag me back. Each leap onwards, he forces a retreat. Enough so that the two wolves catch up to me, one in human form, the other animal.

I duck the lunge from the animal and instead rise to meet the human with the tranquilizer gun pointed at me. He fires off a shot that goes in my flank. I should feel something, anything. But it barely registers as I clamp my jaws on his arm and rip it off.

Blood gushes everywhere, and I leave him to his demise, turning to the wolf. He seems less than a third my size, so when I lift my paw and smack him, he lands head-first against the wall of a building.

I want to finish him off, but my wolf is already moving us back to the shop, and towards Monica. Howls in the distance catch my attention, and I see Dominic's black fur as he's flanked by a few of his vrykolakas. Their stench is enough to turn my stomach, but I'm oddly relieved to have him around.

Even if he's only here to get Lucrezia to safety.

My thoughts are confirmed when his wolves leave him, and surround the redhead of our pack like they're willing to lay down their lives for her. Which, they probably are.

This time though, it's not Lucrezia I'm worried about.

Monica

Merda! I knew one day my impulsivity would get me killed, but even so...

Once Dominic's vrykolakas join the fray, I move away from the battle to assess. That's how I'm first to notice Finn heading on his own, his pace fast, even while Tristan and Daniela join the fight with Lucrezia.

I know where he's heading thanks to Lucas' call – Elle. And since it's my own damn fault she's in danger, I can't just stand by and do nothing. So, I follow Finn. Something tells me he knows I'm there, but he still allows me to continue pretending.

We reach the bakery in time to see Elle being dragged out by another two wolves. *There was a third car.* Rather than taking my cue and making a run for it, that's where my impulsivity kicks in.

Lucas was right, in a way. I did pretend. But I won't anymore. Because who I am has nothing to do with Alessandro Conti's pack, nor with my own indoctrination. Who I am is loyal to a fault – whether to a villain intent on collecting, or to a man who's undeserving of my love. And that...is a problem for another day.

Instead of hanging back, I lunge in the midst of Alessandro's men, digging my canines into one's thighs, even as Finn faces off against the other one. You wouldn't think it with his lean bulk, but his punch cracks the guy's jaw and sends him flying backwards.

Finn grabs Elle under his arm then, pausing only enough to kiss her temple and murmur, "You alright, love?"

She nods, hanging onto his chest with hands that are white-knuckled. "What's going on?"

"That's what I'd like to know." His stare is heavy on me, accusing, and I glance away. That's when I see them – two snipers on the rooftop.

I jump in front of Finn and Elle just as they fire a shot – tranquilizer or not, I couldn't take the chance. It hits me instead, and it's not a harmless dart. The bullet clears my flank and I howl in pain, dropping to the ground and becoming the perfect target.

Even as the guy aims again, a massive shadow drops in front of me. My vision is filled with rusty fur, dotted with specks of grey, charcoal and black.

Lucas?

His growl reverberates in the air, and then he smacks his paws on the pavement and the entire ground shakes, taking the building with it. Since the sniper is positioned right at the edge, he goes off flying to the side and drops like a pancake. The sound of his body hitting cement, of the bones breaking and the flesh tearing, turns my guts.

Lucas then whirls to us. "It's over. We got the bulk of them, and Dominic's vrykolakas are finishing them off."

How... How can you speak?

He spares me a glance I can't read, then focuses on Finn. "Grab Elle and follow us."

To my utter surprise, Lucas drops his muzzle to me and picks me up by the neck, carrying me like a mama wolf does her cubs. We all return to the shop, and I can see now why it's a good thing there aren't any humans around anymore.

The minute we're by the entrance door, Lucas drops me. I allow the change to come over me, leaving me trembling and naked. Daniela moves and lifts her index in the air. One drawn rune returns my clothes, while the other she places on my thigh. The blood stops flowing so freely, and some of the pain goes away.

"This works way faster than my herbs," I whisper. "Thank you."

She smiles at me like I'm part of the family, but I can't bear to see that kindness that'll soon turn into hate. So I refuse to look at her, and instead limp to lean on the door while the rest of them pair off.

"What the fuck's going on, Lucas?" Surprisingly, the outburst is from Tristan.

Dominic's on the other side of the street, holding Lucrezia tight against him, still surrounded by his wolves. Bodies litter the street between us like the set of a horror show. His gaze is steady on us, and I can see the wheels turning at the back of his head.

I'm bewildered at the purposeful distance for a second, before I remember Lucas admitting he banished him from the pack. And yet the extent of their bond is such that Dominic is still here helping out... Shame runs through me, hot and heavy.

"It's my fault," I whisper, eyes still on the ground.

Dani's kind expression slips, replaced by confusion. Tristan reaches for her and moves her away from me, and I can't blame him. He's protecting what is his, as they all are. They had a good thing going before I showed up and messed it all up.

"No," Lucas says. "The fault is my father's. And he needs to pay for his past and present sins, once and for all."

Tristan stares at me, then at Finn. "What do you make of it, meu amigo?"

Finn shrugs. "She protected us, but..."

"But what?"

"She's been lying from the beginning."

I keep my head bowed. "It's true."

"Shut up," Lucas says, angling his body almost as if to stop my words from escaping. "This doesn't concern them."

I straighten then, raising my chin. "Let me own up to my mistakes." When he says nothing, I push past him. "You're right, Finn. I did come here under false pretenses, and I lied. Not because I wanted to hurt any of you, please believe me."

"So, which part is truth?" Lucrezia asks.

Meeting her eyes across the distance, I only read wariness and suspicion. It doesn't stop the truth from tumbling past my lips, hoping she'll understand. "I did come here for Lucas, and I was sent by his father. But not because Alessandro misses him. More because he wants him back to take over the family business, and to use him and his chimera gift."

Pushing past the lump in my throat, I clench my fists.

"This is your fault," Tristan says to Lucas. "You had to think with your dick and put us all in danger!"

"Who was it telling me some sex would loosen me up?" Lucas scowls.

"Not when it's a danger to everyone else!"

"As if you didn't do the same?" Lucas marches on him, and I grab the edge of his shirt in time to hold him back. It's a small gesture, but it seems to cool him off some. At least, I hope so. Because unless it's my imagination, his body is getting...bigger.

I gulp and whisper, "Lucas, va bene. He's right. What I did was despicable."

"Shut up," he tosses over a shoulder. "For once, just shut *up*, Monica." Turning to Tristan and Finn, he glares at them, then extends that to Dominic. "You all put this pack in danger at some point or another. What's the difference?"

"The difference," Dominic says, "is that we did it for love, not a quick roll in the hay."

Lucas lunges then, but Finn steps between them. His hand on Lucas' chest seems to calm him, and I remember what the girls told me about his gift. Seeing it in action is...different. Like the entire fight is drawn out of the situation via one simple touch.

"Enough already!" Lucrezia tugs on Dominic, trying to pull him back, too.

Finn is pensive, staring at us. Then something flashes in his eyes, and he nods to himself. "There is a simple solution."

"Don't," Lucas warns.

He speaks anyway. I guess these guys really love honesty. "You don't want to hear it, but it's nothing less than what you've told each of us at one point or another. Return Monica to your father, let her pay for her mistakes. And let's leave here. You disappeared once, you can do it again."

"Absolutely – fucking – not." I've never heard that amount of rage in Lucas' voice, not even when I told him what I did. And unless I'm mistaken, his body has started shaking.

Finn shrugs, as if he doesn't notice it. But something about his demeanor tells me he did – that he's doing this on purpose. "Mate, you said it yourself. She's nothing to you, right? So, let her pay. Monica's punishment will be the distraction we need to escape your wanker of a father and get out."

Even I can't deny the logic, though it hurts that after all I've done to save Elle he'd turn on me like that. Elle herself is tugging on his hand, whispering furiously, but Finn won't be moved.

Features cold, he steps around Lucas and towards me, gently pushing Elle away. And that's when Lucas loses it.

"Do *not* touch Monica if you value your life."

Finn looks at me, then at him. "Lucas, it's the right thing to do. Tristan? Dominic? A little help."

With more speed and ferocity than I thought them capable towards their alpha, the three move in perfect synchronicity. Tristan and Finn each take one of Lucas' arms, and Dominic walks behind him and grabs him in a chokehold. "Relax, it'll be over soon."

I look at the girls, each staring at the scene as confused as I am. Yet none of the guys are doing any harm. On the contrary, if I didn't know better I'd say they're trying to provoke something. But...what?

"Don't hurt him," I whisper. "Please."

And that's when Lucas *really* loses it. He curls into himself, then with a roar as loud as a lion's he bursts into movement. One hand pushes Finn away, the other Tristan. Then with barely any effort he pulls Dominic's arms from around his neck and tosses him away as easily as a fly.

"Basta!" he growls. "No one – fucking – touches – Monica."

Out of the corner of my eye, I see Luz head to Dom, Elle to Finn and Dani to Tristan. So it only makes sense I find my feet carrying me towards Lucas, step by step. I walk around his heaving form – now taller than me by a head – and glance into his face.

His features are taut, as if the muscles are barely holding the beast within. His nostrils are flaring, and he's mid-transformation. Rusty hair covers his arms, his shirt is hanging off and showing his chest filled with fur. And his hands have turned into massive claws.

Even as I take it all in, Finn gets to his feet, wincing as he rolls his shoulder. "Watch yourself. We might've pushed him a little over the edge."

Lucas is breathing hard in front of me, and the guys around me evidently think I've lost my mind. But I shake my head. "It's okay. I've got him, I swear it."

Finn alone seems to believe me, and nods to them. "She's not lying. We can give them some privacy."

Even as they enter the shop, Lucas' panting doesn't abate. There's something incredibly primal in seeing him like this, all raw and almost unhinged. Memories of me screaming his name, of his body on mine, rifle through me and I can't settle down. My hands itch with wanting to touch him, but I'm not sure if it's the best idea.

Then Lucas sniffs the air.

I open my mouth, about to ask him something, but he's on me. Only, he's no longer half-morphed. The mouth meeting mine is all Lucas, demanding and possessive. The hands pulling me closer are merciless, but without claws. He's pushing me to the wall, grabbing my ass and lifting me up in the air. I can't control my reaction, melting like a damned cat in heat, moaning against him. Our wolves care for nothing other than immediate pleasure.

We're lost in it – too lost. Then there's a breeze, a chuckle.

"My, you really take your job seriously, Monica. We'll take it from here."

He'd frozen between my legs at the first words, but now he's a pure statue. Lucas stops kissing me, his gaze filled with betrayal and hate, then drops me as if I've contaminated him.

Before either of us can do anything, a glow suffuses the air. Then I hear the sounds of a fight, but I've already dropped to the ground, unconscious.

"Monica, wake up!"

The voice is soft, insistent. I blink. Elle is over me, frowning and trying to shake me.

"What.... Lucas!" I look around. "Where is he?"

"That's what we'd like to know."

I meet Dominic's fiery gaze, and gulp.

∞ ∞ ∞

CHAPTER NINE

∞ Coraggio ∞

"What would life be if we had no <u>courage</u> to attempt anything?"

-Vincent Van Gogh-

Lucas

A ringing in my head wakes me up. Metallic taste fills my mouth. A groan escapes me, and I shift – only for the floor to move with me. I'm definitely on something solid, I realize after the initial dizziness. The fuckers knocked me out straight after dragging me to the van. Must've been afraid of something – me morphing? If only I could figure out whatever the fuck that is, then I could stop wasting time here.

Instead, I have to take a deep inhale, while trying to appear immobile. My chest hurts – they kicked me, too. I try to move a wrist, and hear the tell-tale clink of chains.

Interessante...

Bit by bit, I move to a half-seated position and open my eyes. My vision is blurry at first. Whatever kind of tranquilizer they used must have knocked me out for hours. And the more I take in my surroundings, the faster my heart beats.

I'm no longer in Rockland Creek. No, rather, I'm back in my old mansion, in the wine cellar by the looks of it. Father did always like an old dungeon, so when he purchased the villa it conveniently came with a wine cellar, as well as a jail cell. It used to freak my mother out, but Matteo and I played in here countless times as kids.

My hand touches the ground, feeling the worn stone, the echoes of laughter. The walls are older than I remember, and the smell here is filled with mold and rankness. Low lights hang above, casting dim glows everywhere.

Where I'm at is in the cell itself. A cot with straw is set in a corner, and two massive chains are anchored to the ground, and my wrists. The door to the cell is closed, locked from the outside. And by the scents in the air, I catch a whiff of wolves. Guards. And nearby, too.

Merda. How do I get out of here?

Clatter upstairs and the sounds of creaking hinges set my teeth on edge.

"Dov'è?" The sound of a slap. "*Idiota*! Stop sleeping, unless you wish me to burn your eyelids. Where is my son?"

My body tenses. I know that voice all too well. Spent my childhood trying to do well by him. The last time I'd seen him was while cradling my mother's broken body, after she'd unsuccessfully tried to kill him, and instead took her own life. Refusing to do his bidding.

He's the one who sent Monica. He's the one who started all this shit instead of letting the past be in the past.

I know this, of course. But somehow, the anger over his interference hasn't quite gotten out of my system, it seems. So I wait until I hear the door to my cell open, keeping my head bowed as if I'm still not fully in control of my faculties.

His footsteps clatter on the cobblestones – those fancy Armani dress shoes he loves to wear. The self-assured bastard. Rage fills me, but rather than the red haze usually accompanying it, an odd calm spreads over me.

It's almost surreally that I watch myself snap from the ground, break the chains holding me captive, and slam my father against the wall. The hinges rattle on the door, and the wall itself seems to curb.

My fingers grip his throat, squeezing the Adam's apple that bobs fearfully under my touch. "Care to explain what the fuck the meaning of all this is, Alessandro?"

I'm towering over him now, and he's definitely put on some weight. Those eyes are still as cold and calculating as ever, taking my measure even as I could snuff out the life from under him. I hate that I got my looks from him. I hate *him* with a passion. A spasm goes through my fingers, and they clench even tighter.

"You won't do it."

There's a satisfied quality to his voice, as if he still knows me. As if he can still control me.

"You don't know me anymore," I spit in his face. My jaw hurts from the force I'm clenching it with. The calmness is gone, and there is that raging burn inside me to tear his insides out. My wolf growls a soft approval. "A long time ago, I swore to myself I would kill you if I ever saw you again. And now nothing, and I mean *nothing*, stands in my way."

"Except for the guards," he wheezes.

A quick glance to the side confirms three men snuck up, with their guns trained on me. A dark chuckle escapes me as I meet my father's gaze once more.

"I'm not the child from before, *Papà*," I growl. "You think a few men scare me off? Not in a lifetime."

Something shifts in his eyes, as if realizing he miscalculated. "Death no longer fazes you?"

"No," I say simply. "Miscalculated, have you? Too fucking bad. You dare take me from my pack, bring me back here? What, you think they won't follow?"

He laughs. "That is precisely what I'm counting on. If only they *would* follow, so I could add them to my collection."

My body freezes, giving away my surprise. Alessandro chuckles again. "What, bambino, don't tell me they would not make the perfect tesoros for my antiques?"

My fingers squeeze of their own accord, and I watch in cold satisfaction as his skin turns purple. "Sì, Monica said something similar. Is that what this is all about?"

Alessandro's face contorts in a grimace, some semblance of a scowl. So he didn't know she had betrayed him fully. Good.

He ignores my question and instead says, "She will pay for the deception. Always knew she was a good-for-nothing whore."

My fingers clench reflexively on his throat, enough that he starts choking in earnest. Rage fills me more at his words, and this time there is no Monica to pull me back from the brink. Even as everything narrows onto that frenzy, and the eagerness to see him die by my hands almost overwhelms everything else...something nags at me.

A feeling of unfinished business – I need answers. It's a faint grasp at my logical side, but it works. Whatever happens with me, the pack is still alive and well. And if I find out what Alessandro plans, every bit of it, I can figure out how to protect them. Then I can truly help my wolves disappear, so he can never harm them.

With a sharp intake of breath, I force my hand to loosen up. The second he's free, Alessandro shoves me away, his features twisted with indignation. "You will pay for that."

I show him my palms, even as he jerks his head towards his guards. Two of the men holster their guns and walk in, their outfits similar to the ones who kidnapped me. Calmly, I let them surround me and tie new chains to my wrists, saving my sneer for my father.

"So this is what it's come down to? I shouldn't be surprised. The only way you knew how to hold people around you was through threat and violence. And if that didn't work, there was always manipulation."

Alessandro gestures for the guards to leave, and then we're alone again. I guess he thinks some cold metal will keep me from killing him. If only he knew. It would take only one small tug, and he'd be lifeless. I force the thought away.

Besides my need for answers, there is another problem. If I kill him, I will take on the duties for his pack, in the way of the lupo mannaro. Much like Dominic did with the vrykolakas, I'll end up with people under me that I have no desire to rule over.

Alessandro's cold, beady eyes meet mine. "What do you know of it? You were a child."

"I was twenty-five! Old enough to see through your bullshit. You had Matteo wrapped around your little finger. Removing attention to ensure he would be so begging and so desperate, he'd do your bidding without thinking it through."

"You have nerve, to speak of your brother. When it's your fault he died. Had you joined me fully, had you cooperated, I would not have needed him."

Tremors run through me as I try to hold back my fury. "There is only one person responsible for his death, and I'm staring right at him."

Alessandro nods as if I haven't spoken. "We started off on the wrong foot. I will let you sleep, rest. Then we can start anew." He turns his back and leaves, but stops as soon as the cellar door is closed. "And make no mistake, we *will* restart. As many times as we have to."

My shouted curses echo back to me, but there is no one left to hear them. Only the locked cellar door, and the emptiness surrounding me.

Monica

I don't have time to get my bearings or figure out exactly what happened that got me unconscious. Dominic helps me up, then they bring me to Lucas' house.

Despite the pack's cordial demeanor, I have no doubt they see me at fault. If nothing else, the fact I'm flanked by Tristan and Dani in the car, with Dominic and Luz at the front, speaks volumes. Elle and Finn follow behind in another car.

Once we get to the bungalow, they let me in first and spread out in the house. Maybe on purpose or not, each wolf ends up blocking a way of escape, yet still remains within touching distance of his mate. Only Lucrezia and Elle stand in the middle, watching me warily.

I deserve that, more than they know. Before all hell broke loose, all I'd managed to own up to was lying and coming in under false pretenses. Now...

When no one says anything, I clear my throat. "I know what you're thinking, but..." I shake my head. What's the point of lying? "Actually, no. It's true. Lucas being taken is my fault. You all being attacked is also my fault."

Tristan makes a move as if to head closer, but one steely glare from Dominic roots him to the ground. "Explain yourself," he asks instead.

I stare at all of them one by one, and tears fill my eyes. "I... Earlier, I told you that Alessandro sent me here to get Lucas. I'm a fixer in my pack, meaning I get what the alpha needs, deescalate situations, and basically run errands. It's not a glamorous job, but it works when you have nothing else."

"If you're trying to make us pity you, it isn't working," Tristan growls.

"I'm not," I say and bow my head. "I'm only trying to give you a clear picture of what's going on. Anyway, Lucas wasn't responsive, at least not the way Alessandro thought he'd be, and so I had to get creative in finding out more about him."

"And we played right into it," Lucrezia says.

I can't figure out her tone but when I dare look up, her expression is hurt. "I'm sorry. I'm so, so sorry."

"So it was all a lie?" Elle asks, her voice quivering. "You used us?"

"No! I was genuine with you guys, it's just..." My voice quivers. "I may have started on the wrong foot here, to get information, but then I got to know you all and I just felt like... I never wanted to hurt you. He promised me freedom! Freedom to choose whatever I want my life to be, and leave his pack. You don't understand, I've been under Alessandro's thumb for so long and this was a way to get out from it."

"At the expense of others," Lucrezia points out.

Dejected, I stare at the ground again. "I'm really sorry."

"What about Alessandro?" Tristan asks. "You told Dominic he collects. Is that why he sent his goons here, because you blabbed about our gifts?"

I nod miserably. "I didn't mean to. Initially, all I told Alessandro was that Lucas had mated wolves under him. It piqued his interest, but I was too slow to realize why. When I told him about the magic, he wanted me to find out more. I did when I spoke with the girls, but I didn't tell him. The other day, it was a slip of the tongue. All I mentioned was zmeu magic."

At a complete loss, I cover my face with my hands. Monica Delucci, always in control, now crying publicly. Wonderful.

Yet I owe it to these guys to be completely truthful. This isn't about me, not anymore. It's about getting everything out in the open so we can focus on Lucas.

Lucas... My gut churns. What the hell happened? How could we be taken unaware like that? Hormones or not, it's no excuse for letting down our guard. If Alessandro has him now... Gulping, I force the words out faster.

"Alessandro shifted into the occult a few months ago. I didn't get a chance to tell Lucas, but I think that's what started this whole hunt to find him. And... And then it led him to you."

"Because of what you revealed."

A shuffle around has my attention, in time to notice Finn holding Tristan back. My confusion must have shown on my face, because the Irish wolf shrugs. "I'm not on your side, don't get ideas. But Lucas has bonded with you, and whether we like it or not, that means you're part of the pack."

"What?" Tristan asks, staring between me and Finn.

Dani intertwines her hand with his, pulling him back by her side. "You really are thick-headed sometimes, carinho," she says softly. "Did you not see Lucas' reaction earlier, when Finn was threatening to toss Monica back to his father?"

Tristan takes my measure again, this time with a speculative stare. Lucrezia is the one who moves, speaking to Finn. "Is that what your little show was about earlier?"

He shrugs. "None of you could feel it, but it's been getting stronger. Lucas himself is in denial, which made it all the more fun."

"So she's...his mate?" Elle asks.

"Yep." Dani nods, shooting me a wary glance. "Which means, we have to cut her some slack."

"You don't." I shake my head, coming out of my trance. "I'm not... It shouldn't... That has nothing to do with anything."

"On the contrary," Dominic says. "It has everything to do with everything. In this pack, we respect each other's mates, and take care of them. We're family. It doesn't mean we trust you, but it means we'll take care of you."

"At least until Lucas comes back and confirms what's what."

I scan the room, completely baffled. These wolves mean it. Though they're wary of me, wary of what I did, I can feel they would still protect me. All because I'm Lucas'...

But am I really? Yes, he's insufferable, yes he's stubborn and great in bed, but there's no way in just a few short days...

"It doesn't take years," Finn says as if reading my thoughts. "Sometimes all it takes is a day, or a glance."

"And sometimes it *does* take a year," Lucrezia smiles at Dom. She walks over to him, burying her face in his opened arms. Effortlessly.

I gulp, sensing the same kind of love across all the others. "It can't be. I mean, that fairy lady did say something but –"

"Ileana came to see you?" Lucrezia arches an eyebrow. "Wow."

"Why wow?"

Shrugs go all around, but it's Finn who says, "She visited everyone at some point or another. Even gave Lucas a good trashing. She's our matchmaker, courtesy of Dom."

If I expected more explanation from the Romanian wolf, I'm sorely mistaken. He only shrugs. "Maybe Ileana was right, so what?" Dominic says as he rests his chin atop Lucrezia's head. "We have all fallen, and I don't hear anyone complaining." There's a wry tone to his voice, and just like that it takes the tension out of the room.

Lucrezia turns to me again, a suspicious glint in her eyes. "If this is all true, then how do you feel about Lucas?"

"I..." The question catches me by surprise, and I'm nowhere ready to answer it. I can't even fully admit it to myself, let alone these guys.

She nods as if expecting my confusion. "You'd best figure it out, because he's not a guy willing to accept love in his life. Even when it's staring him in the face."

Words fail me, so I keep my silence. But while the pack may be open to me, they're not done with their questions.

"Suppose it's safe to say Lucas' wanker of a father is behind the kidnapping," Finn says. "The question is, why does he need our alpha's chimera powers, and ours on top of it?"

I shrug. "He's greedy. The chimera won't just have his powers, but also channel yours. To someone like Alessandro, it's an invaluable tool he just has to add to his collection. I'm just... I'm just glad he didn't get to any of you."

And then something else dawns on me, and I inhale sharply.

"What is it?" Finn asks. "Your emotions are all over the place."

I stare at all of them, and gulp. "The chimera in Lucas... That is what's been causing all of this! You coming together is not by chance, merda, but now it all makes sense!"

They stare at me like I've lost it, but for the first time in my life, I feel like I've finally gotten it.

∞ ∞ ∞

CHAPTER TEN

∞ Inaspettato ∞

"To expect the <u>unexpected</u> shows a thoroughly modern intellect."

-Oscar Wilde-

Lucas

Sleep is fitful that night. I sit in a corner so I can have a perfect view of the entrance, not trusting my father. I've seen his tactics, and the last thing I want is to be taken unawares. I know he must be pissed at the fact I got the upper hand. And, unfortunately, he now knows the extent of my physical strength.

I glance at the new, larger chains on my wrists. Could I snap them? Claro. But there is no point when I'll be captured as soon as I'm out of here. Now that I'm in the wolf's den, I may as well make the most of it and find out what he's hiding under his sleeve.

Then I can pull out my own aces, and watch the bewilderment on his face.

Soon as I'm done plotting that, my mind wanders elsewhere. Why did he stay here, in the same house after Mamma died? And, even harder to think of, is the grave I dug for her that night. I still remember how long it took me to get the grime of the ground from under my nails. My tears mingled with the shower that night.

For the first time, I allow myself to feel. My head rests against the stone wall and I sigh heavily. *Mamma...*

I must have closed my eyes, because when I blink awake she's there. Translucent, shimmering form, wavy hair, eyes saddened. "Luciano, I warned you..."

She speaks clearly now, no longer in broken words. Perhaps the closeness to her resting place makes for an easier connection. "Mamma, what were you trying to tell me?"

"So many things, mio figlio..." She floats to me and kneels in front of me. Her hand is a whispered caress on my cheek, and I lean into it. "Alessandro failed with me, but he will try to break you."

"He can try, but he won't succeed." I peer into her face then, trying to read the melancholic expression I'm not used to seeing on her. "What is it you're not telling me?"

"You father wants your gift, that is why he brought you here."

"Sì, but why? Is it just my pack?"

"No, son. It is because the chimera blood in you can act as a conduit for all your friends. The vârcolac, the faoladh, the two lobisomens, as well as the girls with the zmeu magic in them. They will come after you, and your father plans to capture them."

"I will not let him do it."

"It doesn't matter what you do, Luciano. If he captures them, he will force the women to breed, to create more of their kind." Tears fill her eyes even as I freeze, stunned. "He has done it before."

"What do you mean?"

"I... Years ago, there were some women he brought into the fold. They had old stregheria magic in them, which Alessandro thought would be useful. He had his wolves take them as concubines, and hybrids were born out of it."

Something nags at me, and slowly the pieces come into place. "Was that Monica Delucci's family?"

My mother tilts her head. "Yes. How did you guess?"

"Let's just say I recently ran into her."

"Ah." Francesca nods. "Monica alone survived, because of her gift, along with one other, Ana. I'm not sure what fate awaited her, I do not perceive all, but Monica became a tool. Your father saw more use in her serving him via her magic."

So what Monica told me was true. Not only did my father enslave her family and ancestors, but he forced the women into a life they didn't want. Dio alone knows what those poor women endured, because I don't remember any of his wolves being kind, let alone gentlemanly.

And Monica...

I try to picture her life as a young child, a young woman, in a pack where that is automatically seen as weakness. Where she had no choice but to use her best assets, to carve out a certain image, and step on whomever was needed to maintain it. To preserve her *life*.

Is it any wonder then that she was so eager to get out from under Alessandro's thumb, that she'd do anything? Even if it meant putting my pack in danger... My fists clench at the thought of her growing up in such an environment.

For some reason, my reaction seems to amuse my mother, who smiles. There's an odd glint in her eyes, melancholy all gone, and I don't particularly like it. It's too similar to Ileana's smug expression.

"Anyone would be mad at hearing such an account," I say to defend my reaction.

"Of course."

My eyes narrow. "That's the tone you used to pacify me when I was a child."

She laughs and floats closer. I can still smell her perfume, and she seems so real I could almost touch her. Hesitantly, I reach a calloused hand towards her – and jump when I make contact with her cheek.

Another smile, sadder this time. "You are of my blood, and the chimera in you is bonding already with the Underworld. Ghosts are not the only things you can touch." Her eyes sparkle then. "And you should not be afraid to let love in, mio figlio."

Before I can respond, she jerks to her feet and glances to the door. Then she turns to me, her eyes panicked. "Keep your cool, Luciano. Do not let him see your power. The sooner he does, the worse it will be." The second after those ominous words, she's gone.

A moment later, footsteps echo and my father walks in. "Good morning, son. How did you sleep?"

I get to my feet and lean against the wall. "Swimmingly."

My sarcasm rains on his parade and he scowls. "I said we will start again this morning. Can we not do that?"

"Claro," I mutter. "Soon as you take these chains off me and we talk like adults." I grin. "Unless you're afraid."

"I do not understand why you must be so obtuse," Alessandro tells me. "I am your family, your blood. It is with me you must stand, not with your wolves. Besides, we can have them all join us. You've managed to get yourself quite the collection."

I grit my teeth at the words. "Family? What family, Papà? Family doesn't gut you open. Family doesn't let you die on the shores of a shitty deal. Family doesn't come to you when it's convenient, and suited only for them. And most of all, family doesn't fuck you over time and time again. So no, we are not *family*. My pack is more my blood than you'll ever be, let's get that clear."

His eyes glitter with menace, his face a mask of restrained fury. For a second, I think he'll strike me. I'm ready for it, ready to return the blow. Instead, Alessandro only says, "You will change your mind." Then he leaves my cell once more, leaving me wondering what kind of a fucking game he's playing.

Monica

"What do you mean?" Dominic asks after my outburst. "Enough with the riddles."

"Not riddles," I say. "Thing is, I was born in Alessandro's harem. He collected people under him, but not for himself. His wife, Lucas' mother, was also a chimera. Her blood attracted various shifters of special gifts. It's nature's call, as these shifters bow down to the apex predator. A chimera takes their subservience, provides protection, and... builds an army."

"How?" Tristan asks.

Daniela has already clued in. "Breeding. The more the special shifters multiple, the more of their kind exist... All under the chimera."

I remember what she told me about her deceased brother, and how he'd been trying to breed the females of his pack forcefully. The recognition must be apparent on my features, as Dani's own shutter at the memory.

There are many apologies on the tip of my tongue – again. But nothing can erase what I've done, what I've caused, and the consequences of it all. So rather than shower her with platitudes, I keep my mouth shut.

"One big feeding machine," Dominic says. "You're saying it wasn't my godmother's magic, but Lucas' own that created this environment where I ran into Luz, Dani walked in, and Elle and Finn collided."

I nod.

"And then you came," Finn points out.

"What? No! I'm not..." I clear my throat. "I'm not part of this equation. I mean, sì, Lucas will need his own mate to bring the cycle closed, but it's not me. Non è possibile. Despite what you may think and what you said, it's *not* possible. That's why you don't owe me anything."

Finn rolls his eyes and ignores my comment. I can't help glancing at Elle, who's purposefully avoiding me. I really messed this up. Shaking my head, I focus on Dominic's orders.

"Dani, Tristan, spread out here and see what you can find about the chimera, or anything else that can fill us in on this new craziness. Until I can reach Ileana to confirm one way or another, we're pretty much clueless to what's real and not." His speculative gaze falls on me. "No offense, Monica."

"None taken," I mutter to the ground. It's only fair they'll be taking anything I say with a grain of salt. After all, I wouldn't trust me either.

Tristan and Dani spread out, and I notice Elle following them, too. I figure right then's a good time to head to Lucas' liquor cabinet, and pour myself a shot – or four. With alcohol buzzing in me, the tightness in my stomach unfurls.

Is Lucas alright? I've been avoiding thinking about his kidnapping. He's big and strong, he can take care of himself. Plus, it's not like Alessandro will hurt him.... Unless, of course, Lucas refuses to comply.

Images of Alessandro's punishments flash through my mind, and the hand holding the glass shakes. Before I break it, I place it back on the mantel and take a deep breath. *Stop thinking the worst.*

It doesn't take the pack long to find something, and any thoughts of Lucas are pushed to the background. I leave solitary post and join them by a couch, hovering on the edge of it.

Dominic immediately waves me closer. "Most of it is in Italian. Do you see anything you recognize in here?"

Finn and Luz move out of the way and I inch past them, scanning the old papers strewn about. There's anything from old Roman texts, to legends, myths, and folklore. Lucas must've been researching his genes, but was this recently?

Something grabs my attention – the edge of paper, with a drawing of a snake tail. I pull it from under the rest... On it is a full picture of the chimera. A massive lion, the head of a goat protruding from its back, and a snake as a tail. Red eyes burn off the page, staring at us.

No one breathes. No one moves.

"Is that.... Can Lucas turn into that, even though he's only half-chimera?" Luz asks.

"Sì," I whisper. "But only if pushed to the brink of breaking. I don't think his wolf would allow it, otherwise. That's what keeps him sane right now. My nonna used to say it was a wonder Francesca, his mother, had not lost her mind and killed everyone."

"Why?"

"The chimera gene, it's normally passed to the female. In such a case, the female becomes the chalice for all the channeling. But she still has to morph, to transform, and let the beast out. Francesca, according to my nonna, refused to do so. She wouldn't put people in danger, and it drove Alessandro mad that he couldn't control her."

Dani leans forward. "Control how, and to do what?"

"Alessandro always wanted Francesca to be his tool. To open the Underworld as he wanted, and make him master of death. She refused, even when he used her children as bait. But not giving in to the transformation had its own price on her health."

"And what of the male?" Dominic asks. "Lucas said if he suppresses it, it can make the process quicker. Like either way, he's screwed."

My hand trembles again, and the picture with it. "I... I think the chimera overruns his wolf. And... Lucas said something, the other day. It was in the midst of an argument, but he said it's already too late for him."

Dominic frowns. "Late how?"

Finn snaps his fingers. "The execution! That's why he's been pushing for the Reapers' extermination."

"I don't follow," Tristan says.

"Lucas is running out of time. Based on what he and Monica have both said, the more a chimera kills, the closer the link to the Underworld becomes. So, think about all the fights we had to get through recently... What are the chances Lucas went over his quota and is actually feeling that pull? With or without his wolf resisting, he must realize he's losing the fight."

Silence answers him, and this time it's me who breaks it. "But what does that have to do with exterminating the Reapers?"

"Because Lucas would want us safe," Lucrezia whispers. "That's why he didn't try to kill the Reapers himself, to try to hang around a little longer. But if something happens to him, if he feels he's about to lose himself, then he'd want us safe."

"Damn," Tristan mutters.

The implication reverberates through my body like an explosion. That's what Lucas had meant – that it was too late for him. So the entire time he was with me, he already knew he was doomed. Yet he never trusted me enough to tell me.

Can you blame him?

No, I can't. I can only admire his will, and the love he has for his pack. I wish there'd been an iota of this in my own growing up, but there's no point thinking about a past that cannot be changed. I owe it to Lucas to clean up the mess I've created.

Only, I don't know how. I stare at the drawing in my hand, and something else catches my eye. The paper is so thin I feel it'll crumble. Yet when I touch it, shift it just so, there's something else just underneath the surface.

I untangle the pentagram necklace from around my neck and wave it counter clockwise over the colorful lines, breathing softly. Hoping I can call forth whatever is cloaked... The paper rustles and the writing that had been hidden appears line by cursive line, like a forgotten secret.

"Uh, guys?"

I feel them turning towards me, but I can't tear my own gaze from the words. "This says the chimera... It says if it's fed, that its soul will belong to the Underworld." The writing disappears as soon as I speak it. "It's not just a matter of saving Lucas from Alessandro. We need to make sure he's protected from the Underworld, period."

"Then it's a damn good thing I didn't listen to him and kill the Reapers," Dominic mutters. "Not that there's many of them left now, anyway."

"I reckon that's a problem we can consider solved," Finn says, then walks over to him and whispers something in his ear. After he nods, they turn to me. "Alright, this is what's going to happen. You need to tell us everything you can about Alessandro and his domain. Then you're going to help us break Lucas out."

"Okay," I say without hesitation. "Does anyone have a map?"

They spread out to look for one. Lucrezia takes that moment to walk closer to me, determination in her every step. When she speaks, her voice is low but firm. "I'll only say this once, since Lucas and I have a history. And because of that, I really care for him. Do you plan to betray him again?"

I meet her gaze head on and slowly shake my head. "No. I... I didn't mean to either, this time. I was stupid, Lucrezia. But the last thing I wanted was to hurt him, or any of you."

She holds my gaze a moment longer, then nods. "Fine. I'll choose to believe you, but Monica, mark my words. If you do anything else to bring jeopardy to this pack, I'm going to order the vrykolakas attack you myself – mate or no mate bond with Lucas. Understood?"

I nod, gulping at the fire in her eyes. If before I didn't understand the bond between her and Dominic, now I definitely do.

As if my thoughts called him up, he struts to our side and wraps an arm around her shoulders. "Everything okay, draga mea?"

"Yeah," she grins up at him. "Just girl talk." To me, she winks and says, "And please, call me Luz. Everyone else does."

Before Dominic can question us, Elle yells, "Found one!"

We take it and spread it on what's left of a table. It takes me a moment to locate Alessandro's mansion, but I point to it. "This is where it is, a few hours away from here. Does anyone have a pen?"

With a sharpie, I start marking around it all the defense systems I remember, including the number of wolves and gifted shifters. By the time I'm done, the pretty map is all filled with my scribbles, and none of it looks good. I'd never paid much attention to it when I was living there, but according to everything I've been able to remember, Alessandro has built himself quite the fortress.

The mansion is protected by three circles of defense, of various strengths. On the outside are the body-builder wolves, the runts of the pack. In the second circle, it's people like those who kidnapped Lucas, along with some of his gifted wolves. And last, inside the house itself, only elite soldiers and the most trained of his gifted warriors.

Dominic lets out a grunt and rubs his hand over his neck. His look of concentration bodes nothing well, confirmed when he says, "It's a fucking fortress."

"Even with your vrykolakas, we're outnumbered," Tristan says. "We need a better strategy."

I remember his army experience, and then it makes sense why they're all nodding to his words.

Dominic says, "What do you suggest?"

Lucas

When I was twelve I held a gun for the first time, to save my father's life. I still don't know if it was the right choice, though it made him damn proud. That same night, he beat the crap out of me for forgetting one very important lesson – the Contis do not show mercy.

My time away made me naïve. Naïve enough to think I could catch some shuteye without interruption. Naïve enough to stupidly believe I was safe in my childhood home.

That all shatters in the middle of the night when the door to the cell bursts open and five thugs burst in. In the distance, I hear a female voice muttering something – some kind of incantation. And then I'm bound, unable to tear the chains nor defend myself.

Their blows rain on me – batons, punches, kicks in the gut. My wolf rages inside me, and the other part, the darker part, thinks of tearing their throats out. But through it all, I'm unable to do anything other than drop to the floor in a mess of tangled bones and limbs.

My breathing is ragged. Blood coats my mouth, and I can't see past my swollen eyes. Yet I can still feel a sense of satisfaction in the air. And then someone moves closer, and the scent of an overly strong perfume hits my nose.

"Tuo padre dice ciao." *Your father says hello.*

The sound of heels clattering on stone announces her retreat. A second later, the door is closed and locked once more. My muscles are my own again, and knives upon knives of pain hit me like a pack of bricks. I drag myself to a corner and heave the remains of my stomach, then rest my pounding head against the cool wall.

"Alright, Papà," I whisper to the night air. "The gloves are off."

∞ ∞ ∞

∞ Fratello ∞

"A friend is a <u>brother</u> who was once a brother."

-Unknown-

Lucas

Hours later, I stir. Must have fallen asleep, as the side of my face leaning on the wall is caked with dry blood. In a corner of the cell, slipped through the bars, is a bowl with stale water. *Like a damn dog.*

Still, I reach for it and splash it on my face in an effort to clean up. My entire body is tense with pain, and I cringe with every small movement. But I won't let my father see my weakness. He sent his men rather than come to me himself because he's afraid.

Bene. He should be. Because after last night, it'll be no holds barred.

I lean my head back against the wall. My thoughts go to Monica. Even in my beat up state, it annoys me that my body yearns for her. It was her voice I'd been dreaming about, her cry that woke me up.

This place... I need to get out. But not yet. Not until I have answers. There's something else going on here. Even so far removed from the rest of the house, I can feel an evil at bay, a sense of something not right. And whatever it is, I have to figure out the truth behind it.

Not for me – that's already too late. But I won't let my father drag anyone else down with me.

Hours later, my wounds feel better. Whether it's the chimera blood or my wolf's resilience, I'm able to move around the cell. When I'm sure no one's around, I bend my knees and aim a few punches at the air. The rattle of the chains is loud, but I need the movement, the pain and tear of my muscles to keep me focused on something else but this annoying yearning inside me.

Is Monica even alive? The last I'd seen, she went falling like a rock. I don't know what that means. If my wolves found her, will they believe she didn't get me kidnapped on purpose? For a moment, I thought she had. I wanted to hate her. But her expression of genuine surprise keeps flashing in my mind, and I cannot deny her innocence in that particular development.

A snort escapes me and I stop mid-punch, stretching out my neck muscles. *Innocente, Monica?* I may have known her for only a week, but there's no way those two words go together.

After I'm done with my warm up, I get back to the ground, and try to analyze the problem from all angles. Without more information, I'm running blind. And while I thought my father would come in the morning and gloat, there's no sign of him.

More time goes by, and it's almost evening yet I still haven't heard peep from anyone. This won't do – I won't be getting in Alessandro's head unless I speak with him. With a groan, I get up from the floor I'd reverted to and kick the cell's bars.

Footsteps come resounding – two wolves, in the black attire I've come to recognize as a uniform. "Dov'è Alessandro?" I ask, but they only sneer at me. I wonder if they're part of the crew that attacked me last night. At the possibility, my fists clench automatically and I want to tear through these walls and rip their faces off. Instead, I take a deep breath and smile coldly. "Tell me where he is, or I'll bring this entire house down on us."

They share a worried glance at my tone, but another voice speaks. "That won't be necessary."

They move backwards and a woman comes into my view. Blonde, curly hair, blue eyes as innocent as a baby's and as cold as the lakes of Hell. Her voluptuous body is encased in a black, sheer lace gown that stops above her knees, right where leather boots start.

"Like what you see?" she asks in a husky voice.

It's my turn to sneer. "Not even remotely." I recognize that tone, and the perfume coming off her. *She* was the woman whispering. My blood boils again at the reminder.

"Had fun last night?" I counter.

She widens her eyes in a mock portrayal of innocence that does not become her. "Why, yes. As a matter of fact, it was rather interesting." Her assessing gaze runs up and down my body, making me aware of my grimy state. "I would've thought you had more....fight."

"Bit hard to rise to the occasion, what with your little magic trick."

A surprised laugh escapes her. "My, my, nothing escapes you, hmm? How very refreshing." She shifts her weight to the other foot, cocking a hip and placing a well-manicured hand on it. "But isn't it a tad old-school to blame the woman for your inadequacy?"

A growl lets loose from my throat. "How about you let me out of here, and I'll show you how inadequate I can be."

"Mm, tempting." My skin crawls at the innuendo, and some of the disgust must show on my expression. She steps closer, the heels of those boots beating a rhythm. "Ah, yes. You prefer brunettes, no?"

My jaw clenches. Whoever she is, she's trying to destabilize me, but I refuse to let this get to me. That resolution lasts until her next words.

"Tell me, how was dear old Monica in the sack? I've only heard good things from here." A coy look to one of the wolves, a smile playing on her lips – the implication couldn't be missed if I tried.

I step closer, gripping the bars. "Whoever the fuck you are, I'm not interested in your petty games. Get my father, or get the hell out of my face."

"Mio Dio," she puts a hand to her chest in mock offense, "did Alessandro not raise you with manners?" Her cold eyes rake me over, then her nose wrinkles in disgust. "No, it's not his fault. Your puta mamma—"

She got too close, and my hand snakes out between the bars and grabs a handful of her hair, angling her face against the bars. "Watch yourself, woman. No one dishonors my mother's memory, least of all a whore like yourself. You can spread your legs for Alessandro all you like, but around me, you better watch that mouth."

I let her go before the wolves can intervene, and she steps backwards, clenching her fists. "We shall see."

The clatter of her boots echoes in the tunnel as she leaves, followed by her guards. That was pointless, and I let my head drop on the metal in frustration. When she spoke of

Monica, and then my mother... I wanted to rip her throat out.

"Grazie, Luciano."

I look back, noticing Mamma's shimmering form again. I don't move from my position, wanting to hear if someone gets close enough. But my eyes drink her in, and all I want is to hold her tight for all the times I didn't get to.

"I'm sorry, Mamma," I whisper. "For Matteo, for that night... I wish I'd done more. Been more."

She shakes her head and walks closer. "None of it was your fault. It was your father's, and mine. If I had told Matteo the truth of our heritage, perhaps he would have listened more. Perhaps not. Lingering on the past is no way to live your life, mio figlio. Promise me that once you are out of here, you will do better."

I look away, swallowing past the lump in my throat. "I promise."

"Bene. Then, will you tell me about her, this woman who rouses your wolf's protective side?"

Monica

"I don't like it," Finn says. "It's a good strategy, but it puts us in danger."

Tristan shrugs. "You got a better one?"

I look between the wolves, trying to gauge which of them I can really count on, and which I cannot. We've been going over this most of the day, in between breaks for power naps and food for sustenance. With each passing minute, my insides have been burning more and more. Maybe it's the alcohol I drank, or just my own guilt, but I feel bile rising up my throat even as I wipe a tired hand over my face.

"Basta, please! While you argue, Lucas is in his father's clutches. And the longer he's there, the less chance we have to get him out."

"Oh, 'cause now you care?" Tristan mutters.

I wince. *Touché.* "I've already apologized for the part I played. And despite what you may think, I'm not going to waste more time with this. Just let me go, alone. There's a strong chance if I grovel enough, Alessandro will let his guard down. I can be a Trojan horse."

"No," Elle says, to my big surprise. She hasn't acknowledged me much in the past hours. "If there's one thing Lucas was clear about, it's that he does not want you back around his father."

"I'll do it, if it means a solution we can all agree to," I add, my tone close to begging. "Please. Let's just pick a way, and go for it."

"Monica is right," Lucrezia says, saving me from digging my own grave. "We have to get Lucas out, and we have to do it now."

Dominic's silent, as are Elle and Dani. Their indecision makes me nervous. And then Dominic moves closer, and rubs the bridge of his nose. The gesture is so like Lucas, something like yearning runs through me and I have to look away.

More and more thoughts of him have been swirling through my mind. I need to get out of here, away from them. This craving inside me, this need to have Lucas nearby – it's about to drive me crazy.

"I need a minute," I mutter and head out. Conversations continue behind me, but I lose track of them as my heart starts beating wildly.

I run into Lucas' bedroom almost blindly and drop next to the bed. As I pull the sheets into my lap, his scent rises from them and I bury my face in them. Musk, and pine, and Lucas. Tears fill my eyes, and my throat clogs. For the first time, I cry for a man.

I'm not a weakling. I don't get attached. I don't do clingy. And yet, less than forty-eight hours away from him, and I cannot keep it together. A moan of practical pain escapes me, and I bend over trying to grasp some kind of semblance.

A creak makes me jump, but it's just Elle entering the room. She stares between me and the unmade bed, and the wary look in her eyes turns sympathetic. She walks into the adjoining bathroom and comes back with a wad of toilet paper.

"You've got mascara everywhere," she says as she hands it to me.

A surprised chuckle escapes me and I try my best to blot at my face, wincing when the paper comes out all dirtied. Elle lingers nearby, looking everywhere but at me.

"I'm sorry," I whisper for the millionth time. "Please believe me, I didn't mean to hurt any of you. I've lived for so long caring only after my own survival, that being around so many selfless people, it's....enlightening."

She snorts then. "Selfless? Please. We're all selfish. All the guys had a brawl or another with Lucas at some point for each of their women, and Lucas himself has done more than one stupid thing in the name of his pride." A soft sigh escapes her. "So have I, for that matter."

After a brief moment of hesitation, she sits on the bed next to me and reaches for the top of my head. Slowly, gently, she pushes my hair back and caresses my forehead. "I know what it's like to miss your mate."

"He's not my mate," I mutter, even as I blow my nose into what's left of the tissue and new tears arise. *Merda.*

"Keep telling yourself that," Elle laughs. "I thought it was crazy, at the beginning. Being human, or what I thought was human, this whole thing with mates and falling in love at the drop of a hat was the stuff of fairytales. But... I've found myself, in this. If that makes sense."

I sniffle. "It doesn't."

"It will," Elle says. Then she stands and holds out her hand to me. "Come on. They're almost done agreeing on something, and you don't want to miss it."

Despite all the crap I pulled, she just comforted me, spending precious moments reassuring me. *Is this what having a real family feels like?* My throat clogs and words fail me, so I simply choke out a small, "Thank you."

Elle smiles. "What are friends for?"

I take her hand then and get back up. The time for wallowing is gone, so we head back into the living room area. The tension has gone up a notch, with the unbelievable feeling of something happening.

"I agree with most of the plan," Dominic is saying, "but not with putting the girls on the front lines."

"Dom, come on!" Dani yells, confirming my suspicions we stepped into a new kind of war zone. "Enough with the protectiveness. Luz isn't some piece of glass, she's stronger than you know."

Dominic's demeanor changes then, his muscles growing tight and his eyes blazing fire. "When you live through the pain of losing your mate, then talk to me. Until that time, Dani, keep your mouth shut. In Lucas' absence, I call the shots, yeah or no?"

She glares at him for a moment longer, then takes a physical step backwards and bows her head. "Yes."

Dominic surveys everyone else for a long moment, as if daring further defiance. *How the hell did he and Lucas last in the same pack for so long?*

Eerily enough, Dominic's words bring us all back into focus. "Lucas kicked me out of the pack and never brought me back in. If any of you have a problem with me leading this, now's the time to say it."

No one speaks again, and I hold back my sigh of relief.

"What I was going to say," Dominic goes on, "is I don't agree with putting the girls on the front lines. However, I realize we need some magic to push us forward, so what I propose is we find them a safe spot around the mansion, somewhere high up where they can be protected by my wolves. The vantage point will allow for more precision with their magic attacks. Luz can play with the elements, Dani and Elle with the runes, sticking to fire as much as possible. Anything for maximum damage, distraction and occupation. It'll give us the advantage, and then we're in and out."

Silence descends on us all at the solid plan. I have to say, I didn't expect it of him. He seemed so...hotheaded, to hear him so logical is almost a role reversal.

Finn snorts, meeting my eyes over the map. I chance a smile, our own private joke. Then he turns to Dominic. "I like it."

"Me, too," Elle whispers.

Tristan nods, and I do too. Dani bites her lip and bows her head. "Sorry, Dom. I owe you an apology."

He takes a deep breath and reaches for Luz' hand. "All good. Now, let's go save ourselves an alpha, yeah?"

We follow him out the door and pile into two cars like before. Only this time, I'm not feeling constrained or like I'm about to head to my execution. On the contrary, I feel like I truly belong. For once, I'm working with others towards something, rather than on my own. And that feeling...it's worth all the freedom in the world.

Lucas

"I like her," Mamma says after I've caught her up to speed on how I met Monica. "Though I don't agree with your choice of wooing her, at all."

Her frown makes me bark out an incredulous laugh. "Mamma, it's not like she made it any easier for me."

"Hmm. So, you care for her, then?"

The word has me wince and I backtrack. "No more than I'd do for a stranger. She's just a woman."

"Sì, just a woman," she repeats docilely. "If only you would stop lying to yourself."

My scowl doesn't deter her, so I switch topics. "Shouldn't you be teaching me how to get out of this? Shower me with wisdom?"

It's her turn to laugh. "Oh, Luciano, I am selfish. I am not here to teach you, but simply to steal a few moments with you. It is the most I can do, and the most I'll ever have to treasure for the rest of eternity."

Her eyes fill with tears and leave my post by the cell door. "What is it, Mamma? Why do you cry?"

"Your father, he... It is sacrilege, what he did. You cannot–"

Before she can finish, the clatter of heels starts again and she disappears. I turn to my door, scowling as the blonde woman from before shows up again. "There, let's try this again. My name is Ana, and I have a gift for you. Your father was selfish not to show you right away, but I suppose he had his reasons. Just like why he didn't tell you of his new bride."

Ana... My mother mentioned that she'd been taught alongside Monica. And Monica herself had once alluded she didn't get along with her cousin. This explains why.

My eyes shift to Ana's left hand. Monica's words... *Your father remarried...* Sure enough, there's my mother's wedding band on her finger. "How dare you wear that!"

"I dare because I am the new lady of the Conti mansion." Ana takes a step closer. "And you will do well to step in line. Your father does not tolerate people badmouthing me. Why, the last one had his tongue cut out."

"That sounds like Papà," I smirk. "He never did have much control – or taste, apparently."

Her eyes flash with indignation, and I make a show of redirecting my attention to the ceiling. If I don't react, maybe she'll take the hint and leave before I pull her apart limb by limb.

The ferociousness of that yearning has me pause in my thoughts. Enough so that I miss what she says next.

Before I break the place apart, Ana smiles almost cruelly. "Come on in, darling."

More footsteps resound, heavier almost. A man.

Another wolf? Some piece she has on the side who's going to torture me?

If only... Because the reality is a million times more impossible, and unreal. The person who turns the corner isn't a stranger. I would recognize those red curls and honey-colored eyes anywhere, even if his skin tone is a lot paler than I remember.

I stagger backwards, catching Ana's satisfied expression out of the corner of my eye. But all I can focus is the boy...who should be dead.

Matteo, my younger brother.

CHAPTER TWELVE

∞ Fretta ∞

"Nature does not <u>hurry</u>, yet everything is accomplished."

-Lao Tzu-

Monica

Rain coats the roads slick, making Dom's speed even more dangerous. But we're pressed for time, and some things gotta give. I stare out the window, lost in the landscape passing by. Mountains filled with fog loom in the distance, dark and ominous.

A shiver races up my spine, and I'm reminded of my earlier sickness. We all raided Lucas' fridge while brainstorming, but that food won't hold us for long. I only hope we find him – and in time.

My nonna always said chimeras are unpredictable. She used it to explain Francesca sticking with a man as monstrous as

Alessandro, and I still don't understand what possessed me to believe a single word out of his mouth.

But Lucas...will we be too late to save him? Can he hold on and avoid the Underworld until we get there? If anything, my greatest fear is he'll give in to his murderous urges and kill Alessandro, crossing that last barrier and having no one to pull him back from the brink.

Dominic pokes his hand out the window, signaling to the car behind where Tristan, Dani and Elle are. In the rearview mirror, he meets Finn's gaze. "I need to make a quick pit stop and talk to my pack."

Moments later, he pulls over and heads into the woods. I see nothing at first, but once I squint I can detect the outline of dark shapes moving about. Yellow eyes tinged with red appear out of the darkness. I can only count ten, but surely there must be more.

"Is that all of them?" I ask.

"No," Luz says. "Most of them are somewhere in the woods. Others are in town, chasing Reapers."

"I thought Dominic said he didn't agree with Lucas' plan of executing them."

"He doesn't," Luz says softly. "But between letting the vrykolakas prey on humans, or rogue Reapers, he picked the lesser of two evils. If the urge takes them, the Reapers are free game. Otherwise, they've been ordered to stay put."

"With all the humans gone from the area," Finn says, "it's not like the Reapers have any more victims to turn. Soon enough, they'll be extinct either through in-pack fighting or because they've run out of ways to survive."

I can't figure out what to say to his sentiment. From what I've seen of those particular wolves, I don't feel sad that they'll soon be dead. But, who am I to judge?

"They've agreed," Luz whispers, a hint of relief in her voice.

"How can you tell?"

For a moment, I think she won't answer me. But then she says, "Each mate bond has its own quirk, because of the nature of each wolf. It's always a deep connection, with an added bonus. With me and Dom, it's both being tied to his pack, and able to link up mentally."

"For Elle and I, it's more sensing where the other is."

"And Tristan and Dani?"

Luz laughs. "They can tap into each other's thoughts."

"That's...scary."

Luz turns in her seat to look at me. "It is. But it's also really, really worth it." After a beat, she resumes her position and stares back out the window. I think she'll let me off the hook, but nope. "Speaking of... Have you noticed anything weird lately, especially now that Lucas is gone?"

"Weird how?" I don't think I want to know the answer to that question.

"Oh, you know... Weird thoughts, dreams, yearnings you can't explain?"

"I..."

When I'm unable to finish, Luz chuckles and grins at Finn in the rearview mirror. He's smirking into his palm. "Sooner or later, you may as well stop denying it, love."

I force my eyes to stay glued to the window, and Dominic's returning form. "I don't know what you're talking about."

Dominic re-enters the car among boisterous laughing from my two companions. "What's so funny?"

"Nothing," I mutter.

Luz whispers something too low for me to hear, and all he does is smile. Then he leans forward and kisses her forehead, before addressing all of us. "We're good. Half of them will stick around here to cover our backs, and the other half will follow us. They'll be able to keep up, so should arrive on Alessandro's grounds at the same time as us."

Relief spreads through me at the information, even as he puts the car back into gear. It doesn't take us long to get to the edge of town.

Only, as we get closer, something in my gut starts churning. At first it's just an odd pain, almost a prickling sensation.

Then the wave gets stronger, starting a bout of nausea and a throbbing in my head. The closer we get to the edge of town, the worse it gets. Before I can warn anyone, I'm doubling over and panting, moaning in pain.

And then Finn, next to me, yells, "Stop!"

We come to a screeching halt, and I almost bang my head against Luz's seat. Another screech of tires at the back confirms Tristan, Dani and Elle have also come to a standpoint.

Dominic meets my gaze in the rearview mirror, then turns to Finn. He's as green as I am, his fists clenched on the bench next to me.

"Care to explain?" Dominic asks.

"The air tastes weird," he pants. "Filled with...something."

"Magic," I whisper.

Dominic frowns my way. "How do you know that?"

"The same way I do," Finn says. "She feels it."

Already, I'm opening the car door and stepping out. The fresh air helps a tiny bit, but my knees still wobble. When I try to move closer, the nausea hits me again and I double over.

Everyone else has gathered around, and Finn's filling them in on our theory. Meanwhile, I grab hold of the pentagram around my neck and try to center myself. My hand digs into my jacket pocket, and the lavender pouch I have there for such occasions. One breath, two, and I straighten.

The necklace feels warm in my palm, and I can only hope whatever this is, it's something we can surmount. I shake my head, smacking my forehead with my palm. "I should've known Alessandro's men would have a backup plan. Stupid, stupid me."

On a hunch, I bend over and pick a rock, tossing it towards the sign that proclaims *Thank you for visiting Rockland Creek*. There's a sizzle in the air, and the rock turns to dust on the other side. Silence drops behind me, all conversation coming to an abrupt end.

I turn back to the car, my shoulders slouched. "We're fucked. And so is Lucas."

Lucas

"This is... It's not possible."

Dimly, I register Ana opens the door to my cell, and Matteo walks in. He's not a ghost. No shimmering from this one. He's as real as could be and just as young, given he died years ago.

He stops only a foot away from me, and I shakily lift a hand to his cheek. When it touches, the coolness registers, but I don't care. It's my brother, my little brother...

Tears sting my eyes as I pull him into my arms, holding on tight. He hugs me back, shaking in my arms with pent-up emotion. Ana watches on, an unwelcome intrusion into our little get together. Upon seeing my glare, she leaves, but makes sure to lock us both in. Ovviamente, trust runs rampant in this mansion.

I push Matteo back, cupping his cheeks and dropping my forehead to his. "How is this possible? I held your body as you died, I felt your soul..."

He closes his honey eyes and breathes out slowly. Then he opens them and steps back from me, pacing as though he can't keep still. He rakes a hand through his fiery hair, looking still the same – same age, same hair...

"Matteo, talk to me," I plead.

He sighs then and stops pacing enough to meet my gaze. "Papà brought me back."

For a moment, I stop breathing. The words make no sense. I know my father is selfish, but there is no way... *He didn't...*

And then Mamma's words ring in my head. *What your father did...*

Matteo rakes his hair again. "He missed you, missed me, missed having a family. So, he brought me back." He shrugs with a small smile.

"That's not possible," I finally say, my voice flat. "He isn't God."

"No... But he's *a* god. Or, some type, anyway. How else do you explain this?" Matteo looks to the ground. "Besides, isn't this a good thing? I want to be here, *vivo*. Alive. With you."

Yet something doesn't ring quite true. Matteo believes what he's saying, but there's an odd hue to the color of his skin. It's not quite alive, not as it should be. So what exactly did my father do?

My hand shakes again. "How did he bring you back?"

"Ana, his new wife... She's nice. She also comes from a long line of witches. When she realized how sad Papà has been, she promised to make him happier. And, since she can't have kids of her own, she brought him back, well, us."

Claro. Because there's no way that bitch has any other ambition.

The innocence in his expression kills me. "We can be a family again, no? Now that you're here."

I lift my wrists, chained, to show him. "Do you think this is what family does to one another, Matty?"

He shakes his head, and his hopeful expression falls. "I'll talk to Papà. He's just... You know how he gets."

"Sì, I do." A sigh escapes me. "Did he even tell you how Mamma died?"

Matteo looks down. "Yeah, because of me."

The rage is swift and cutting. "Lies! She died because of what *he* did, what *he* caused. Matteo, can't you see he's using you?"

"He's not!"

He moves backwards against the bars, denial apparent in his body language. "Papà only wants us to be back together, as a family. You have to help him, Lucas. Per favore... Do it for me."

I drop to the cot in a corner, so weary I can't stand anymore. "What does he want from me?"

"You wouldn't be doing it for him, Lucas. It's for me. I need... Well, the way they brought me back, it's not right. I need to get something from the Underworld, and then I'll be okay. Alive, for good. Returned from the dead."

The eagerness in his voice drains the last of my strength. "Go upstairs, Matteo. Go upstairs... And bring Papà to me."

He leaves, and it's only then I let the tears fall. Nothing has ever broken me than my poor brother begging, pleading for my help... And not realizing he's playing straight into our monster father's hands.

The droplets fall on the floor silently, feeling like it's pieces of my own soul that are ripped apart. I cry unashamedly for Matteo's innocence, for the peace Alessandro robbed him of... And for what I'll have to do to correct it.

Monica

We've wasted hours trying to find a way out, but whoever did the spell is good. Too good. Every inch of the ground is covered, and so is the other side of town. And I have an idea who's behind it. "This is Ana's work."

"Who's Ana?" Dominic asks.

"My cousin. She used to be Alessandro's mistress, but when I left, had become his new bride." I wrap my arms around myself in a pointless effort to keep warm. What's chilling me is not the air, but the indifference I remember from her as Alessandro doled out his punishments. "She's good. Ruthless. Exactly what Alessandro values."

"There has to be a way out of this," Elle says. "If it's a spell, it can be broken, no?"

I shrug. "Her magic is pretty strong. She's one of Alessandro's collectibles."

Elle grins then. "Trust me, zmeu magic is stronger."

"Can you find out what spell she used?" Dani adds. "Or anything about it?"

I mull it over, then nod. "I can try. She's too smart to give it up, but there's someone else who may slip up." Stepping away, I pull my cell and dial Alessandro. The phone rings, and rings, and just when I think he won't answer, he finally does.

"You have balls calling me, *traditrice*."

I gulp at his tone. If he's calling me a traitor, it's because he knows the full extent of my betrayal. I've seen him angry, and in a rage, and it's never been something I wanted directed at me. Not again, at any rate. The few times it happened were enough, and taught me an unforgettable lesson.

Remember he cannot harm you. You're far away... And you need information. Focus. I take a deep breath and ask, "Is Lucas alright?"

"*Luciano* is perfectly fine, at home where he belongs. And if you had one iota of brains, you could've been here too, free. Instead, I plan to ensure you'll die a miserable death."

"Whatever you say," I mutter, and glance at the sky. The darkening clouds will bring more rain... Could help us. Or not. "I thought the great Alessandro Conti fears nothing."

He bristles on the line, and a low growl seeps through.

"And yet you felt the need to imprison us in the town, so we can't come after Lucas? A bit overkill, don't you think?"

He laughs then. "Ana's idea of a backup plan, cara. Unlike you, she knows where her loyalties lie."

"Sì, too bad we have zmeu magic on our side here. It'll be a piece of cake getting through, you know that?"

"Not even zmeu magic can stack up against the power of the elements, cara. Enjoy trying."

He hangs up, and I close my eyes in relief. It worked. "I'm coming for you, Alessandro." Grinning, I turn back to the wolves. "I have it!"

Only, we're not alone anymore. A familiar figure is floating nearby Dominic, her immortal face solemn. I head back in time to hear the end of Ileana's warning. "I know you think this is something you can face, but there is a lot at stake."

"Da, I get it," Dominic says. "And we'll be careful."

"I don't mean for them," Ileana says with a sweeping gesture towards the pack. "I mean you, dragul meu."

Her proclamation seems to frazzle him, and that in itself makes me wary. I've never seen Dominic shaken, and I don't like the fear filling Luz's expression.

When I head closer, the tension is broken and Ileana glances my way instead. "So, the circle is complete."

"What circle?"

She shrugs, more forlorn than happy. "The mating circle, my dear. You each have your mates now."

"And you never had anything to do with it, right?" Finn asked. "Why let us believe it?"

Ileana tilts her head. "Because it is easier to blame the unknown for a mistake, than to own up to it yourself. And, I do enjoy playing matchmaker occasionally."

Dominic speaks again, seemingly calmer. "Will you help us get out of town?"

"Nu," she says in Romanian. "But you don't need me. Your newest addition has already figured it out."

They all turn to me, even as Ileana takes that moment to disappear, taking her warnings with her. "Is... Should we be worried?" I ask.

Dominic shakes his head, reaching out for Luz's hand to squeeze. "No. Tell us what you found out."

I pull out my cellphone and say, "Alessandro says no zmeu magic can stand up against the elements. Ana was always really good at one particular spell that secures an area with the four cardinal directions and respective elements. Of course, back then she was doing it on a smaller scale, but I guess everyone evolves eventually."

"So how do we break it?" Dani asks.

"We need to find the four points – north, south, east, west. Each one of us will have to conjure one of the elements there to negate whatever's already in place.... And we have to do it at the same time."

The girls all share a look, then nod. "We're in."

Dominic whistles and one vrykolakas comes out of the woodwork, stepping closer. He points to me and says, "Protect her with your life." To Tristan and Finn, he adds,

"The rest of you, go with your mates, and I'll go with Luz. No way we're leaving them alone to do this."

"Alright," Tristan says. "But exactly how are you going to make sure you're doing it at the same time?"

"Flare guns." Elle grins and pops out a few from the back of Finn's truck.

"Alright." Dominic nods. "Everyone shoot up a flare when you're in position. Once the last one shoots, wait for exactly five seconds, then do whatever it is you girls do."

No one complains at the plan, and we spread out, each taking one area. The vrykolakas by my side scares me, and I hesitate for one moment. He comes up to my hip, his bulk large and ominous. Yet rather than open his jaws to eat me whole, he sits down and tilts his head in a way that's almost...cute.

I've heard from Lucrezia how these beasts used to eat humans' hearts, and have venom in their canines to incapacitate. So for me to even think it can be cute, obviously means I've lost my mind.

Step by careful step, I head into the direction of the southern point. With each moment the wolf follows me in silence, I get more comfortable, until I'm finally moving at my regular speed. A flare goes up behind and I figure Luz has already found the northern point.

Keeping my eyes on the ground, I struggle to find the damn area – and then I do. A pentagram symbol etched on a tree, and the scent of blood nearby. With a wince, I pull out my flare gun and shoot up in the sky.

Then it's a waiting game. After a beat, another flare goes to the east.

I pull on my pentagram necklace, centering myself again. Whispering words of comfort, drawing in deep breaths of nature. I only need a wisp of earth to complete my part here, and it should be easy enough to conjure it.

You are connected, through the wolf and the stregheria... Never forget it.

My quiet prayer of thanks goes to my grandmother, for her wise words from so, so long ago. *Grazie, nonna.*

Then the last flare goes to the west. I count to five, and on the fifth number, I place my palm to the tree and summon the magic of my ancestors. Despite the work for Alessandro, I've never had to use it to such an extent.

Yet I feel more than my magic. Through the connection to the tree, I sense the water Luz found, the air symbol Dani ran into, and the fire for Elle. Each one of them, and their zmeu magic, lights up the connection at the same time I do – then lightning strikes the four parts of the circle.

I'm blasted backwards, and by the time I come to with the vrykolakas near me, it's to find the tree completely obliterated. Their extra dose of magic must've made up for my fainter abilities. *Let's hope this worked.*

Wobbling, I head back to the cars. One by one, each of the girls returns, appearing just as worn out as me.

Once we're all together, Dominic says, "Care to do the honors?"

I pick up another rock and toss it into the distance towards the town sign... And watch with satisfaction as it lands on the other side, completely whole. Grinning, I turn back to my companions. "Let's go rescue an alpha, sì?"

∞ ∞ ∞

∞ Tempo ∞

"Time is what we want most, but what we use worst."

-Buddha-

Lucas

With each passing hour, the wounds inflicted on my body heal. My mind though, that's another thing. I can't get over seeing Matteo. Reconciling this new picture with the kid who died in my arms, whose touch I felt as his soul departed... It's beyond me.

For the second time in my life, it feels like the rug's been pulled out from under me and I have no leg to stand on. Darkness consumes this place, and has consumed my father. And he's trying to drag Matteo into it again.

I'm no fool, though. There is no way the great Alessandro Conti feels regret. No, more than likely he wants what he's usually after – control. Over Matteo, and me. I have no idea what use he has in mind for my younger brother, but I need to get him out.

Drained is a poor word for how I feel. For the last hours, all I've done is turn the problem in my head, without finding a solution. If I escape with Matteo, without knowing the implications of his resurrection, Alessandro will come after us. I cannot lose my brother again, not if there is a chance to save him, to give him back the life so unfairly taken from him.

When I sense a presence in the cell, I look up with accusing eyes. "Mamma, is this what you've been trying to tell me?"

She stares at me, eyes filled with tears, but says nothing. I get back up, clenching my fists and feeling that trembling in my body again. My muscles rip, and the change almost overwhelms me. Mamma comes to me and places a hand on my shoulder.

I turn to her, frustrated. "Why won't you say anything?"

Her contrite expression clues me in. Something changed between last time and now, and she cannot talk to me anymore.

"Is it because I'm getting closer to the Underworld? But I haven't killed anyone, and if anything, that fact should be opening the communication between us."

I stare into her eyes, filled with so many unspoken words. Once more, I'm being robbed of answers, of the only person who can provide them. And because I've been too stubborn and have no mastery on the chimera, I cannot work it properly.

Frustration rolls through me again. And then steps echo again outside my cell, and a red haze unlike any previous ones fills me. I gently push my mother away, and face off to the gates. Out of the corner of my eye, I notice her disappearing, but don't let it affect me. Feet width apart, fists clenched, I'm a hunter waiting for its prey.

And when Alessandro walks in, I lunge on him. My chains snap, and this time I yank chunks out of the wall with them. Then I'm flying at him, my fist connecting with his jaw, time and time again. We slam into the wall and I'm unleashed, a flurry of fists and snarls that makes the place tremble.

My father has no chance to fight back. I'm the tornado he should've expected, the fists of the gods coming down on him with all the power of a tsunami. He is useless – pathetic.

"Fight me, bastardo!" I yell back. "Or is it only the weak you like to manipulate?"

By the time six of his men pull me off him, my forearms are filled with rusty hair, and I'm panting hard. It feels like I'm halfway, stuck between morphing and my human side. My wolf is nowhere, instead all I get is the chimera. The fucking chimera singing in my veins, demanding I take a life.

Just one more.

One. More.

And this one, I would relish. The taste of his blood, the feel of my claws ripping through every inch of his chest, pulling out that cold, unfeeling heart – that is what I crave. That is what I *need*.

I lunge again, pulling three of the men with me, then someone tosses a chain against my throat. My neck muscles cord, taut, and I turn to my right. Ana's cold gaze meets mine and she tugs on the chain like a leash.

"Basta," she says softly, and the men step away from me. Or rather, her. It takes me a moment to realize why. She doesn't appear as innocent as she did before. Instead, her robe is almost undulating with darkness.

Ana tugs on me again, and with a jerk of my head, I snap the chain out of her grasp. Alessandro is helped up by two more wolves, which he shoves away, wiping blood off his chin. "Have you lived among savages, boy? All I've tried is to connect with you, and this is how you repay me?"

My fists have found their target. His nose is bloody, and he's sporting a black eye and a bruised jaw. His suit is spattered with more blood and ripped in parts. Satisfaction tears through me, but not enough to dilute the rage.

"How dare you bring Matteo back? Have you so far lost your mind that you really think you can bring us together?"

He slants a look to Ana, who shrugs and bites her thumb. "Scusi, caro. I couldn't resist."

Rather than get mad, Alessandro snorts and judging by their sickening camaraderie, I get the feeling this is a twisted game they play. One I refuse to be a part of.

"You committed a despicable act," I growl. "If Mamma was around, she would be ashamed of you."

Alessandro shrugs. "She never was very proud of me. Then again, you get what you pay for."

"You fucking—"

The wolves around him form a semi-circle, and the movement makes me laugh. "Scared much? For once in your life, you should be."

Alessandro pushes past one particular guy and steps until he's only a foot away from me. It's a show of force, but I can tell he doesn't mean it. His fear coats the air – I guess Finn's gift does come in handy.

"Don't ever talk bad of Mamma again," I hiss at him. "You don't deserve to even say her name, after what you did."

He spreads his palms in a gesture of helplessness. "Luciano, basta! Enough with the old grudges. Your mother was a complicated woman, and she drove me insane as much as I did her. What happened that night was an unfortunate incident. One we have to move on from."

"Sì, I can tell you moved on real well," I scoff with a scornful look at Ana.

Alessandro scowls, his expression almost pinched. "Watch your tone."

"I don't take orders from you anymore, remember?" With deliberate movements, I tear into the chain cuffs around my wrists, watching his expression pale as they turn to dust in my hands. "You wanted me strong, wanted to raise the chimera? Well, congratulations. You have managed, *Papà*. Now what?"

"So you're done with your tantrum and ready to listen to reason?"

I frown. His satisfied stance tells me he's got something coming. "Send your goons out of here, and I'll listen."

Alessandro nods at them and they leave, but Ana stays behind. I can't resist another dig. "How easily you replace quality with quantity, Papà. Used to be you cared about a good thing."

Ana takes a step towards me, hand raised in a slap, but I catch the wrist and stop her. "Raise your hand at me again, and you won't live to regret it."

She blanches at my furious tone, and staggers backwards to Alessandro's side. The sight of his pudgy arm around her trim waist makes me want to puke. "Now, now. I want you two to get along, if we are to be a family."

"You are deluded," I mutter.

"Not so, mio figlio. This entire time you could have escaped, yet you stayed. Why?"

My fist itches with the need to punch him again, but I manage to hold back. Channeling my inner Dominic is not the way out of this. "I thought there might be some logic to your craziness. Something behind all this. Something more than... you losing your mind."

I shake my head, feeling drained all over again. "How could you do this to Matteo? *How*?"

"Matteo died too young, you know it as well as I do. And I found a way to return him to his former glory. You should be thanking me, not judging me for it."

"But I do!" I glare at him, stepping closer. "Do you not see you've robbed him of the afterlife? How can you live with yourself after this?"

Alessandro holds my gaze for another moment, then smirks. And laughs. Maniacally. A similar expression is on Ana's features. "What the fuck am I missing?"

"You never do change, Luciano," Alessandro says as he rights himself. "Very well. Let me drop the charade, since it seems you outgrew the time of fairytales. I don't care about your brother, or you for that matter. What I do care for is your gift. Now, the way I see it, I have what you want. You do something for me, and I'll let you have Matteo, to do with as you wish."

I thought I'd heard it all before from him. I guess I was wrong. Ana's cold smirk confirms they're not joking about this, and that it was their plan all along

"And what makes you think I'm not going to go out there now and drag him with me?" My gaze drops to the remnants of the chains. "Not like you can keep me here."

"One, because he wouldn't believe you. You see, your fratello *does* believe in fairytales, and even though his last life ended rather unhappily, he is so very eager for more." A mocking chuckle. "He definitely does not get that from me. And two, because *un anima* – a soul – taken unwillingly will disintegrate and haunt the earth forever, rather than return in the afterlife."

"What are you talking about?"

"My, you really are clueless for such a powerful hybrid," Ana snorts. "After death, the soul travels to the Underworld. When its existence there is troubled, there is no way to bring him back to the world of the living other than bonding him with someone."

My gaze goes between them. No way my father volunteered for the experiment, which means... "He's bonded to you," I say.

Ana grins wider. "Indeed. Which means any attempt on my life will impact his. And if something happens to me or you try to unwillingly bring him back to the Underworld, to return his peaceful ever after, it will backfire. Matteo will haunt the edge of the earth forever and never find peace."

My fists clench and unclench. Processing this, not acting on it, not killing them when the chimera wants their blood, is hard. Sifting through the rubble and the words trying to find the deeper meaning is even worse.

They bonded Matteo with this witch, and there is no way to undo it. He's stuck on Earth, in a half existence. My poor brother...

Alessandro watches my every move, that glint of calculation in his eyes. "And of course, there is your pack. You do this for me, and I will release them from Rockland Creek."

"What do you mean, release them?" I take a step forward. "What did you do?"

"Tsk, watch yourself," Ana says. "It's only a little spell, designed to keep them confined there. But I could just as easily blow them up to pieces if you don't behave."

"See, mio figlio, over here you are no alpha. And if you do not submit to my demands, I will send the full force of my wolves on them, and make sure to breed your females *extra* hard."

Bile rises up in my throat. "You make me sick."

"Difference of opinion." Alessandro shrugs. "What will it be?"

There isn't much of a choice. I became alpha not because of the power or control, but because it called to me. It's the same reason I've played nice. It's the same reason why I won't leave my brother behind to suffer a worse fate than before.

"Unlike you, I don't let my pack pay for my mistakes," I finally say. "What is it that you want with my gift?"

Alessandro claps his hands in delight. "Meraviglioso! It is simple really. I want you to go to the Underworld and retrieve an object for me. In so doing, you can find a little something that will ensure your brother regains his full life, and no longer needs to be bonded to Ana."

"And what is this object you require?"

Ana steps forward, an eager glint in her eyes. It's only then I notice she's been twirling something in her hand – a coin of some kind. "There is a man there, soon as you enter. It is he who drives the souls to their final destination in Hades' realm. His name is Charon, and what you will procure for your father is his staff."

I shouldn't be surprised anymore, and yet... "His staff? That's what you want?"

"Yes," Alessandro says. "Easy, sì?"

There must be more to it, but I'll leave that for later to figure out. "And what about Matteo's cure? Where is it?"

"Matteo knows," Ana says. "I will give him proper instructions before you head in."

"So, do we have ourselves a deal?" Alessandro asks. "Ana here is a great witch, but even her spells do not last forever."

I glare at him. Forcing the words past my lips feels like the ultimate betrayal, because it's an agreement I don't wish to give. "You can go to hell, Alessandro."

"I knew you'd see it my way." With barely contained satisfaction, they leave my cell, not bothering to chain me again. They've ensured other restrictions are placed on me, though. Ones I cannot escape through sheer brute force.

Merda!

Monica

I'm half-dozing at the back of the truck on the way to the Conti mansion. At some point, I fall fully asleep and wake up in a cellar. A man is on a cot, spread over and with his arm over his head, covering his eyes. Bits of chains are scattered on the ground, and the walls around look like they've been pummeled down.

"Merda." He sighs and stands, only then noticing me. "Monica? What—"

I'm just as shocked. How can I be here, with Lucas, when moments before I was in Dominic's truck?

And then my eyes drink him in, starved from being distanced. He'thinner, though it's only been two days. And there are bruises I can see through his ripped shirt, and a bloodied lip healing. In short, he looks like a mess. "What happened to you?"

Lucas jumps up at the sound of my voice with a panicked expression. "Are you dead? Dio, I swear if he hurt you, I will tear him apart!"

"Che? No, I'm—" I glance down at my shimmering body and hands, frowning. "I'm not sure what this is, but I'm not dead. We're on our way to you."

Lucas pauses midway towards me, taking my words in. "We? Who's we?"

"Me and the pack. Dominic and the vrykolakas, too."

"Merda!" He crosses over to me, grabs me by the shoulders and shakes me gently. "You can't, Monica. Tell them to turn back, all of them! Alessandro wants you here, he wants to use you as leverage against me."

"We can take care of ourselves, we have a plan."

He shakes his head. "My father is a monster, much worse than either you or I could have imagined. You have to turn back. Promise me you'll tell them."

"I'll tell them... but none of us will turn back. We're committed to rescuing you."

Lucas lets me go then and paces the ground in frustration. "I don't need a rescue! I need a damned *miracolo*."

Since I still don't know what's going on, I figure I might as well find out more. So I chance getting closer, and touch his shoulder. "What is it, Lucas? What did Alessandro do?"

He freezes at my touch, and his breathing shifts. Then he's pulling me close, kissing me like I'm his water. It's what I've been craving, yearning for. His touch, his skin close by, his mouth on mine. My body hums at the closeness, and my wolf purrs in satisfaction.

I vaguely wonder if he'd been feeling it too. There's an urgency to his touch, to his kiss, like he knows time is running out. Not just for us, but for him, specifically. That's what makes the alarm bells ring in my head, albeit sluggishly.

We end up on the cot, me on top, tangled in a mass of limbs. I don't even know how it's possible, when it looks like I'm some apparition to him, but I chalk it up to his chimera. What I do care about is his frantic heartbeat. I recognize this mechanism, I've used it enough times.

So despite wanting more of him, I pull back gently from his masterful touch, and cup his cheek. In his lap, with his arms on my waist, the gesture feels close, intimate. "Talk to me. What's going on?"

Lucas says nothing for long moments. So long, in fact, I fear he won't open up, much like before. But then...

He drops his forehead to my chest, not in a sensual gesture, but in one of defeat. "Alessandro brought back my brother from the dead, and he's leveraging him against me. Him, and all of you. I cannot... I won't let him hurt any of you. I failed before to protect what was mine, and I will not do so again."

There's so much pain in his voice, so much hopelessness that I'm not used to, not with him. Lucas has been a rock, a pivoting tornado since I've met him. To see him like this...

I drop my mouth to his, gently kissing him. He nips at my lips, then the embrace grows in intensity. My fingers roam through his hair, and he pulls me even closer, then releases me abruptly. I can hear footsteps in the distance, a clatter of boots and heels. Two men, and a woman. I can already guess who she is.

"Why did they beat you up?" I whisper urgently.

"A measure of control." He stands, running a hand through his hair in agitation. "You have to go, Monica. Before they come here."

"I don't even know how I got here! Let alone how to get back."

He sighs, caressing my cheek reverently, like he'll never see me again. "Just close your eyes and think of your body. It's bound to work, none of this is permanent. Just... temporary." He opens his mouth as if to say something else, but the footsteps get closer. "Tell everyone to stay away, tesoro."

I don't know what to say to make it better. It feels like I'm losing him, and I'm not even grasping the full story. So I fill the silence with empty words, hoping he gets my meaning. "Hang in there, Lucas. Just... hang in there, please."

The last I see of him is his resigned expression. Then I close my eyes, and think back to the smells inside Dominic's truck, and the mission I have to return to. When I open them again, I'm back to reality.

Finn's staring at me intently, and I gulp. *How much of all that did he catch?*

"Pretty much all of it." He grins. "You're having Lucas dreams, and you still deny you're his mate?"

"More than that," I whisper, ignoring the second part of his question. "I don't know how, but I was physically with him... And we're going to get there too late."

∞ ∞ ∞

∞ Salvezza ∞

"Work out your own <u>salvation</u>. Do not depend on others."

-Unknown-

Monica

"Not if I've got something to say about it," Dominic growls and guns the engine. Next to him, Luz dials a number and tells someone – I'm guessing Tristan – to step on it.

"Will the vrykolakas be able to keep up?" She asks Dominic.

He nods tightly, then meets my gaze in the rearview mirror. "How did that happen, you seeing him?"

"I don't know. One minute I fell asleep here, the next I was with him in Alessandro's mansion. I... Lucas thought I was dead, because I looked like a ghost. But I wasn't."

"How do you know?" Luz asks.

A blush spreads on my cheeks. "Umm, because he could touch me." Thankfully, I'm avoided further embarrassment when Dominic shifts into a deeper question.

"How did Lucas look?"

I shake my head. "Not good. He was beat up, but didn't say much about how it happened."

"Beat up?" Finn frowns. "With all of his powers? That makes no bloody sense."

"Unless someone with magic restrained him," Luz points out.

"Those wankers!" Finn curses, at the same time Dominic lets loose a few string curses in Romanian. Not that I speak the language, but his tone is unmistakable.

"What else?" he asks.

I think back to the dream – or interaction, whatever it was. Lucas' hands on me, his mouth on mine, all of it makes my body hum. But that's not what I need right now. My wolf craves the real thing, but first we have to help him escape.

"You still want to pretend you're not mated?" Finn points out again.

When I glare at him, I notice I now have the attention of everyone else in the car. "What do you want me to say? That I miss him? Because dammit, I do! With every inch of my soul."

"Good," Dominic says coolly. "Then you should be able to take that and focus it. Turn it into a weapon. Tell us everything that can help us, otherwise we're going in there blind. That's the only way you can help out Lucas right now, Monica."

"Okay, okay." With a sigh, I push aside the memories of our urgent fumbling and instead focus on the words. "Lucas seemed really drained. I don't think it was from the beating. He was just... I've never seen him like that. His dad brought back his brother from the dead. I think... I think he's going to use it as leverage on Lucas, and that he's going to willingly do what they want him to."

"Which is?" Finn asks softly.

"We didn't have time to get into it. There were footsteps and Lucas was adamant I had to get out before whoever it was returned."

"Can you guess what they'd want of him?" Luz asks.

With what I know of Alessandro, only one possibility comes to mind. "They probably want him to open the gate to the Underworld."

Dominic mutters some more Romanian curses under his breath, and I feel the car speed even more. We must be way over the limit, but I'm not about to tell him to slow down. Instead, my thoughts go back to Lucas, to the utter helplessness I'd seen in him.

How I wish I could've taken it away...

I've tried so hard not to care for this guy, when in reality I've been hooked since the moment I walked into his office. If I'd ever dared to hope for a match, a mate, he would've fit Lucas to a T. And now that I risk losing him...

My chest hurts and I inhale deeply. Finn reaches over the seat and holds my hand, squeezing it. "I know that feeling. Elle was taken from me, too, and I got her back. We all owe Lucas something, and there's no way we're letting him go without a fight."

"I appreciate your words, but there may be more going on here than even I realize. Especially with Lucas' brother back... I can't even fathom how Alessandro made that happen."

"Whatever it is, we can fix it," Luz says.

"You say it like it's easy... Lucas himself seemed so resigned, he begged me to tell everyone to turn away. And you don't know Alessandro."

"No," Luz agrees. "But I know Lucas. And nothing – no one – stands in his way. Least of all his father."

Lucas

Seconds after Monica disappears, my father and brother step in, as does Ana. Footsteps echo in the distance, like a security group coming together. Even if my estimations of their numbers are off, it's clear I'm not going anywhere.

I only hope Monica brings back my message to Dominic, and he makes the right choice for the pack. It was obviously a rather stupid move on my end kicking him out again. Not that it hadn't come to a boiling point, but the fact is his loyalty was always to me. Something I was irreversibly blind to.

When Matteo skulks inside the cell too, something inside me cringes. Accusation lingers in his eyes, and I can only imagine what Alessandro told him about the bruises and cuts on his face. Sighing, I hold out my hand.

"Matty, come here, ti prego."

He shakes his head at my pleading and steps closer to our father. The stubborn jut to his chin is one I recognize all too clearly. Alessandro grins wickedly, something that goes completely missed by my younger brother. Another wave of helplessness threatens to descend on me, but I refuse to show it. Not to them.

They think they can control me.

They think I give a shit.

I don't. But Matteo is an innocent, and I won't let their perverse greediness have him pay the price for something that's not his doing. If there's even a small chance I can give him back the life he was robbed from, then I will do it.

A sigh escapes me, and I try again. "Matteo, our papà has asked me to go with you someplace. A darker place. To get you something that will... It will ensure you'll be back, for good, with us. You asked me to help you before, remember? So, will you come with me, fratello?"

Matteo shrugs and finally moves towards me, reluctance in his every heavy step, his head bowed and hands in the pockets of his jeans. "Fine, but don't expect me to talk to you after the way you beat him up."

Over his head, I glare at our father, but say nothing. Instead, I focus on Ana. "Do your worst, witch."

Ana steps forward and heads to the far wall of the cell. She places her palms on it and moves them in a crisscrossing pattern, muttering something under her breath. I can see a pentagram bracelet dangling from her wrist, the symbol similar to the one Monica wears.

Despite being here, surrounded by all this shit, the little reminder brings me back to having her in my arms. It had felt good – too good. The way she read me, cradled me, I haven't known that in a while. Great sex, sure. But bone-deep caring? I'd never let my emotions progress past the physical stage. But with Monica...

I shake my head. *Gotta focus on what's important right now, not get airheaded.*

Ana is muttering some more things, and for a second it feels like the entire room has a heartbeat. There's elation coming off her in waves, which I can sense thanks to Finn's gift. I'm so very tempted to use the vârcolac strength from Dominic and Tristan's abilities to grab Matteo and get out of here...

One look at my father reminds me of his words. He will carry them through, even if it means killing his own freshly bedded bride.

Scowling, I can only wait and bide my time. The scent of blood hits me hard, and I notice one of Ana's hands is dripping. The wall she's been holding on to is now pulsating black, undulating and rolling like a live mass.

Every hair on my body rises in protest. I may not know how to use Daniela's magic, but even I can sense when something is so utterly wrong, it should not exist right now.

Ana turns and heads closer to me, again twirling that coin in her hand. "It is done," she says. "All it needs is the blood of the chimera to open." As she passes by me, she tosses me a knife.

I wish to hell I could slice her throat with it, but not yet. For now, I will bide my time, and get Matteo his innocence back. After, once he's safe, I'll finish this up.

So I move away from her and my father, and cut my palm. Blood trickles down, coating the blade and I thrust it into the darkness of the wall. It gets swallowed up and no clatter of noise echoes back.

For the first time, it sinks in what I'm doing. Mamma's stories of the Underworld, and what awaits there. I'd had nightmares as a growing young man of its fiery depths and everything they hide. Of becoming enslaved to it, like Cerberus was to forever guard the gate.

And now, in spite of everything I've done to steer clear, I'm about to head right in.

"You ready?" I ask Matteo, forcing my tone to be light.

He nods, and though he appears brave I know he's afraid. I hold my hand out to him, and this time he takes it despite still being annoyed at me. His palm is clammy, and I bite back any further words of reassurance.

Over my shoulder, I add, "Isn't there a payment for Charon?"

Alessandro grins and tosses me a coin. It's lighter than Ana's, but with the same type of design – a man's face, pointing in two separate directions.

"That should do it," my father says. "Now, off you go." As if he's sending us to fucking school.

I hide my rage and turn back to the portal. My blood has made it shimmer silver now, as if that would make it more inviting to cross. It doesn't. But then a tendril of that portal sneaks on the ground and wraps around my ankle. Iciness spreads through me, followed by an emptiness as swift as death itself.

Monica

It's easy to recognize when we enter Alessandro's territory, because we go from the wild of the land to something completely put together. After a few kilometers, we get closer to the mansion's grounds.

In the distance, I see the house cradled at the bottom of a valley. Old-school Victorian style, all white and ivory, it's meant to impress, and it does. As we get closer, I know we'll see the Roman-style columns at the front, luscious gardens, and luxurious opulence inside. A forest runs alongside the road leading there, providing ample coverage.

Dominic pulls the car over before we go any further, and Tristan does the same behind us. We all pile out, and Dani draws a rune in the air that makes the vehicles shimmer, then disappear.

"It won't last long," she says, "but it should be enough to get us in unnoticed."

Dominic nods, then surveys us all. "Alright, people. We stick to the plan, no improvisations. Luz, if anything happens, call this off, grab Dani and Elle, and get the hell out of here."

Lucrezia's stubborn expression tells me that order is wasted on her, but she says nothing. Dominic pulls her into his side, as if to draw strength from the swift embrace. "If everything goes well, we'll be back here before the sun rises."

"And if it doesn't," Finn says, "you girls do as he said. *No* exceptions."

No one nods, or agrees. We're all on edge. In the woods around us, I feel movement and turn – but it's only the vrykolakas. Half of them hang back, and I know they'll be around to help Luz. The other half dutifully line up behind Dominic.

He nods, as if that's the signal he'd been waiting on. "Here it goes." With a kiss to Luz that breaks my heart, he turns away and morphs. Tristan and Finn say their goodbyes too, and then it's just me they're waiting on.

I look at each of the girls and whisper, "I'll make sure they get back to you safe." It's a promise I'll do my best to fulfill, even if it costs me my life. I figure after all they did, and what they've shown me is possible, it's the least I can do.

Then I turn to morph, but Elle calls out. "Monica?" When she has my attention, she smiles. "Go get your Lucas."

I don't bother correcting her. There's no point, given everything else I've lived in the last days. So I let the transformation come over me, and join the guys. As we run, keeping to the shadows, I'm thankful for the dark night that coats us all.

And then something hits me – from the inside. Like an icy wind that knocks the breath out of me, and I drop to the ground, howling in pain. Within moments, the guys are surrounding me, but only Finn chances a prod with his muzzle.

Dimly, I hear him talk to Dom in my mind. *It's Lucas. She's feeling something that's happening to him.*

How is that possible? Tristan asks.

The same way it happened to all of us. Dominic lays down by my side and drops his head on mine. *I need you to get up,*

Monica. The more we linger, the more chance there is to lose him. Help me get to Lucas, and I will make sure he's safe.

It takes all the strength I possess and a heavy dose of will to push myself to a standing position. My muscles tremble with the effort, and I'm chilled to my insides. *What the hell is going on?*

Dominic shakes his head. *We'll find out when we get there. Can you move?*

Barely, but yeah. Don't worry about me.

And then we're running again, and I'm using that pain to fuel me, because I know I need to get to Lucas.

Vrykolakas flank us from every corner, and we storm the mansion like ninjas in the night. Grunts and muffled screams echo as the vrykolakas' venom kills the guards, and then we're still covering ground. Magic has hidden us this far, helping us get by the outer circles almost undetected, and I know the girls are doing their job. But now we're in Alessandro's territory.

It's amazing seeing Dom's brute strength and how Finn and Tristan work together without even checking. They have each other's backs, and when outnumbered, I have theirs. We move with a synchronicity that surprises and leaves me in awe, all at the same time.

Once we're deep inside the mansion, I take lead since I know the place like the back of my hand. The minute guards see my branded chest, they frown in confusion, hesitating.

Alessandro must have not told them of my betrayal – a mistake that will cost his life.

It takes us much longer than I'd thought to get through to the last portion of the house. I lunge on one of the guards, while Finn finishes the other. Turning to my human form, I hold onto the wolf's throat and ask, "Where is Lucas?"

His eyes shift to the cellar doors, and I get up. Daniela made sure we'd all be clothed when switching forms. And although I'm not sure it's a good idea to go in human, Dominic, Finn and Tristan also shift.

"You lead," Dom says. "We'll be right behind you."

I nod and step down the stairs. A murmur of voices drifts upwards.

"Do you really think he'll do it?"

"For his brother, Luciano will do anything."

I appear in the cellar just as they turn to leave. Alessandro and Ana. Behind them, Lucas' body is sprawled on the floor, pale and near an incinerated wall.

"Well, well. The traitor returns."

At the sight of Lucas' pale body, I lose it. I lunge at Ana, shoving her further into the cell. She trips over her heels and barely holds herself standing.

"What did you do to him!"

Behind me, Dominic and Tristan move on Alessandro, restraining him so he can't help his witch lover. I'm unhinged though, the wolf in me boiling with fury. I grab a fistful of her hair and yank it back. Ana winces in pain, but I don't hold back from punching her in the stomach.

As she doubles over and flops to the ground, I say, "What. Did. You. *Do*?"

She glares up at me, her makeup smudged. "Something you should've had no problem doing, cara. It's not my fault you have scruples."

With a howl, I fall atop her, straddling her and smacking her head on the floor. My hands go to her throat, and I want to squeeze every bit of life out of her. Then Finn's there, pulling me back, and his gift calms me while his arms restrain me.

I glare at him. "She deserved it."

"Not arguing there, love. But if you kill her, we'll never know how to reverse it."

Without answering, I yank myself out of his hold and crawl over to Lucas, touching his cold hand. The same one that held me mere hours before.

"There's no pulse." My eyes are filled with tears when they meet Dominic's. "There's no pulse!"

He grabs Alessandro by the neck and lifts him up. "Now, you have one chance. You're going to let us follow Lucas wherever the fuck you sent him. And then I'm going to make sure to bring him back and let him have his revenge on you."

He tosses my old alpha against the walls, rattling the entire building with the force of his attack. It feels good to see Alessandro scared. So, so good.

It's then I notice Ana staring at something. It must've fallen during our struggle, and by the look on her face, she wants it. Desperately. As I pick it up, it's a faded coin. I rub the dirt off it, and find the profile of a man facing two ways. My nonna's old teachings come back to me and I recognize it – Janus. *The god of doors and arches... Could she have used this to open the portal?*

With a smirk her way, I pocket the coin. *Might come in handy later.*

"Get him and the witch, and let's go up. Monica, help me with Lucas."

I follow Dominic's orders. We get out of the cellar, but the entire time I'm torn between keeping an eye on Ana to make sure she doesn't toss some magic at us, and Lucas, whose cold arm is now wrapped around my shoulders.

"We'll get him back," Dominic whispers as we walk through the mausoleum. "I promise."

Thing is, I've had enough broken promises to know not to count on them.

∞ ∞ ∞

∞ Inferi ∞

"No one should brave the <u>Underworld</u> alone."

-Edgar Allan Poe-

Lucas

"Luciano? Lucas!" Matteo's voice snaps me out of my daze. I come to, realizing I've been on my feet and staring into space for a few moments. How long exactly, I can't pinpoint, but it must've been bad enough to get my younger brother to talk to me.

We're in some kind of dark forest. Behind us, there's a path that grows increasingly more obscure. And ahead, a little past where Matteo is yelling at me from, the path goes downhill towards a cave.

I glance down at my body, noticing I'm shimmering just like Mamma. Matteo, on the other hand, is still as pale as ever, perhaps even more so. I frown at him. "Why do I look like a ghost?"

He shrugs, and continues walking. Apparently now that I've answered him, I also lost his attention. "Hey, do you even know where you're going?" I call out.

That stops him in his tracks. *Idiota.* I love my brother, but his antics are getting on my nerves, as is his naivety. So I stride over and turn him around by the shoulders. I'm jarred by his stricken expression, and the tears falling down his cheeks.

"Matty, what is it?"

He sniffles and wipes at his face clumsily in an effort to appear less affected. "I just...You weren't moving at first, and then you did but you weren't, well, you, and I thought... I thought... that you died." The last is said on a whisper.

Without a word, I pull him into my chest and hug him close. "I'm still here, fratello." Father did a number on him, removing him from his peaceful slumber. But add on top of that our dysfunctional family, and I'm not surprised he's even more on edge than of his living.

"Then why are you so...shiny?"

I snort and let him go, ruffling his red curls like I used to. "Probably because Mamma gave me her special gift."

"Is that why Papà sent us down here together?"

I sigh then, all trace of lightness gone. "Sì, claro." Rubbing the back of my neck, I look around. "You've been here before, Matty?"

"Yeah," he says, seemingly unaffected. "We go that way." He points towards the downhill slope, and I follow in his tracks. Now that we're alone, I'm having a hard time finding the words. I've been so focused on Alessandro and his shit that I haven't even allowed myself to enjoy having my younger brother back. How does that feel for him, I wonder?

"Matty?"

"Yeah?" He focuses hard on the path ahead, but I can hear the catch in his voice.

"I know it's weird, being back, but... You know I'm happy you're with me, right?"

He stops then and turns to me, his expression forlorn. "Are you? Papà said you beat him up because you didn't want to be forced back into the family."

The bastardo... Of course he took my words and twisted them! I sigh and step closer, grabbing his shoulders again. "Matty, Alessandro and I have never seen eye to eye. You know that. Remember back before you died, how I also nearly beat him up?" When he nods, I continue, "That's why he has bruises. Because I don't agree with what he did – he disturbed your sleep. It's unnatural, no matter which way you look at it."

His eyes fill with tears and he tries to push me away, but I hold on tighter. "Matty, *aspetta*. That doesn't mean I don't love you, and I'm not happy to see you! You're my little brother, and you have no idea how much I missed you and how much I blamed myself for what happened."

My words seem to be getting through. At the very least, he stops trying to struggle out of my hold. "I wasn't even at your funeral, because Mamma died shortly after. I... It's been hard, Matty. I'm glad you're back, but I'm deathly scared of losing you again. I don't think I could survive it."

The truth of the words reverberates through me, something I haven't let myself feel. Much like my feelings for Monica. How much have I really buried, and how much more will have to go sideways before I'm able to man-up and admit everything?

When I let Matteo go, there's a tentative smile on his lips. "I'll be okay, Lucas. With a big brother like you, how could I not?"

I return the smile, even if it feels forced. Something about Alessandro's eagerness to have us down here tells me this won't be easy. None of it. As we start walking again, we're side by side like the hikes we used to take as kids. Only, of course, this time we're heading into the Underworld itself. I try not to let that dampen my spirits.

"How does it feel, being back alive?"

Matteo shrugs. "Strano... Like I'm there, but not there, you know? Like part of me is missing."

"Ana said you'd know what we need from down here to make you whole again."

He falters in his steps. "Well, sort of. Charon will know, and if nothing else, I figure Mamma will."

I remember Charon being the guy in the boat who leads the souls around. Hopefully, he'll be less of a bastard than our father, and give us some straight answers.

We get to the cave and Matteo goes in first. I hesitate, then follow him in. The moment I step through, my body vibrates, and the shimmering grows more intense, almost reddish. Then it's gone, and I'm back to a regular silver color.

Matteo's wide eyes meet mine. "Is that normal?" I ask him.

"No... I've never seen anything like that. The souls that come through aren't, um, well they're not formed like you. They're little orbs. Like these ones."

I take in the surprisingly well-lit area we're in. The cavern walls have a rugged yet smooth surface only man could have designed, and little shiny orbs are floating all around. That's what Matteo is referring to. I shudder at the thought of the humans reduced to such...remnants.

Matteo notices it. "They're not so bad, you know. But, maybe, let's not stick around too long. Charon's boat is that way."

As we continue onwards, I take in our surroundings. I've no idea how we'll even get out of here, but maybe I might just be able to see Mamma, and she can tell me what she couldn't in the land of the living.

Now that I'm here, the exact same place I didn't want to be, I wonder if I'll even be allowed to go back to the living. My nightmares of the Underworld are ever more real in my mind, and so is the gut feeling that I'm running out of time. Too fast.

As if to prove my point, some of the orbs don't linger above our heads, rather surrounding me close – too close.

"I think they're attracted to your gift," my brother laughs from ahead.

Matteo's steps never falter. I lengthen my stride so I can be fully by his side and nudge him, trying to make the most of the time we have together. "So, did you meet anyone while you were down here?"

He shakes his head, though a blush sort of coats his cheeks. "Not really. I mean, some of the people here have been around for ages, so even the girls who look like my age are ancient."

I snort. "And? You got something against older women?"

He wrinkles his nose and I laugh. "Alright, point taken. No mummies for my younger brother."

"What about you?" he asks. "I overheard Papà talking about some Monica. Who is she?"

"She's..." Damn, I dug myself into a conversation I don't want. "She's a friend."

Matteo snorts. "I've seen your *friends*, Lucas. They're model-worthy. Is she just as banging?"

I roll my eyes. Even years in the Underworld haven't robbed him of his much-loved slang. "Sì, she's pretty."

"Pretty?" Matteo wrinkles his nose. "Come on, give me a bit more."

"You don't give up, hmm? Bene. Let's see. She has hair like a raven's, and eyes as blue as sapphires. When she gets mad they flash with lightning. And her body, well, it would put a goddess to shame."

Matteo whistles at my description. "Wow, you've got it bad!"

"Got what bad?"

"Being in love, duh!"

I nearly trip over my own two feet. "Fratello, you've lost your brains down here. I'm not in love. I don't *do* love."

Matteo laughs even harder. "Claro, whatever you want to tell yourself."

Too soon, the hilarity ends as the space around us grows somber. My eyes scan the area, waiting for an ambush. "Why did it get darker?"

Matteo shrugs. "Don't know. I don't remember much from the first time, but I know around Charon's boat it gets like this. Some people whisper it's because he's blind, and he wants to take the light out for unsuspecting souls, too."

I glance at him. "What do you think?"

"I think... I think that what's scarier is not Charon, but the dog past him."

"Cerberus, you mean?"

My thoughts drift back to the old legends I grew up with. A three-headed dog that protects the gate to the Underworld. Incidentally, one created by the same father of the original chimera. *I wonder if there are also mini versions of that particular monster running rampant somewhere in the world of the living...* The thought isn't comforting. At all.

Matteo nods, snapping me back to reality. "He's massive, Lucas."

I laugh, trying to sound brave. "Don't worry, I'll protect you." Even as I make that promise, my gut tells me nothing will be simple this time around. And for the first time, I miss my pack, sensing their loss like a physical blow.

All the past conflicts, I've had them to rely on. Now, I'm on my own. And while this is my blood family, my mess... I miss the family I chose.

Monica

"You cannot save him," Ana taunts me.

"Lucas can save himself," I toss back at her. "But thanks for being a bitch and meddling with things that don't concern you."

She tries to laugh, but I push her into a chair next to Alessandro. She's been talking crap the entire way to the library, and I'm tired of it. Mainly because I really, really want to slap the shit out of her.

Once we have Alessandro and Ana secured with rope – and a blindfold and gag for her to avoid magic use – I leave Finn and Tristan to keep an eye on them and join Dominic. I make sure to take her pentagram bracelet, too. He's talking with Lucrezia, and their whispered fight has me antsy.

After we caught Lucas' dad, Dominic's vrykolakas secured the mansion and we called the girls back here. The outside is a mess – Alessandro has a lot of loyal wolves that were recalled by some who managed to escape us. So, really, we're under siege in a Victorian-era house with more secret passages than a castle, meaning we need to get out of here, and fast.

But we can't until we figure out how to get Lucas back. All we've managed to put together is that somehow they sent him and Matteo to the Underworld. Ovviamente, only Lucas' soul travelled, and his body was left behind because he was still alive. Whereas Matteo...

"What's going on?" I ask Dom and Luz, avoiding the sight of Lucas' pale form on a sofa.

I don't know how much longer I can stand seeing him like that. If someone would have told me I'd be pining for a stubborn alpha with a streak of crazy chimera blood in him, I would've laughed in their face. And now... I just want him back. Clenching my fists so I avoid going to him, I force attention on my companions.

They stare at each other for another beat, then Lucrezia folds her arms over her chest and lifts her chin in a gesture I've come to know as defensive. "If you go, I go."

"Out of the question," Dominic says.

"Just because *your* blood is royal, doesn't mean you get to order me around. I've humored you enough, but this is where I put my foot down."

I groan, loud enough to grab their attention properly this time. "Guys, please. I'm tired, I'm hungry, and Lucas looks dead enough to make me lose my shit. *What* are you talking about?"

"Dominic wants to go after him, in the Underworld, and I want to join him."

"Great, I'm in," I say. "I didn't know it could be that simple. How do we do that?"

Dominic glares at me. "It's *not* that simple. I'm only *guessing* that I can go, on account of me having both strigoi and wolf blood in me. My vrykolakas have no soul, meaning, technically, I can do this. But you and Lucrezia don't have the half-dead in you."

"Except I already died," Luz reminds him softly. "Which means if nothing else, going back there should be easier for me. And Monica is linked to Lucas, so there's that. Plus, your vârcolac side has its downsides, or have you forgotten? If you get tempted down there, if anything like what happened with Radu happens again, you may lose your soul, period. Which is why you need me there."

"Oh." It dawns on me then that they're both afraid to let the other go. "Why don't you let me go, alone?"

"No," Dominic shakes his head. "Lucas would kill me if anything happened to you."

"I doubt that."

He throws me a glare intended to shut me up, then turns to Lucrezia again. Their bickering resumes, and I give up and head back to the rest of the pack while they reach a conclusion. Tristan and Dani are keeping an eye out on the prisoners now.

"Where did Finn and Elle go?" I ask.

"To check out the area, and make sure we didn't miss anyone inside the house," Dani says.

"I may owe you an apology," Tristan adds. "For being a bit of a bastardo."

"Just a bit?"

He shrugs. "Maybe more than a bit."

I grin. "Apology accepted."

Dominic and Lucrezia come back then, and she's grinning. "We're on, but just the three of us."

"You're not seriously going after him in the Underworld?" Dani pales.

Alessandro hears us and starts laughing, but I ignore him. "We are, and we're going to get him."

"And how can you be so sure?" he drawls, desperately trying to gain our attention.

It works, if only temporarily. I pull out the coin I'd been hiding and shove it in his face. "Because I have this. And your precious Ana isn't the only one who can play with the occult when the need arises."

His eyes glitter with menace, and I get a bad feeling about leaving the rest of the pack behind. To Dani, I whisper, "Get Lucas' body somewhere safe... Maybe even back to the cellar, after we leave. If anything happens, if you guys need to take off and his body is harmed, we won't ever be able to bring him back."

She nods. "Consider it done."

Then I join Lucrezia and Dominic, already by the door. "Let's head back to the cellars. It'll be easier to re-do the spell in a spot it's already been cast in."

We head down, the silence eerie in our steps. Dominic mutters under his breath about Lucas and his crazy family.

"It's too bad you didn't get to meet his mom," I say softly. "She was a beauty."

"Lucas never talks about her," Lucrezia says.

"I've only ever heard him talk of her once," I admit. "I think... Her loss really affected him, and the fact he could do nothing to stop it. I'm not sure he's ever gotten over it."

"Speaking of losing people... We're omitting something else," Dominic says. "We said we'll bring Lucas back, but what about his younger brother?"

The door to the cell squeaks as I push it open, and walk to the incensed wall. My palm presses against it, caressing it and getting a feel for the energy underneath. On a whisper, I say, "There was only one coin."

"I don't get it." Dominic steps near me. "What's the link with the coin?"

"Janus is a god we know in the old stregheria way of life. He's the deity watching over doors and arches, but a lot of people think in terms of houses. Or, he's also the same one who looks over portals. Like between worlds."

"And the Underworld falls under that?"

"Sì," I say. "So knowing how to tap into that power while having stregheria magic that is linked to the old ways, it's a pretty high. From when we were young, Ana's been into the occult. It's why my nonna refused to teach her magic at some point, but Ana just went off on her own. I guess she figured out a way to do the ritual while channeling Janus' forces, and that's how she sent Lucas to the Underworld."

"That's great," Dominic says, his tone dripping with sarcasm. "Gotta love more witches into the occult. But the question is, can you replicate the ritual?"

"I think so," I say. "But something like that would need chimera blood to open properly, to lead directly to the Underworld. Which is one thing we don't have. But since Lucas got beat up in here, I'm hoping we can scrape some blood somewhere."

"Alright, good. And his younger brother?"

"That's what I can't figure out," I whisper. "If they used Matteo to leverage Lucas, why send them both to the Underworld? Ana bragged that Matteo is bonded to her, and that's what keeps him alive. If that's the case, then sending him there is counterproductive."

"Unless..." Luz shares a look with me. "Unless Matteo was a trap, and never intended to actually survive."

Dominic straightens from a corner he'd been inspecting closely, presumably in search of Lucas' blood. "You've lost me. What are we saying?"

"That Matteo isn't coming back. They sent him to the Underworld so Lucas can witness him die – again," Luz says.

"And there's only one reason why they would do that." I feel sick at the realization. "To force Lucas' change to full chimera, once and for all. *And* make sure he would do their bidding in the Underworld."

"But with Matteo gone," Dominic points out, "they would lose their leverage."

My heart beats faster as more of the pieces fall together. "No, on the contrary. They would use what has happened *as* leverage. Either Lucas remains in their servitude, doing whatever they wish of him, or they pull Matteo and his mother's souls from the Underworld, over and over."

"That's horrible!" Luz says.

"What happens to a soul when..."

Dominic doesn't have to finish his sentence. "It gets displaced, and haunts the earth forever, until nothing is left."

"So you're saying Alessandro would force Lucas to work for him, and if not would threaten to destroy his brother and mother's souls?"

"Yeah," I whisper.

Dominic growls. "If Lucas doesn't kill this fucking bastard, it'll be my pleasure to do so when I return."

∞ ∞ ∞

∞ Sfide ∞

"Accept the <u>challenges</u> so that you can feel the exhilaration of victory."

-George S. Patton-

Lucas

One thing I always remember from my nightmares of the Underworld is the darkness – gripping, living, and thriving like an evil being. There is none of that here, only never-ending walking, and souls. So. Many. Souls. Despite them, my steps are assured, unafraid.

Perhaps the reason for my calmness is Matteo, and trying to be strong for him. He had no one the first time around, and it's my duty as his older brother to be there for him. Or, maybe, it's because I expected some kind of effect on me. The chimera to completely overtake me, the need I'd been feeling to rip through me.

None of that happens and, in a way, it makes me even more wary. In other ways, it calms me down. Not as much as I need it, though.

When we emerge from the dark tunnel, it's in a larger cavern. Or, what I think is a cavern. It takes me a moment to realize the ice I see in the distance is actually a lake. A faint light emits from above amid dark clouds, like the barest of moons. Not that it's possible, but the illusion is grand.

Matteo glances over his shoulder. "That'll be Charon, up ahead. Let's get closer." Without waiting for me, he bounces ahead, completely unafraid.

I shake my head and follow behind, toying with the coin my father threw me. Its rough surface feels like sandpaper against my fingers, an odd reminder that I can still feel something.

As I step forward again, something shudders through me. I stop in my tracks, taking stock of every shadow around me. There is no witch here to cast a spell, no one trying to pull one on me. So where the hell is this coming from?

My insides feel icy for the barest of moments, and all breath leaves my body. I bend over, hands on my knees and panting. My chest constricts, my lungs seize – and then it's gone. The only aftereffect is a tingling around my fingertips.

"Che diavolo..."

The only possible explanation would be something happening to my pack. We've been interconnected since

Lucrezia officially joined us, and it has only gotten stronger. I'd felt the depth of that connection when we lost her – however briefly – and suffered a new kind of hell on my own, isolated from my pack.

But I'd told Monica to warn them off. Did she play into Alessandro's hands, and fall prey to his machinations? Or... There is, of course, the possibility I felt Monica's own pain. But that's ludicrous, and would imply a much stronger bond than we currently have.

A chuckle escapes me, and I straighten from my crouch. I don't have time to linger over the odd sensation. Matteo waves me over urgently, and I head towards him.

The boat comes into view first, gliding over the somber lake. I would've expected it to be black, but it's a rich mahogany that glints a little, almost begging to be touched. Curved at the front and back, it gives the illusion of a crescent moon on its side from a distance.

Nearer, of course, it's a different story. I can see the curve I thought was smooth is actually rough, as though something bit into it. Scratches cover the sides of the boat, as though from many hands. And then there's the broken design right under the bow.

Before I can make it out, a figure shifts in the shadows and we come to a stop. Matteo's slightly trembling next to me, now. The man is dressed all in black, with a long cloak over shaggy clothes. His face is partially hidden, but as I come closer I see a hairy chin, with a long beard falling to midway down his chest. It's unruly and peppered with dirt. And his eyes – Matteo said he was blind, but surely he cannot be when I feel him looking into my very soul.

His lips move and a toneless, empty voice echoes around us. "What do the living come seek in the Underworld?"

I don't miss a beat. "A cure for my brother, *signore* Charon," I say. If he knows what else I'm here for, we're doomed from the start. Best I get to the heart of this jungle for Matteo first, and deal with the staff later.

"A cure? There is no cure here. I am the ferryman of the dead. The living cannot come on this land."

I produce the coin Alessandro gave me, tossing it towards him. "Not even with this payment?"

His long, thin fingers catch the coin mid-air – ovviamente, he must be playing the blind angle. Then he tilts his head to the side, feels around the coin with frail fingers, and his expression changes. It's a small transformation, almost easy to miss, but I catch it. Not fast enough to decipher it, though.

"Very well," he says smoothly, and moves aside. "Step onto the boat."

I let Matteo go first, then follow. Surprisingly, the boat holds us just fine. I would've expected with how ragged it seems, that we would all sink. Instead, it simply centers itself. And then it starts moving, as though pushed – or pulled – by invisible hands.

Matteo stands at the opposite end of the boat from Charon, so I move closer to him. "I thought you said Charon would know where to go."

"Yeah, but forget about asking him – he gives me the creeps," he mutters. "Let's just find Mamma, she'll know."

"What makes you think that?"

He frowns at me. "Because Ana said she would."

"Ana said..." I trail off, narrowing my eyes on him. "Matteo, how much do you realize of what Papà has done to you?"

"What do you mean?"

I'm starting to lose my patience. This isn't the strong, intelligent brother I'm used to. It's like he's only half himself. "This cure they sent us down here for. Do you even know why you're alive, in this state?"

"Ana said she bonded with me."

"Did she say why?"

"Because she loves Papà and hated seeing him sad," he whispers, as if reading off a card. They're words I've heard before, spoken in the same tone.

I remember Monica's tapping, that first day we met. How it had entranced me, almost hypnotized me. And she practices the clean side of stregheria. What are the chances Ana, with her powers heightened by the occult, actually has full control of those faculties? And what's more, why push my brother towards Mamma?

"I hate this," I mutter.

Matteo's expression is filled with sorrow. "I'm sorry. I don't mean to be a burden, Lucas."

"You're not, fratello. I will find your cure, but on my own terms. Not Alessandro's." Without waiting for his reply, I head to the front of the boat. If Charon heard any of this, he gives no sign of it. "You lied, before. Otherwise you would not have accepted the payment and broken the rules of this land. Am I right?"

He says nothing, instead placing both hands on his staff. His back seems straighter, as though he's fighting against himself to retaliate.

I have no such qualms. "Do you know where I can find this cure, yes or no?"

Charon caresses his staff. "I do." He stares into the darkness of the lake for a long moment, and another. "And perhaps I will tell you. But first, answer me this. How did you come upon the coin?"

"A witch from above gave it to me."

Charon turns his head to me, and I stand immobile. After a beat, he nods, once, and his beard moves. Out of it fall pieces of – bones? I don't even want to know. *Stay focused on this. Forget Monica, forget the above, this is about Matteo and nothing else.*

"Very well. The cure you seek is on the other side, where the dead converge. Bordering Elysium, the final resting place of the virtuous, is a small river. You will hear its call, it cannot be ignored."

He pauses then, and I fight the impulse to shake him for the remaining information he's withholding. "And what of it?"

"If your brother drinks from it, he will be cured in the only way he can be."

"Thank you," I whisper, and head back to Matteo, tugging him under my shoulder again. "You'll be alright, fratello. I swear it."

He settles against me. "I believe you, Lucas. You always looked out for me... Of my living, and even now. I'm tired... So tired." When Matteo rests his head on my shoulder, I don't shake him awake. I let him sleep, because I've got a feeling we'll need all our energy for what will follow.

Monica

"This place gives me the heebie-jeebies," Luz whispers. "Is it just me?"

"No," Dominic says. "It's not."

We've been searching for the last half an hour everywhere around this cell to try and find some of Lucas' blood. I peer under the cot for the fifth time, just as we hear noises from the entrance.

"Stay here," Dominic orders and heads out.

Luz watches him leave, then goes back to searching. A moment later he comes back with one of his vrykolakas.

"Did something happen?" I ask, noticing his frown.

"No. He's just here for added protection. And if you're right and our physical bodies will be left behind, he'll stick around to guard them. Apparently the outside is being handled, curtesy of Dani and Elle's magic." He glances at Luz. "Sure you don't want to stick around and help them?"

"Nope," she says as breezily as if he asked her out for coffee. "I'm good with my decision."

"That's what I was afraid of," Dominic mutters and goes back to searching.

I sink again next to the cot, feeling around blindly underneath. *There must be something!* The moment after, my hand hits something wet. I pull it back and find it coated with blood.

"Is that it?" Luz asks.

"Maybe? There's no way to be sure it's Lucas', but we might as well go with it."

I stand up and, holding my dirty palm to the side, I reach for the coin stolen from Ana and wrap that same hand around my pentagram necklace, meshing the two metals together. Step by step, I head closer to the incinerated wall and take a deep breath.

"You guys might want to step back for this," I tell them. "It's not like I make a habit of playing with the occult."

Once I get the go-ahead from Luz, I focus my attention on the stone. This close to it, I smell sulfur and something else, something unidentifiable. It's enough to make bile rise up my throat, but I refuse to back down.

My mate – potential mate – is beyond this wall, and if I don't get to the damn Underworld before he loses his soul, I'll never find out if we're meant to be together or not. So yeah, that's motivation enough.

Another deep breath, and I tap into what Ana used to brag about as a child. *I can feel the evil, Monica!...It's so empowering!...Your darkest dreams, brought to the surface, used as a fuel for whatever you want... Just wish with me, that's all. It's that simple. Open yourself up...*

My being rebels against the idea, but I push past my natural distaste of the occult in favor of what must happen. *I better not regret this.*

The hand around my necklace tightens on it, letting the sharp points dig into my skin until it pierces, and hot blood trickles down my hand. Then I bring my bloody palm to the wall, and slap it on – coin and all.

"Janus, master of all doors, I call upon thee," I whisper. "My mate is past this, and I need to get to him. I'll pay the price in blood or life, whatever you demand, but I *need* to get past this."

I close my eyes when nothing happens, and a hot wave of despair threatens to overwhelm me. I place the other palm against the wall, the one tainted with Lucas' blood, and rest my forehead on it.

Thinking back to the rage that filled me with Ana, and the power I'd relished under Alessandro's command. Every dark thought, dream and wish that crossed my mind, I feed on it, letting it fill me and –

A beat pulsates in the wall. Something vibrates under my right hand – the one with Lucas' blood – and the darkness of the wall turns to silver. I step back with wide eyes, nearly bumping into my companions.

"I did it!"

"Great," Dominic says, looking like he's about to throw up. "Let's go, then." He turns to his wolf and whispers, "This is as far as you go, camarade. I'm on my own from here. Watch over my people, and our bodies, please."

He's first in line, crossing through and followed by Lucrezia and me. Once we're on the other side, it takes me a minute to adjust. Our shimmering forms are the only light.

"Merda, the portal is gone!" My whisper echoes too loudly around here, but I turn to Dominic and Luz and notice they're also ghostly form, like me. "Okay, no panic. The faster we move, the faster we get out. And, um, we'll figure that part out later."

I pocket Janus' coin and head down the path that leads to a cave. They follow, keeping an eye out just as I am. Where could Lucas be? He can't have been down here long enough...

"If I remember my mythology correctly, we're about to run into Charon," Luz says softly. Her face is lighted by some orbs above us – souls, I think.

Dominic grabs her hand, throwing her an odd look. "Is it just mythology you're drawing from?"

She looks away, and it makes me come to a stop next to them. "What?"

Dominic's expression is tense under the lights. "Since you've been back, you're having dreams just as much as I am. And you scream about rivers and ghosts, but what you're really seeing is this, isn't it?"

Luz bites her lip, fighting back tears. "Don't be mad, Dom."

"Ah, draga mea," he whispers and pulls her in his arms. "I should have known. You were gone for days, of course your soul would have followed its natural path... But why? Why would you come back down here? What if they don't allow you to leave again?"

"They will," Luz says softly. "We'll all get out of here."

It dawns on me, then. "The portal didn't just need a chimera's blood. It also needed one who'd been in the Underworld... That's why they used Matteo. And I inadvertently used you, Luz, didn't I?" She nods, and it breaks my heart. "Why risk it?"

Luz shrugs. "Because we don't leave behind any of our own, and going against that would be a horrible way to fight for a better future."

I sigh, wiping my forehead. The air here is stifling, or maybe it's just me. "Bene, we'll just have to be extra careful. I'm pretty sure whoever runs this place doesn't take kindly to people just waltzing in and out. Even if you were protected and didn't die per se at the time... Let's not chance attracting too much *attenzione*."

We come to a stop, having exited from the cavern into a larger one. A lake glints in the distance. "I don't even know what we're supposed to do. If we're right and Matteo is doomed, then what else did Alessandro ask Lucas to do?"

"I guess we'll find out soon enough," Dominic says. "I just hope we get to do that without encountering the worst the Underworld has to offer."

We get closer to the river, but there is no boat. None that I can see, anyway. The faint glow above us barely illuminates more than a foot ahead. There's also no Charon.

"Must be a busy day for him," I mutter. Then it dawns on me. "Merda, we probably just missed them!"

Dominic looks around, sniffing the air. "I don't like us being in the open like this. Let's find shelter."

Just as we turn, I hear a growl.

"No..." Lucrezia's whisper is filled with panic. "He can't cross the river!"

But *he* had. A massive shape emerges from the shadows we had just left. A shape with three canine heads, each bigger and uglier than the last, and a massive snake as a tail.

Lucas

The boat journey finally comes to an end. We disembark, and as I pass Charon he says, "I will see you again, young wolf."

Ignoring him, I follow Matteo out. As we cross the new path, I hear grumblings from afar. "Where's Cerberus?" I had half-expected to run into my great-great...whatever he is. Just because we share a gene doesn't make us family, I guess. He's more likely to kill me, than anything.

A shiver runs through Matteo. "Maybe he went out for a walk. Whichever the case, let's count ourselves lucky enough and get a move on."

We continue walking for a bit, passing various scenes. Souls are everywhere. Some weeping, some raging. They're not in orb form anymore, more like humans – except for the shimmering aura around their bodies.

In the distance, a large mountain looms, with a red cloud hanging around it. Lightning strikes every so often, illuminating a massive boulder that seems to be going further and further up the path. It might be my imagination, but for a second there it seems there's a small figure trying to push it upwards... *Surely, I'm hallucinating.*

The deeper we go, the hotter it gets. Matteo doesn't appeared bothered by the change in temperature. More and more, the sense of not belonging creeps up my spine, demanding I leave. And then, on another hand, my chimera yearns for something. I can't quite understand it, but whereas above I was so quick to rage, down here... I'm almost domesticated.

Matteo grabs my hand when I stop again, staring in the distance. "Don't hang around, Lucas. The more you look, the more questions you'll have, and we risk never getting out of here."

I allow him to drag me away. Moments later, we pass another field, and I stop dead in my tracks. I wouldn't have, except... Souls of dead women are picking blossoming marigolds. The yellow flower, Mamma used to tell me, can raise the dead, and point spirits in the right direction. As if that wasn't enough to reason to become a statue, one woman amid all the others draws my full attention.

"Lucas, come on!" I let go of Matteo's hand and move closer, my heart pounding hard.

In the distance, the woman with red curls turns around and smiles at me.

"Mamma?" I choke.

Matteo is frozen next to me, his mouth gaping. But I don't hold back, I run to her and pull her in my arms, inhaling her familiar smell.

"Oh, Luciano!" It takes me a while to realize she's crying – and not tears of happiness. "Why have you come?"

I pull back, searching her features for an explanation and frowning. "To save Matteo, Mamma. Whatever Alessandro did, this is one thing I can help with."

She turns to him then, and the tears come even faster. Only I hear her whispered words, and they root me to the spot.

"There is no salvation for him, and Alessandro knew it."

∞ ∞ ∞

CHAPTER SEVENTEEN

∞ Mostri ∞

"There are very few <u>monsters</u> who warrant the fear we have of them."

-André Gide-

Monica

I thought I'd seen enough monsters working under Alessandro Conti. But, nope, fate is still surprising me. As I stare into the dog's murky eyes, the massive canines, I instinctively move backwards until I bump into Lucrezia's shoulder.

Cerberus is *huge*. No, even that is an understatement. I used to think Lucas in wolf form was massive. But this creature...this *mostro*...is easily ten times that bulk, if not more. His fur is a muted grey mixed with brown, and each of his heads has floppy ears, with eyes the color of a muddy lake. One that would swallow us whole.

And those teeth... The large canines, or fangs, are the length of my arm. His paws are bigger than my head, and the claws digging into the sandy shore we're on are thick. Sharp. Very dangerous-looking. As if the entire package wasn't enough, his tail swishes back and forth, drawing my attention to a brown snake. Though smaller than the heads, it's every bit as intimidating.

In short, we're faced with our worst nightmare.

Dominic stirs first, though I sense he's steeling himself against it. "Go find the boat guy," he says through gritted teeth. "I'll handle the dog."

"Dom—"

"GO!" He yells at us, with something akin to desperation in his voice.

I recognize the sentiment. He doesn't want to lose Lucrezia again. But neither am I willing to let either of them get hurt. Rather than move, I share a glance with my newfound friend and she nods.

We pretend to step away, watching as one of Cerberus' heads follows us, while the other two are aimed at Dominic. He's laughably small in comparison to the massive monster, and I seriously fear for his life.

"Got a plan?" I ask Luz, trying to hide my doubts.

"No," she whispers. "I never ran into Cerberus before...before I was pulled back. I never even crossed the Styx." Her wide gaze lands on the river, and she gulps.

"Okay, okay." I scan the area for some kind of weapon to use, but there's nothing. We're surrounded by emptiness, walls and rough sand under our feet. I'm not sure my magic will do anything here. With a sinking feeling, I realize Dominic had a point. "Let's find Charon, then we can get your mate," I tell her.

Luz follows me reluctantly, turning every few seconds to keep an eye on Dom. From afar, it almost seems like they're talking, him and Cerberus, but I know differently. What I'm seeing is a hunter getting ready to snap its prey in half.

Eyes wide and urgent, I search across the surface of the river. And then I see its bow first, followed by the rest of the mahogany boat. "Lucrezia, that must be him!"

The man leading it takes his sweet fucking time getting nearer, and we're both ready to jump in and drag him to us. When the boat finally hits shore, he lifts his bowed head in our direction.

His eyes are hollow, and a shiver rakes down my spine. The staff is his hand looks ugly, worn and downright grimy. There's also an odd power humming underneath it.

"More living souls?" he snorts. "What are you—" He stops as his glazed eyes linger over our heads, in the distance where growls can be heard. In an instant, he's off the boat and pointing the staff at us threateningly, and with surprising accuracy for someone so blind. "How did you get Cerberus on this side?"

"I thought he's supposed to be blind," Luz whispers.

Charon hears her and sneers. "My lack of vision does not prevent me from seeing things. What did you do?"

"We didn't *do* anything," I toss back at him. "The merda dog came out of nowhere and attacked us. Now, are you going to stand there or call him back?"

"No one commands Cerberus," Charon says. "No one but the lord of this place."

"Yeah, we'd rather not run into him," Luz mutters, her eyes darting around. "Can you take us away from him, to where you left our friend?"

Charon's expression returns to indifference. "I know not what you speak of."

"Cut the crap, ferryman," I get up in his face. "Another living soul passed by here, with a young man who was stolen from the Underworld. Where did you take them?"

Charon stares in the distance, then a growl from Cerberus draws his attention. The massive dog is slowly stalking towards Dominic. He shifts to his wolf form, and a breath of relief escapes Luz. So we can still have our wolves here – bene. That'll come in handy.

Abruptly, Charon says, "Perhaps I can take you where you wish to go. However, payment must be made."

I lift the Janus coin and show it to him. "You can get this, but only after you've returned us safe to this shore."

He lifts his nose in the air as if breathing in the coin, then shakes his head. "No." Turning to leave, he doesn't count on the bolt of lightning Luz tosses at him.

When I turn to her, the red curls around her face look like living snakes, and her eyes are flashing more gold than green. I'm not even sure how her Solomonar magic transcends the Underworld, or the fact we're shimmering forms. Maybe it's the anger visible in her stance, or her love for Dominic. Whichever the case, she's a force to be reckoned with.

Charon is immobile, his staff held tightly in his hands. Slowly, slow enough to make me grit my teeth, he turns and scowls. The mask of politeness drops and he spits at her feet.

"You..."

"I am a Solomonar," Lucrezia takes a step forward, "and under protection of both wolf and zmeu."

"You have also been here, before. What makes you think you can escape again?" His tone is too cool to be considered nice.

But Luz doesn't budge. "You cannot touch me, Charon, and neither can your lord. Now get us the hell out of here, or else you'll have more than the edge of your robe charred."

A brief moment of anger, hesitation, then he steps back and frees the way to his boat in silent acquiescence. Behind us, Dominic's yelp echoes and we see Cerberus toss his wolf form away into the wall.

"DOM!" Lucrezia yells. Before I can stop her, she's running across the sand, one hand extended and black lightning crackles everywhere.

I can't move, afraid Charon will take off on us the minute I turn away. Luz seems to be drawing energy from the dark clouds above us, and I can only pray it's enough to save Dominic. I don't know how to help other than focusing on the ferryman.

"Where did you take them?"

He shrugs. "Elysium, where else."

"And were they looking for something?"

Charon's lips thin out, and he refuses to answer. Shouts from behind drag my attention. Luz is dancing out of Cerberus' bad aiming, even as Dominic drags himself to his feet and launches himself on one of the dog's massive paws.

Cerberus flicks him like a fly and he smacks again into the cavern wall, landing with a heavy thud I feel under my feet. One of his claws must have nicked Dominic, as blood spills everywhere. Luz finally draws on lightning again and this time it hits the ground in front of the monster. Its three heads shake in tandem, blinded by sand and light.

Luz reaches Dom in time and drags his now human form back to the boat. I run halfway towards her and help her, moving as fast as we can to escape before Cerberus regains his vision.

Charon makes no move to come to our aid, but neither does he try to leave. By the time Cerberus is done shaking his heads, the boat is moving, and we disappear in the darkness of Styx. The monster's roar of rage follows us for long, long moments, but he doesn't try to come after us.

Lucas

Mamma walks ahead of me, murmuring to Matteo and holding him tight. We're still in the fields of Elysium, and I can't make myself leave. I also can't get her words out of my head, so finally I join them.

"Mamma, what did you mean?"

She lets Matteo loose and he dances further on, sticking within the general area but not quite listening. He nods at a few passing ladies as though he knows them. Mamma's eyes tell me more than she'll say aloud in front of him, and my chest seizes.

"No..."

"Mi dispiace, Luciano," she whispers, coming to a stop. "Your father knew. He knew the risks, and he did it anyway. There is no way to raise the dead, period."

"There must be a way to save him."

"There is not. That is what I was trying to communicate up above, mio figlio. Before that witch's spell blocked my ability to speak to you."

Claro, I should have known... I shake my head. "Mamma, please. You've been here for years. You master the chimera. There has to be a way to ensure Matteo regains his life, what he was robbed of."

"There is none, Luciano. Binding him to a living body is the only thing that kept him in this form for so long. Death cannot be beat."

I think of Lucrezia, but she didn't truly beat it. She was protected by me, and Tytus. Whereas Matteo had no one, not even Mamma at the time.

"All of this...for nothing?"

She nods, her eyes filling with tears. "There is more, Luciano. I wish I had been able to protect you both from it, but I could not. Alessandro wants to use Matteo as leverage. Each time you refuse to listen, he will threaten to break Matteo's eternal peace again. There is only so much the soul can take without fracturing and forever... being..." She trails off, and on a whisper she adds, "I expect he planned to use me, too, were it not for my gifts that can fight off that witch's magic."

I want to hit something. The intention must show on my face, as Mamma shakes her head. "Anger is useless, my son. Alessandro has won."

"NO!" My shout makes more than a few heads turn our way, and I force myself to lower my voice. Anger still reverberates through every word. "There *has* to be a way, Mamma. We cannot let him win!"

"You can kill the witch," she whispers. "But he will find another. He always does."

"Then I will kill *him*, period."

"And darken your soul even more?"

I take a step closer, feeling like I'm young and foolish all over again. "Do you think I care, Mamma? I want you both safe."

"And I wish happiness for you, mio figlio."

A frown creases my brow. "Happiness? How can I have happiness when your very existence and my brother's is threatened by a monster?"

Mamma looks at me, and a small, hopeful smile plays on her lips. "Monica," she says simply.

Her name alone drives an arrow through my being, and my fists clench and unclench. Her scent, her laugh, her moans of delight... I want that. I do. But I also want my family safe. I push it all down, and clench my jaw.

"She cannot give me what I seek, Mamma."

"I know," she says softly. "Because you have tied yourself to us, and closed yourself off to the world. And that, Luciano, is Alessandro's greatest success. For once, I am done letting him win."

"So you'll help me fight him?"

"In a way, yes." Her words are filled with something I cannot decipher. "There is a river here, Lethe, that begets forgetfulness. It will also bring rebirth. A chance for Matteo to have a new life, one where Alessandro cannot follow. That is the best way to keep your brother safe, and ensure he truly does have his happily ever after."

I glance over my shoulder, finding Matteo talking to a younger girl in the distance. He's smiling, completely unaware of our conversation. "I've only just gotten him back... Is there no other way?"

"I am afraid not."

"But you'll be safe, then? Your magic will still protect you?"

Mamma shrugs, glancing away. "If Alessandro tries and my magic fails, Hades won't let him. A regular soul like any other, the lord of this place doesn't care. A chimera whose blood and gift can open the Underworld and create a revolving door? He would care."

I run a hand over my face. "Matteo..."

As if summoned, my brother comes back to us. "Jeez, who died? You both have one of those faces."

I gulp past the lump in my throat and ruffle his hair again. "No one, fratello. But we're going to make a pit stop." It's only as I say the words that Charon's earlier statement makes sense. *If your brother drinks from it, he will be cured in the only way he can be*

Fuck. Me.

Monica

Dom isn't hurt too badly, but it's clear even to my untrained eye that we're going to need more manpower. "How exactly are we supposed to get past that when we return?" I whisper.

Dom glares back at where we left Cerberus. "I don't fucking know, but that thing is *strong*. Only something as strong as him can fight it off." Another curse, and he adds, "I should've brought my pack with me."

Luz runs her hand through his hair, and kisses his forehead. "It's okay. We'll be okay."

"Yep," I add, not convincingly enough. "We'll just cross that bridge when we get to it."

Luz finishes patching up his bloody side with part of her sweater. Dom winces as she presses on the tender slash. With a groan, he stands and faces Charon. "Where are you taking us?"

"Where your females asked."

He refuses to acknowledge us now, and it bugs me like I can't say. Lucrezia whispers something to Dom, and he stares at me. "What about Lucas? Do you feel anything? Sense his presence anywhere?"

I close my eyes and try to feel.... There's no need to even try. The moment I think of him, I can sense his presence nearby. It's almost tangible, within reach. Only problem is, it's not in the direction we're going.

When I open my eyes, Dominic reads the confusion and scowls. "I thought as much."

He grabs Charon's shoulder, forcing him to turn. But the damn ferryman is ready. He shoves the staff into Dom's chest, sending him blasting into the Styx waters. He disappears under the surface, even as Lucrezia attacks Charon.

"Bring him back, you bastard!"

The boat comes to a stop, and Charon uses the same staff force to toss us off. The blast sends us flying onto the shore we'd been heading towards, and we land with a heavy thud. Luz gets up almost immediately, cursing Charon to hell and back as she paces the shore length, crying for Dom.

The ferryman is observing us, perched on the boat. I show him Janus' coin. "Guess you didn't need this? I thought doors would be important for someone of your profession."

He smiles then, and it looks so wrong on him I want to puke. "I already have one." The boat withdraws, disappearing into nothingness.

"Dom! Dom!"

Pushing away my panic at being stranded in the Underworld, I join Lucrezia. There's a form floating in the water, and we get knee-deep and pull him back to shore. Dom's shimmering is still intact, and even his wound seems to have stopped bleeding.

But when he opens his eyes they're no longer blue – but yellow, tinged with red.

"Oh no..." Luz whispers and backs away, as if afraid.

I don't understand why, at first. And then Dominic stands, and the way he's moving is *wrong*. He takes stock of our surroundings, and turns to us with a cold smirk. That's when I clue in and follow Lucrezia in backing away, because I've seen those eyes before. In the soulless vrykolakas.

Lucas

In a daze, I follow Mamma as she walks ahead with Matteo. With each passing step, we leave behind the fields of Elysium and head towards a smaller mountain.

The anger burning inside me has only racked up a few notches. I'd known my father was planning something, and I even had a feeling it was meant to leverage my gift. But this...

Losing Matteo once broke me. I cannot stand by and lose him again, not now that I've had him back and been able to talk to him. But is it fair of me to think selfishly, when keeping him here would only threaten his very existence?

I look at them, Mamma holding Matteo's hand, and my heart squeezes painfully. The journey here was for Matteo, and no matter what it costs me, I will see it through. For my young fratello. But I *will* make Alessandro pay for this, for all the suffering he put us through. He will learn what real torture is like at my hands, if it's the last thing I do.

Mamma comes to a stop in a garden filled with pale flowers. I join them around a corner, noticing a small cave on one side, and a river passing right by it. Its murmur, that I'd heard walking here, grows louder and louder. Without even realizing it, my feet bring me closer.

Then Matteo's hand is on my arm, holding me back. "Watch it, big bro. That's Lethe, the river of forgetfulness. Don't let it drag you under."

I shake my head and come to my senses. Still, the alluring murmur doesn't relent in the background, constantly trying to grab my attention.

Matteo glances between me and Mamma, noticing our grave expressions, and his smile falls. "What is it?"

I take a deep breath and place both hands on his shoulders. "Papà lied to you, Matteo," I say softly. "There was never a cure for keeping you alive."

"What?" He shakes his head, moving away from under my touch. "That's not true. He told me. He said we'd be a family again. Mamma –"

He turns to her, but she's crying softly, her cheeks bathed in crystalline tears. "Mio figlio, we have all been played. For the second time. Your father is not who you think he is."

"But he promised!" Matteo cries.

"And he broke that promise," I hiss, "intending I be the one who delivers the news. What he did with Ana is only temporary, not meant to last. Only long enough for me to know what it's like to have you again, to joke with you, and to fucking lose you all over again."

I blink back my own tears, forcing myself to be strong, even as my younger brother falls apart in front of me. He drops to his knees, hunched over, and I join him on the soft grass and pull him in my arms. "I'm so sorry, Matteo. Ti prego, forgive me... Forgive me..."

Rocking him back and forth, I inhale the scent of him, knowing I'll never be able to hold him again. His sobs break my heart, and I look up to find Mamma just as close to breaking down. One hand muffles her cries, but it's impossible to hide the tears on her face, and the pain I feel through Finn's gift.

"I will make him pay," I whisper to Matteo. "I swear it, fratello. He will pay for all of this."

Eventually, Matteo sniffles and pulls back. His gaze falls on Lethe. "Am I meant to drink from this, then?"

Mamma joins us on the grass then and grabs his hands in hers. "Sì. The gods will help you forget, and you'll get a new life. If you stay here, your father will only try to draw you into the living world again, on false pretenses. Nothing will save you, and your soul will eventually disintegrate." Another sob, and she adds, "But I will keep you safe this time, if you come with me."

My heart thuds more wildly. "Mamma... Not you, too!"

She smiles softly at me. "It is time, Luciano."

"You said Hades would protect you!"

"Yes, but I am weary of Alessandro's games." Her gaze falls on Lethe. "It will be nice to forget it all, to restart a new life." She touches my cheek, then Matteo's. "But I will never forget you two, my sons. You will always be with me."

Something in me breaks then, and I grab her hand to squeeze it hard, as if by that feat alone I could keep her with me. "I need you."

"No, Luciano. You don't, not anymore." She stands, pulling us both with her, and it feels like my legs won't hold me up with each word she says. "I only wish I had met this Monica of yours. She sounds like someone perfect for you."

"Mamma..."

"Take care of yourself," she whispers and leans in for a kiss on the cheek.

I pull her into my arms, and Matteo, inhaling their scents for the last time. I'll never have dreams of them, only memories that will fade with time. And that kills me. But I wasn't born a coward, nor a wuss, and I will stand by them. If this is the best thing for them, I have to accept it. No matter how much it kills me.

One last sob, one last kiss, and Mamma backs out of my arms. Matteo looks up at me, fear all over his face. I force words past my numb lips. "You'll be good, fratello. It'll be a new life. A better, safer one."

He nods, and whispers, "Don't forget me, Luciano."

"Never," I whisper back.

Mamma takes Matteo's hand, and they step towards the river. She leans in first, cupping some of the water in her palms and giving it to him. Matteo sips at it, his gaze never wavering from mine. I force a smile. "You're the bravest, Matty."

Then Mamma drinks, too, and waves my way. "Be happy, Luciano. For both of us."

Their smiling faces are the last thing I'll remember. A moment later, their forms shimmer a bright silver, and trickle down into the river, disappearing in its depths....and taking my heart with them.

∞ ∞ ∞

CHAPTER EIGHTEEN

∞ Dolore ∞

"No one ever told me that <u>grief</u> felt so like fear."

-C. S. Lewis-

Lucas

After the last of their essence, of their soul, is gone, my legs fail me. I drop to the ground, head bowed and fists clenched. I'd felt tired in my father's mansion, even hopeless. But here, right now, despair fills me to an extent I've never experienced.

I throw my head back and roar at the black sky, then slam my fists on the ground hard enough to make it shake. None of it helps – nothing will bring them back, not now. But the raw pain in my chest won't let up. And the chimera, more than ever before, demands retribution. Demands blood.

As does my wolf. While before he'd been at the back of my mind, now he's right there with the chimera. For a lupo mannaro, family is everything, whether it's a chosen pack or blood. So why in hell would I be called lord of death, pack alpha, when I cannot protect those I love?

Failure rolls over me in waves, weighing my shoulders. None of this feels right. And none would have happened if I had killed Alessandro, rather than try to outmaneuver him.

"Who goes disturbing the peace of my souls?"

My glassy eyes lift to find a man in the distance. He must have entered the Lethe sanctuary quietly, as I did not feel his presence. Now, he's standing a few feet away from me, watching me with an arched eyebrow. Black hair streaked with silver falls to his shoulders. Stormy blue eyes meet mine, and he's dressed in a simple tunic and dark pants. When I try to stand, he lifts one hand and I find I am unable to move.

Yet though he controls my body, he cannot stop my glare. He circles me, inspecting me assessing me with a gaze that grows ever more speculative. "Hmm. I thought your kind were extinct, chimera."

"We are," I grit out. "My mother just drank from Lethe."

"I see." One more glance at the river, then he drops his hand and extends it to me instead in a shake. "I am Hades. Welcome, son of Francesca."

I find I'm able to stand then, and do so without touching him. "Great. I need to get going." There is nothing left to do but get out of here, and return to Alessandro so I can have my vengeance. Shaking hands with a god is not nearly a priority when compared to that.

Dimly, I remember Alessandro asked me to take Charon's staff, but I plan to do nothing of the sort. Not unless I need the blasted piece of wood to get out of here, but otherwise, it'll be the chimera he gets back, in all its fury.

Hades' rich laughter follows me. "Not so fast, young wolf. You come here seeking something for your father, no?"

I freeze. "What makes you say that?"

"Nothing goes in my realm unnoticed. Nor has the fact your friends followed you here." I turn back to him, slowly. The fire in his eyes reminds me I'm standing in front of *the* lord of the Underworld, and that alone deserves some respect. With Finn's gift, I can sense the power emanating from him, coupled by a rich annoyance.

"Three lives have followed you here, easily disposed of if you dare to remove anything that is mine," Hades says and pauses. "That includes another life. Remember that."

My newly reckless temper chooses that moment to poke its head. I take a step forward, already preparing for an argument – and then light clapping echoes around us, and we're bathed in a light almost too bright.

The scent of cinnamon assaults my nostrils, and I frown, squinting towards the illumination. "Ileana?"

Hades arches an eyebrow until the brightness dims, leaving behind Dominic's godmother. She glances around the Underworld but says nothing, her expression odd – almost longing.

"Che... What are you doing here, Ileana?" I ask.

She shrugs, and smiles. "Paying a little visit to an old friend." To my surprise, she inclines her head towards the lord of this place. "Hades, good seeing you."

"And you," he murmurs, though his voice is different now. Huskier, richer – the kind you use for someone you know and care for. "Is your presence gracing me for business, or pleasure?"

Ileana laughs, her twinkling sound as annoying as it is beautiful. "Oh, you can wish, my mercurial god. But no, I am only here to put this lost wolf on the right path."

"Indeed," Hades says and returns his attention to me. "I do believe you were about to attack me, were you not?"

I hesitate, torn between logic and feelings. Logic finally wins, and I mutter an apology. "Scusi. My head is not...thinking clearly."

"Forgive him, Hades. For old times' sakes. Surely you remember what losing loved ones feels like?" When the god remains silent, Ileana's sunny eyes meet mine. "Dominic needs you, as does your mate. It is about time you stop fooling around."

"Monica's here?" The thought both elates me and infuriates me, though I ignore Ileana calling her my mate. I told her to stay safe, to keep my wolves safe, and she couldn't even do that! And Dominic... Hades had mentioned three. "Did Lucrezia come, too?"

"Of course," Ileana says. There is a warning somewhere in those words, and in the way she tilts her head to the side, almost as if subtly pointing in the direction away from Hades. I sense an odd urgency in the air around her. "Shall we go and find them?"

That, more than anything, moves me from my trance. If my wolves are here, I owe them safety – and getting them out the Underworld. There is no time to wallow in self-pity, to cry over Matteo and Mamma. Those few moments, before Hades interrupted, are all I'll ever have. They are gone, and it is for the best – for *their* best. I lost them once, and survived. All I have to do is take these memories and shelve them in my mind, closing the chapter for good. And, this time, the chapter *will* remain closed.

Doesn't mean I have to like it. Doesn't mean I have to forget them. But I do have to move forward... And get the three people who risked their lives back to the world of the living.

Once that's done, I can have my vengeance on Alessandro. The thrill of it brings life to my frozen limbs, and I take a step forward.

Ileana rolls her eyes and grabs my arm, pulling me onwards faster. "Nice seeing you, Hades. Until next time!"

To my surprise, he does nothing to stop us. And yet, we're barely out of the garden when his voice carries over. "Remember what I said, wolf."

When I check over my shoulder, he's gone, and the reply to *shove it* dies on my lips. I follow Ileana in a daze, lost between the realm I'm leaving, the possibility of seeing Monica again, and wondering why in hell Dominic would follow me.

"I am sorry about your family," Ileana whispers.

I glance at her out of the corner of my eye. "Is there anything you don't see?"

She laughs. "Some things do escape me, yes, but not many."

"Claro. So you and Hades...?"

"Childhood friends."

I shake my head at the impossibility. "He's a Greek god. You're a Romanian immortal. Scusi, but what's the link?"

"Immortal school," she says with a twinkle in her eyes.

I give up on trying to figure it out and instead say, "Where are they?"

She points to a path. "Straight up ahead. And I do believe your help will be needed. The sooner, the better."

I move away from her, then stop. "You wouldn't happen to know how we get out of here, period? Once all the fighting is done, I mean."

Ileana smiles. "You already know – follow the marigolds."

"Marigolds? Surely not the ones I saw in Elysium?"

"No, that would be pointless if you wish to remain alive," she says. "There are many paths in the Underworld, but only one with marigolds that leads to the living world."

Despite my confused frown, she adds nothing else, so I change my line of questioning. "Is there a particular reason you didn't want me to go in depth on Luz's powers, back there?"

"Let's just say, for the sake of maintaining status quo, that it would be best if Hades doesn't know what escaped his Underworld once. And what will a second time."

"You mean because Lucrezia is a Solomonar, now?"

"Among other things," Ileana murmurs. "Your father is not the only one fond of collecting." I can tell by her tone it's as much as I'll find out, so I quicken my step instead, away from her.

I don't have to verify to confirm she's gone, disappeared wherever it is she usually goes to. As for me... *Mamma. Matteo.* I close my eyes, then inhale deeply and clench my fists. Morphing the despair into anger turns out to be easier than I thought.

Monica

You would think seeing someone develop sort of a split personality would be scary, at least. What it is, is downright devastating. Dominic's red gaze doesn't move off us, like he's ready to tear us limb from limb. His mouth twists in a smirk completely unlike him, and he starts gaining on us.

"Um, Lucrezia?"

She shakes her head, eyes wide with panic. "This isn't him!"

"Can't you do something?"

"No!" she cries. "The only element I have to draw on here is lightning, and I won't hurt him."

"Fine," I grumble, still backing away. The more we try to add distance, the wider Dominic's grin gets. "Any idea what caused this?"

"The river must have done something. Like when he was fighting Radu, and he got drugged."

"Who's Radu?" I say as we keep inching away slowly, as if faced with a rabid bear. Which, Dominic kind of looks like. If we turn tail and run, we're screwed.

"Funny you should mention me, human."

Lucrezia freezes and turns around. Facing us are three guys, each more messed up than the last, their forms shimmering silver. The one who'd spoken is half-naked, some worn jeans on his hips. His hair is shaggy, eyes glassy, as if he's on some kind of drug. The one in the middle and the one to his side wear leather top to bottom, which gives a dangerous air to their overall appearance when toppled with cropped hair and mean eyes.

"No..."

"Friends of yours?" I whisper to Luz. She looks ready to bolt.

"On the contrary," she says. "Enemies I've already fought once. Shit." She glances between them and Dominic behind us, and we try to position ourselves to keep an eye on both groups. Which, sadly, means we end up having the Styx at our backs.

The middle one grins. "We got some unfinished business, Red. Let's wrap things up, yeah?"

Luz snaps out of her daze and narrows her eyes. "I'd like to see you try, Jared." I'm a bit reassured she's no longer looking like a panicked doe, but newly scared because we have no way out.

"I'm going to enjoy this," the last one grins, showing brilliant white teeth. He'd be sexy, with the chocolate tone of his skin and the muscles underneath rippling, if not for the deranged look in his eyes. "I'm Cade, baby."

Meraviglioso. Three psychos, all of them who know Luz, and obviously aren't afraid of Crazy Dom, and all intent on having a piece of us. As if guessing my thoughts, the three men move. The one called Cade heads to me, licking his lips.

Then he lunges on me, shifting to wolf midair, and I don't think. I don't wait to see if they can actually inflict harm, given they're the souls of the dead. I just *do*. Letting my wolf take over, listening to her as we roll, avoiding the hit. Cade nearly lands in the river, but instead bumps into Dominic.

Luckily, Dominic doesn't seem to differentiate between enemies and he starts going crazy on him, leaving me time to turn to the other two. The one called Radu grabs Lucrezia's arm, but she holds out her free hand and draws upon lightning.

It zings from the clouds above, and Radu screams in pain as part of his hand gets charred. Hmm. So they *can* be hurt. Taking aim, I jump on Jared's back, my claws digging into his flesh and splitting it open, expecting it'll do the trick.

And then...it heals.

"Merda!" I back away, trying to put some distance between us. Only this time, Dominic is there too, cutting off my escape. "Um, Luz?"

"I know!" she snaps, eyes darting around for an escape. There is none. We're stuck on a shore with her mate in some weird altered state, and three ghosts that won't die. We couldn't have planned a failed rescue attempt better if we'd tried.

And then, a miracle.

Something steps out of the shadows. I tense, expecting another enemy – but his face emerges into the dim light and

I nearly drop to my knees in relief at the onyx eyes I know so well.

"Get the fuck away from them," Lucas snarls. His appearance makes the three wolves stop, and even Dominic seems to hesitate, tilting his head at an odd angle.

Lucas runs, picking up speed, jumping in the air and transforming to his wolf form. He lands next to me and Lucrezia, and immediately strikes out. His rage comes through in every hit, merciless, ruthless. One paw smacks Radu, clawing at his throat. Cade and Jared jump on his back, but rather than be deterred, Lucas seems to only get bigger.

And then Dominic jumps on him with a roar.

"Dom, no!"

Lucas

My fucking beta again. In his quest to come get me, Dominic has managed once again to rile up old enemies. Fucking hell, but this never gets easy. It takes all my energy and will to toss him off me without actually hurting him.

Lucrezia throws me a grateful look, and I yell at her. "Fix him!"

She nods and moves to Dominic, Monica protecting her back. My raven-haired beauty seems frazzled, but our eyes lock and hold across the distance, for all of a second. So many thoughts run through my mind, but there is no time for any of them.

Instead, I focus my attention on the three losers facing me. And then, the chimera comes again. Demanding blood, demanding a life.

I remember what Hades said though – any life I take will put my own pack in jeopardy. I don't even notice my body getting larger, but I feel the pain, the rage, the loss of Matteo and Mamma fill me up.

And then my paws are massive, the wolves are smaller. I head to the water and put my paw in it. I could cross it, I know I could. If I get big enough. Channeling Dominic's strength, Tristan's ability to morph his body...

I test it again, this time growing larger still. One glance at Luz shows she's hugging a normal-looking Dominic, and I'm guessing whatever Sleeping Beauty kiss she bestowed upon him did the trick.

The three enemies get back up, and I don't have time for their shit. Rather than let Monica deal with them, I smack them with one massive paw, and they go splashing all over Styx, unconscious. If nothing else, I'm guessing the river will keep them out of my way.

Taking advantage of the small breather, I allow my body to morph back into human. The minute I'm normal, Monica runs into my arms, hurtling into me with such force I step backwards. "You're alive!" she whispers in my neck, her grip tightening.

Over her shoulder, I notice Luz help Dominic up. While they talk, I force my attention back on Monica. "Sì, I'm fine."

She pulls back at the tone of my voice, her gaze wide. "Where's your brother? Alessandro said he sent you both down here."

A muscle ticks in my jaw. "He did. Matteo..." I look away, swallowing hard to get the lump in my throat gone.

Monica's hold on me loosens, and I taste her pity in the air. It's enough to ignite my dormant anger, and I unclasp her arms from around my neck and push her away. "It's *fine*. I'm not a child, nor do I need your pity. I've made sure Matteo's safe, now, and so is my mother."

She bites her lip, her emotions all over the place. "How?" she finally asks.

"They drank from Lethe, the river of forgetfulness, and went to be reborn. My father cannot use either of them as leverage now."

Dominic and Lucrezia pick that moment to join us, catching the last bit of my words. "I'm sorry to hear that," Lucrezia says.

I nod her way, then hold out my hand for Dominic to shake. "Thanks for having my back down here. Did I hurt you?"

"This? Pfft, you wish." Dominic snorts, wincing as the side of his body bleeds again. "Cerberus' hits hurt a hell of a lot more."

"You ran into him?"

"Yeah," Luz says, and fear tinges the air around her. "He's, um, pretty much as bad as all the stories say."

I shake my head in disbelief. "How did you even survive him?"

"Dominic distracted him, and I used lightning to blind him," Luz says. Her focus flickers between me and Monica, noticing her silence. "We should probably head back, then... To the world of the living, I mean."

"Sì," I nod. "It's about time. Why did you even follow me down here, when I told Monica you all should head back home?"

"The pack never leaves anyone behind," Dominic says while meeting my gaze. "No matter what."

So much has happened, it's hard to remember why I tried to exile him again. I open my mouth to say so, but Dominic waves me off. "Later. Let's focus on getting out of here first, yeah?"

He shuffles ahead, still leaning on Lucrezia, leaving me and Monica behind. I take stock of the river – no sign of the three *cretini*. "We should follow them, try and get as far away as we can."

"Bene," she says in a subdued tone, completely unlike her. Then as if I'm not even there, she tries to pass by me.

Before I can think it through, my hand shoots out and I catch her by the elbow. Despite trying to read her expression, she won't acknowledge me until I force her chin up. "What's with the silence, cara?"

"Nothing," she mutters. "Can we go?"

When she tries to move, I only tighten my grip on her. "No, not until you tell me what's going on."

Monica finally meets my gaze then, her own dulled as if she's trying to hold back emotions. "I got your message, loud and clear."

"Message? Ma di che diavolo are you talking about, Monica? What message?"

She turns her head away, but not before I see a tear slip past her lashes. When I reach to wipe it away, completely confounded, she lashes out. Shoves me away, scowling at me. "Stop! You didn't say it in so many words, but it's obvious my display of any emotion that doesn't equate with sleeping in bed is too much for you. I get it, Lucas. So, you win. I'm tired of games and this back and forth. Let's just get out of here, and then we can go our separate ways."

She tries to pass me again, and I almost let her. Almost. I snap out of the stunned moment of surprise enough to grab her wrist, then pull her body so it crashes against mine. "You want to talk about games and back and forth, and hidden messages?"

Monica scowls, and that stubborn tilt of her chin is what does it. I grab the back of her neck so she can't move and drop my mouth to hers unceremoniously, unapologetically. It's been too long since I felt the fullness of her lips, the softness of her body pressed against mine, and I want more. So much fucking more. But not here, despite how desperate I am.

"Not here," I repeat against her lips, pulling away with much effort. "Come with me, let's get out of here, and then talk properly." When she says nothing, I add, "You want me to beg? Fine. Ti prego, tesoro. Just come with me."

She searches my gaze for a long moment, then nods in silence. I take it as a good sign, then grab her hand in mine and follow in Dominic's footsteps. He and Lucrezia have arrived at the farthest point of the river, but there is no Charon or boat anywhere.

"We don't have time to wait for the ferryman," Lucrezia says.

"Too bad. I owe him a bath in this river," Dominic mutters.

"It might be best he's not here," I add. "Given my father sent me down here to get his staff."

"His staff?" Lucrezia frowns. "Why?"

"Hell if I know."

As my gaze roams the river, looking for a way across, Monica says, "It's for the doors. Charon's staff can open portals to different worlds, different realms. What Ana was able to do in Alessandro's cellar, she can do it again, but all over. It would be...unlimited power, wielded by someone with no care for innocents."

I squeeze her hand in mine as another thought strikes me. "Did you coerce Ana into opening another door, or how did you get in here after me?"

Monica shrugs. "Got a bit creative. Found some of your blood in the cell, and I did the spell." She shivers. "Would love to avoid that particular one again."

"We may be able to," I add. "Ileana said we can get out of here if we follow the marigolds."

"Ileana was here?" Dominic asks.

"Sì, apparently she and Hades are childhood friends. Know anything about that?" He shakes his head, and I sigh in defeat. "A mystery for another day. Alright, I have a plan for getting us across, then all we need to do is find the marigolds."

Taking a step back from Monica, I allow the change to take over me. Like before, I picture myself growing larger, large enough to be mounted, then open my eyes. It seems I achieved the proper size, more or less. So I force my body into an awkward bow right in front of my pack. "Hop on my back!"

They do as I ask, and I enter the river. The coolness of the water chills me to the bone, but I force my paws to swim through it. I've been half-expecting some kind of creature to drag us under, but we reach the other shore without incidents, all within moments.

It's only once I let everyone get off that I bother scanning the area, and notice we're being watched. Charon awaits us, stepping out of the shadows with his staff in hand. And he's not alone. Three heads lift in our direction, mean eyes and growls announcing his arrival – Cerberus.

∞ Battaglia ∞

"You may have to fight a <u>battle</u> more than once to win it."

-Margaret Thatcher-

Lucas

Letting my form revert to human, I step in front of my pack. "Stand behind me," I mutter to them, already walking towards Charon. Something changed in him, but what?

Then it dawns on me. The ferryman is no longer pretending to be a statue. Instead, his expression is filled with anger. "Cerberus here tells me you didn't come just to return your brother. No, you came for something of mine, isn't that right?"

Fucking Alessandro. "No, not anymore. It was a misunderstanding."

My gaze shifts between Charon's ancient form and Cerberus' massive one. One of the heads stares at me, but the other two are focused too much on my pack. I need to figure out a way to draw his entire attention to me.

"Be that as it may, I cannot let you leave."

The wolf in me points its head, followed closely by the chimera. I don't know which is more indignant, but that boiling anger I've gotten used to, is right there underneath the surface.

"*Let* me leave?" I scoff. "What makes you think you can stop me?"

Charon only stares back, and Cerberus' second head refocuses its attention on me. So far, so good.

"Hades himself cleared me," I growl. "Will you go against your master?"

"He will thank me for protecting his domain, I have no doubt about it. And I am sure he will understand whatever befalls you, especially given you were after my staff."

I take a step closer. "I told you, I'm not after it anymore."

Charon shrugs. "Too late. A challenge was drawn, a line in the sand, if you will. You can leave here, you and your little friends... Once you pay the price."

"I don't have another fucking coin."

"It is not a coin I seek." He points a knobby finger towards the massive the dog. "Fight Cerberus. If you win, you get to pick the staff *or* leaving with your lives."

"All of us?"

"Yes."

Only the promise I made to Mamma – to find happiness – holds me back. "And if I lose?"

Charon snorts. "You join Cerberus, enslaved to the Underworld."

Ovviamente. If I want Alessandro's death, there really is no choice – winning, above all. Mi dispaice, Mamma. I nod to Charon. "We have a deal."

"No!" Monica cries behind me, tugging on my arm. "Do you not see what that monster did to Dominic? Lucas, it's suicide!"

Her scent envelops me, the fire in her eyes, the touch of her hand – I want to kiss her. But I push it aside, and instead back away from her. There will be time for that later. For now, I need to do my duty and get us the fuck out of here.

My eyes shift to Dominic, still leaning on Lucrezia. *Find the fucking marigolds, amico.* Without me having to explain further, he nods. His expression is resigned. He knows if I fail, he needs to be ready to get the girls out of here. They will not pay for all this... Not when it can be avoided.

With that settled, I move closer to Cerberus, drawing him away from the others. Three massive heads follow my every move. I remember what Mamma told me, about the history behind our chimera gene.

If she was right, his lineage and mine are from the same god. Only, he's the original monster, whereas my particular gift has been watered down through thousands of generations. Does that make us related, in a way? *Possibilmente.*

Except he's older, has had more practice, and doesn't need to fear me. Whereas I'm...a rookie. One who can't even fully morph into the monster form because I've been fighting it far too long.

Clenching and unclenching my fists, I say, "I know what Charon thinks, but I never intended to steal anything. My father pushed me into this. Surely you know something of that?"

One head tilts to the side, and the other snaps at it. The middle one's gaze never wavers from mine, and I feel like a small insect under a microscope. That thing is enormous. Not even my wolf will stand against it... But I have to try.

When Cerberus says nothing, does nothing, I sigh and morph. My wolf form takes over, and I dig into my ability to enhance my size, becoming as large as I can – roughly still a few heads smaller than Cerberus. Then I tap into Finn's ability of sensing moods, hoping Dominic's vârcolac strength can help me out.

What's confusing is the scents around the heads. The middle one is assessing me, the other two are eager – for my blood? Suffering? Death? It could be either or.

I don't get a warning. One moment they're watching me or fighting with each other, the next Cerberus moves. And for a massive dog, he's too fucking fast and barrels into me like a freight train.

Monica

"Lucas!" I take a step forward, but Lucrezia reaches for me.

"You can't intervene," she hisses. "First off, Lucas is an alpha. He can take care of himself. And second, you heard the terms."

"Does it look like he can take care of himself right now?" I point in panic to Cerberus practically wiping the floor with him.

Lucas slams into the wall of the cavern, and drops heavily to the ground. It trembles with his weight. Then he pulls himself up, shakes his massive head, and goes back at it. It's like watching a train wreck happening and being unable to stop it.

"We have to do something!"

Dominic snaps his fingers. "No! *Focus*, Monica. What did Lucas say about the marigolds? We have to find them, then we can get out of here without you using any magic."

It's almost painful, tearing my eyes from Lucas to look around, but I force myself to. There are no damn marigolds anywhere! And then... I notice Charon's positioning. By all intents, he shouldn't be standing where he is, as he's smack in the path of their fight. And yet he makes no move to get out of the way, almost as if he's covering something.

I'm done wasting time. Instead of trying politeness, I straight up march to him and shove him. Underneath his foot, crushed but still alive, is the tiniest marigold. I bend down and pick it up, then glance behind him. What I thought was a shadow in the wall is actually a narrow opening, more than likely leading to the outside. And at its foot, hidden under a boulder, is another marigold.

The marigolds lead the way, Lucas had said, or something to that effect. Well, that answers that.

I turn to Dominic and wave the flower. "I hav –" Something hard lands a blow on my back, and I fall to my knees. Pain zings in my ears, down my back, a throbbing that feels like it's splitting me, but I don't let go of my prize.

I do, however, manage to angle my head despite the pain and glance behind. Charon is standing over me with his staff, fuming. "You could not leave it be, could you?"

Lucas' roar echoes, covering the rest of his words. My gaze is drawn to him, and across the distance I see him pinned under one of Cerberus' paws. But his roar wasn't for himself – it was for me. I can read the rage in his eyes even from afar, and I feel that pull again. To help him. Is that what he feels, is that what enrages him so?

Movement out of the corner of my eye draws my attention back to Charon. The staff is poised my way now, and I remember its deadly power from before. The bottom of it vibrates, and the energy slowly moves up. I'm frozen, staring at him, and praying to the Goddess I don't get blasted to ashes.

"Monica, duck!" Lucrezia yells, and I don't think.

On instinct, I roll over and grab a handful of sand, tossing it towards Charon. I propel my body away from him, even as a shot of lightning runs over me and smacks him in the chest, tossing him a few feet away.

I scramble back towards Dom and Luz, panting and clutching the marigold. "Thanks for that."

"Don't mention it," she says, frowning over my shoulder. "What the hell was that about? Are you okay?"

When I try to stand properly, I waver forward, almost falling flat on my face. "Don't think so. He hit hard, but I'll deal with that later." I open my palm, showing them the flower. "I found the marigold. It was under Charon's foot."

"That guy is really starting to get on my nerves," Dominic growls.

"You and me both."

"Did you see the rest?" Luz asks.

"Yeah, there's a path that leads over there. See that big thing that looks like a shadow? It's actually a fissure in the wall, big enough for a person to pass through, or a group, but one at a time. There's a marigold at the bottom of that spot."

"Fuck!" Dominic yells and he sprints across the shore. It takes me a moment to realize why, and for my vision to focus.

But then I notice Charon getting up, and his staff rising in the air. Only it's not aimed towards us, it's aimed towards the exit. Dominic tackles him into the wall of the cavern and they wrestle for the staff, whose energy shoots upwards. Luckily, none of the cavern bits that fall from the top damage our only exit out.

For a moment, it seems like we have the upper hand. Dominic even has Charon by the throat. "There's no way a ferryman can withstand a vârcolac's strength, right?" I ask Luz.

She nods, but her frown tells another story. "True, but I don't know why he's hesitating." Then her expression goes ashen, and she turns towards Lucas. "You've got to be kidding me!"

"What?"

"Come with me!" She yells and as we run over, she adds, "Hades told Lucas that if a life or anything of his is taken from the Underworld, one of us will pay in return."

"Merda!" We quicken our step, and reach Dominic in time to pull him off Charon.

While Luz explains to him in whispers about Lucas, I keep an eye on the ferryman. Already, I know this won't go well. He's got us at a disadvantage, and Lucas can't help us out. The sounds of the fight echo in the cavern louder than I care for.

Then Lucas whines – and I lose my focus, turning towards him. One of Cerberus' heads has bitten into his flank, and he pulls away with a large chunk of skin and muscle. Lucas drags himself away, but it's clear he's massively injured judging by the blood staining the shore.

Bile rises up my throat, and then Charon moves again. I turn to him and punch him, but it doesn't do much other than daze and piss him off. As he stumbles away, Luz waves me over.

"Charon won't stay down, and we need to make sure we can get out of here. Help me secure the exit, and we'll stay and guard it."

While keeping Charon in our sights, we start backing away towards the fissure in the wall. About halfway there, I chance a look across – and find one of Cerberus' heads focuses on us. Then the other turns, too. And the third. Like a nightmare on wheels, he starts running in our direction.

But Lucas isn't done yet. Somehow, even while bleeding heavily, he gets up and grabs hold of Cerberus' tail, pulling on it. The various wolf gifts in him must be helping, because he seems to actually drag the massive dog backwards.

We scramble faster to the wall and Luz draws a rune in the air, while I quickly grab my pentagram necklace and use the marigold juice to draw a protective shield into the ground. I've only ever done it once, with a different flower as a child, but I'm hoping it works.

The charm in my hand warms, hinting at the magic, and I breathe a sigh of relief. With Dominic behind us, and Luz' magic as well as mine, we bought some time. Enough that when Charon tries to hit us again, his attack reverberates off my faint defense.

Yet Lucrezia's magic won't hold for long, and mine will fade with every attack. "We won't last long," I mutter.

"We can do this," she retorts. "Dom, how's your wound?"

"I'll survive," he hisses, leaning against the wall. He's holding onto his bleeding flank, jaw clenched in pain. "Just let me know when it's time to rip his throat out."

"Let's hope it won't come to that." But it will. If I don't do something, we'll have no choice but to get back into the fray with Charon, and I can't have that. If Lucas is out there fighting for all of us to get out alive, then I can damn well do the same.

So I do the only thing I can – I shift to wolf form and lunge at Charon, or rather, his staff. If nothing else, it'll give him less power and more of a survival chance for Luz and Dom.

The moment it's out of his grip, I'm aware of a pain in my flank. Blood seeps everywhere, but I don't let go as I keep moving. A deafening roar fills the cavern, and I search out Lucas, fearing he'll have lost the fight.

No... he didn't.

Matter of fact, what I'm seeing is him enveloped in a reddish light, then the wolf form I'm so used to shifts, enlarges. The head becomes that of a lion, and a dark, red mane emerges from the fur like cascading water. Its fiery hue burns bright, even this far away.

The sharp muzzle of a wolf expands into the glorious jaws of the king of the jungle, its massive canines glinting in the darkness of the cavern. The fluffy tail swings once, twice, and on the third move it becomes slick and scaly, with the head of a brown snake at the tip. It hisses, and its blood-red eyes meet mine over the distance, causing a tremor to run through me.

But the change is not yet done. Lucas throws his head back and roars again, the sound echoing across the ground and shaking the walls itself. Charon seems immobilized, his jaw slack and staring in the distance, though he cannot see. However, same as the rest of us, he can hear.

"I'll be damned," Dominic mutters.

Lucas' roar becomes angrier, forceful, as if he's in pain. A similar rippling sensation runs through my own body, causing me to stumble. I realize in that moment the iciness

I'd felt before, when we were trying to rescue him, was truly because of our connection. I can deny it, I can fight it – but the bond between us is set. Our wolves knew it way before we ever did.

Gulping, I stare at Lucas, wanting nothing more than to approach him. Cerebus' proximity keeps me at bay, though. The three heads are fully focused on Lucas, watching as he paws the ground in agony. What more is there?

I get my answer another second later, when the burn inside me eases. At the same time, a hunch protrudes out of Lucas' back, gaining and enlarging like a pus-filled wound ready to burst. And it does – another head rips out through the rusty fur, two angry-looking horns atop it.

The chimera! He's actually fully morphed!

Lucas rears his heads, now as tall as Cerberus himself. None of this should be possible. He doesn't have the full blood of the monster in him, and yet... He is alive, he is whole, and the Underworld has not taken him.

As if to prove it, Lucas slams his massive paw on the ground, and this time pieces of the ceiling drop down all around him and Cerberus – and us. Charon escapes one by chance, thus moving closer to Dominic.

The vârcolac snaps to attention and in one quick move, has him in a chokehold. "Now, enough with the dirty tricks, old man. You're going to let us leave, else your precious staff will be disintegrated."

Charon grumbles something, but puts up his hands in defense. The chimera's appearance seems to have subdued him. Dominic still holds onto him while I keep the staff secure, chancing a glance at Lucas.

He is majestic. What was not a fair fight is now fully one, and Lucas charges like the proverbial bull defending his territory. Each head of Cerberus' that comes at him, he swipes at with a hooved paw, or flat out slams into.

Cerberus may be older and wiser, but Lucas is young and fast. And he carries all the strength of his wolves in him, on top of the chimera change. Everything seems amplified, and he manages to back Cerberus closer and closer to Styx.

Eventually, with one powerful punch, he tosses Cerberus to the ground, and the movement makes more cavern pieces fall on top of him. The massive dog is unconscious – enough to buy us time.

No longer limping, Lucas heads over to us, transforms to human form and yells, "Let's go!"

Dominic tosses Charon away, and I hold onto the staff until we're all running through the fissure. Lucas comes after me, and I toss the staff over his head, and hear it land in the softness of the sand outside.

Then Lucas' powerful punch hits the wall, causing a collapse of stone behind us, effectively stopping anyone from following. Even so, I feel Charon's eyes on us until we are fully surrounded by darkness.

Lucas

Being back in human form after that transformation feels like my skin is too tight, my muscles too strained under my shirt. But I don't have time to wonder about it, or complain. Nor do I have a moment to figure out how the hell it is I was able to master that transformation, and get out of there alive.

Squeezed between two extremely tight walls has never made me claustrophobic. This time, it does. "How much longer?" I hiss.

"Almost there," Dominic yells back.

He's first in line, followed by Lucrezia, Monica, and me pulling up the rear. The order was unconscious, but I realize we both thought of putting our girls in the middle to protect them, lest anything attack us from up ahead, or behind.

Monica. I reach ahead of me, and my hand touches her shoulder. Since we're advancing painfully slow, my touch draws her attention.

"You were amazing, tesoro," I whisper. Annoyingly, it carries over and I know the other two heard it. Luckily, they don't say anything.

"Grazie," she says back just as softly. "You... I've never seen anything like it."

A surprised laugh escapes me. "What, a shifter with two heads?"

"Well, now we know why you always walked around like you had something up your ass," Dominic retorts from up ahead.

I scowl at the darkness, even though he can't see me. Also ahead, I hear Lucrezia's soft chuckle. "And you're still an ass, amico."

"Takes one to know one."

I roll my eyes, but my tone comes out just as playful. "Indeed." Even as we keep moving, my hand reaches for Monica's. I can feel her eyes on me again, but she says nothing. A moment later, I intertwine our fingers and something feels...calm. My insides are soothed, and I can breathe almost easily.

In silence, we keep walking until light escapes from up ahead. Dominic's hand lifts up in the air, and he waves us through. "Easy, I think we're crossing something."

I only notice it once Lucrezia goes under. A shimmering silver curtain in the middle of the path. Once she's through, she disappears completely, but my gut says it's only to reappear in the world of the living.

Monica turns to me. "Ready?"

I nod, and let her pass first. Then I glance behind. Maybe it's a moment I need to say goodbye to Matteo and Mamma, or maybe just to pull myself together after the craziness of the last hours. But I take one last deep breath, say a quick prayer for my lost loved ones, and cross over.

∞ ♦ ∞

My body hurts – I wiggle my fingers, my toes, then my eyelids flutter open. The first thing I see is the worn ceiling of the cell I spent the last days in. Then the stench of blood reaches my nostrils, and I jump up.

Monica, Lucrezia and Dominic are stirring on the floor, their bodies seemingly also in pain. And just outside my cell door is a wolf – a vrykolakas. He's dead, his limbs ripped apart and his blood coating the ground.

I can sense something is wrong. And not just with this particular death, but with our people. It's like the connection I'd had with my wolves has returned tenfold, clamoring for my attention.

"Fuck," Dominic mutters, groaning as he stands. He sees the dead carcass, and drops a few choice Romanian words. "Alessandro must have escaped."

"How much protection did you put on him?"

"Our best, and some of my own," Dominic says.

"There's a barrier here," Lucrezia says as she stumbles to the cell door. "I think they must've locked us in here to protect us. It's zmeu magic."

"Can you diffuse it?"

By the time my question is spoken, she's already drawn a rune in the air, and there's a soft pop like a balloon. Lucrezia then pushes the door of the cell open, and turns to us.

Dominic's impatience is apparent in the way he's bouncing off the balls of his feet, and I lift a hand to calm him down. "Alessandro and his fucking tricks." I glance behind at Monica. She's holding the side of her head like it's pounding – I know the feeling well. "You've done more than enough. This isn't a fight you need to join... I will understand if you choose to leave."

She gives me a look tinged with hurt. Merda. I hadn't meant it like that, only that I want her safe, but it's too late to take it back.

Monica only says, "I'm in. What's the plan?"

"It appears our only option is a stealth attack."

I let Dom and Lucrezia go up ahead, and Monica follows. Once they're past the stairs, I know I don't have long. I grab her wrist and pull her towards me. She was halfway up one stair, so the movement destabilizes her and she falls into my arms.

Exactly where she belongs.

Cupping her cheek, I claim her mouth, not bothering to explain myself. It's almost idiotic what that one kiss does to me, when we've done so much more already. But it reaches deep in me, in my soul, with the soft promise within it.

"Lucas!" Dominic's furious whisper echoes down the stairs, and I pull back from Monica.

"Later," I whisper.

She tries to smile bravely and says, "Try not to get killed. I'll want an explanation of that...later."

I nod, and we rush up the stairs together. Four people against an army. Somehow, after Cerberus, the odds seem almost favorable.

∞ ∞ ∞

∞ Vendetta ∞

"Before you begin on the journey of <u>revenge</u>, dig two graves."

-Proverb-

Monica

That kiss... If I didn't know any better, there was way more to it than just a thank you. But, the battle waiting for us doesn't leave much time for questions. The moment we're out of the cellar, any chance of a stealth attack goes out window.

Wolves line the walls – Alessandro's. Almost as if expecting us. A quick count tells me five, but more could be around the corner. Lucrezia moves by my side. "We'll take care of this," she says to the guys. "Go!"

For once, Dominic doesn't argue, and I know part of it is because he now trusts I'll have her back. I can only hope to do her justice. We quickly become separated, but what Lucrezia doesn't have in size she makes up for in speed.

Runes fly right and left, and wolf after wolf drops. I take care of two, and we hit the last one together then grin at each other. "Let's find the rest."

We search room by room, figuring that Alessandro must've imprisoned the rest of our pack. Yet the more we look, the less we find anyone. It's like they all disappeared. Finally, on the second floor, we get to Finn and Tristan.

They're both pacing the room, seeming ready to destroy the place. When they see us coming, they jump towards us – and smack into an invisible wall.

Lucrezia approaches it gently, then turns to me. "Do you know the root of this?"

I glance at the ground, and notice the ingredients no one else would. Salt, some kind of herbs, and a drawn pentagram. With unabashed joy, I kick them out of the way. The disturbance is enough to break the barrier, and the guys break free.

"They took Dani and Elle somewhere!" Finn shouts, his cool demeanor long gone.

Tristan's already pushed past us and gone down the hall, alerted by some mysterious sense. When we rush after him, we're surprised to find him immobilized at the end of the corridor. His awed murmur reaches us. "That's my girl!"

When I peer out the window that gives onto the opposite side of the house, I realize what he means. The entire East wing is afire, and only two girls could've done that. We take off even faster, battling wolves as we come across them.

"What the hell even happened?" I ask Finn as we run.

"Ana happened," he mutters. "She managed to do some kind of blood magic, undid her bindings and before we knew what happened she had us. Elle and Dani weren't around, so we didn't know where they'd been taken this entire time."

Once we get out of the house and are running on the grass towards the girls, different kinds of shouts get to me. I let the others go ahead, and backtrack instead to –

"Lucas."

There's no way my senses are leading me wrong. Something warns me I need to be elsewhere, with one particular guy, and I listen. I let the others go ahead and emerge into the gardens, just as Alessandro lifts his gun, takes aim, and pulls the trigger.

I don't think, only jump – and then everything goes dark.

Lucas

One moment, I'm facing against my bastard father. He'd run away as soon as he heard us coming, heading to his getaway car. I was ready to face him – and then he pulled the gun. After what I'd just seen in the Underworld, what I'd realized,

I'm not ready to die. But I don't cower, instead staring at him and waiting to see if he'll pull the trigger.

And then he does. Only, there's a blur of movement to the side and Monica's there, taking the shot in the stomach. Everything slows down, and my vision narrows on her body jerking to the hit, then falling, falling...

I lean forward and catch her before she hits the ground, and by so doing drop on my knees, cradling her in my lap. Behind me, Dominic lunges on Alessandro, immobilizing him.

"Monica!"

Her blue eyes are filled with pain, meeting mine for the briefest of seconds before they flutter closed. I'm not sure if she fainted or if that's the last time I'll... – I don't *want* to know. If before I felt boiling rage, there is a coldness inside me that's practically arctic, filling my very soul.

"Dominic, leave him," I order.

He glances at me, his face torn between pain and determination, but eventually steps back. "Come get her, please."

As soon as he inches towards me, Alessandro takes off on a run. Dominic makes a move to follow, but I say low, "He's mine, amico. Come take Monica. Please. I don't want her to get cold."

Dominic does as I ask and I transfer her to his arms, caressing one lock of hair back from her face. Then I bend and kiss her forehead, before straightening to my full glory. "Whatever you hear," I tell him, "don't come. Tell the others."

It's easy to find Alessandro. The scent of fear and cowardice leaves a trail I take no pleasure in following. I reach a garage on the far end of the property, and hear an engine starting and sputtering.

When I round the corner, Alessandro looks up from behind the driver's seat. Whatever he sees in my face makes him scramble for the keys, desperately trying to get the engine to work.

I step closer still, until I'm right in front of the car. It's an old Ford model, probably the least flashy car I've ever seen him drive. The bumper touches my legs as I get as close as I can, then slam my palms on the hood.

Alessandro jumps, and I hear the clatter of the keys as he drops them. He's no longer the alpha, and he knows it as well as I do. "Your reign is over, *Papà*."

His mouth opens as if to say something, but he doesn't. "Get out," I tell him. When he doesn't move, an inferno of iciness pricks my skin, and my hands turn into claws. I dig deep into the hood, the metal bending and falling apart under the pressure of my grip.

Smoke comes out of the engine, and I declare myself satisfied enough to straighten, and walk around to the driver's door. I yank it open, then drag him out of there by the scruff of his shirt, my claws tearing at the material.

"Luciano, mio figlio –"A groan of pain escapes him, and I faintly realize my claws must have dug into his chest.

Not that I particularly care.

Rather than kill him then and there, I keep walking, dragging him behind me, until I'm back to where Monica is still lying in Dominic's arms. He's surrounded by his vrykolakas, and Alessandro's wolves are facing off against them.

"Who is it you fight for?" I roar at them, and they stop in their tracks. Multiple pairs of eyes go from me, to Alessandro in my grip. Some dare raise their guns, which only makes me laugh. "Go ahead, try to shoot. We'll see what happens."

No one actually pulls the trigger. "See, Papà?" I let him go, and he stumbles away from me, his shirt filled with blood, his eyes wide with fear. "Not everyone is as stupid as you are. Hurting the woman I love? Not your brightest moment."

"She is a wh—"

I didn't intend to punch him. It's like my fist moves of its own accord, finding his jaw and watching as he falls to the ground, spitting out blood. My claws have ripped into the flesh of his cheek, leaving behind a grotesque scar.

"This image is familiar," I say softly. "Only it used to be me on the floor, and you standing over me feeling like a man for hurting a child. Doesn't feel good, getting a taste of your own medicine, hmm?"

He says nothing.

"Alessandro!"

A blur of blonde hair tries to pass by me – Ana. Without even thinking it through, my hand reaches for her and grabs a fistful of her hair. She tries to spit out curses, to undo my hold, but it's useless.

I pull her to my chest, my claws at her neck, my eyes on Alessandro. Is that his heart breaking I feel? I doubt it. Nor does it matter, not after everything he did.

"Your fucking spell," I whisper in her ear, "put my brother through more suffering, all for your fucking greediness. In *my* pack, that is punishable by death."

"You can't—" The rest of her phrase ends in a gurgle, and I remove my hand. Blood drips off my claws, as her inert body falls to the ground. Her slashed throat bleeds all over the grass, turning it a deep red.

I step over her, inching closer to my father. He gulps, his eyes flickering from Ana's corpse to me. Then he pulls out a handkerchief from his suit pocket and wipes his mouth. I recognize the move – he's trying to find an angle to play. Then he stands, holding the material to his cheek to stop the bleeding. "Is that what you're after, boy? An apology?"

I laugh again. "Oh, no. An apology would not undo any of what you did. Like letting Matteo die so you could have your stupid deal. Like pushing Mamma to kill herself, because she wouldn't bend to your will. Or bringing my younger brother back to life, only so you could use him as leverage to force me into doing your bidding." Another laugh. "Didn't work out, though, did it? They're both gone, him and Mamma. Reincarnated. You cannot touch them – ever again."

Shock coats his features, followed by fear. "Sì, you have nothing on me, Alessandro. I went to the Underworld, and I came out victorious. Stronger than you could have ever guessed. Which means *nothing* stops me from taking your life. Here. Now."

He doesn't get a chance to plead, and I don't hesitate. I reach for his throat, and in one swift move crack his neck. He has killed enough, and now no one else will suffer at his hands. With a disgusted snort, I let his body crumple to the ground.

Unseeing, I turn to the wolves who used to honor him. "You are dismissed. Consider this your freedom returned, to do with as you wish. I have no desire to be your alpha." Some leave, then, but a few linger behind as if waiting to see how it plays out.

I don't care. The only one I care for, has still not moved. On knees that grow increasingly weaker, I stumble towards Monica and gently pull her into my arms.

Dimly, I'm aware of the rest of my pack coming around me. They're all there in silent support, a real family. One I wanted her to be a part of, so she could know the healing possible when you have good people around you.

Why didn't I tell her that? I had plenty of opportunities.

I've said it once, and I'll say it again – I'm not some idiot puppy about to fall in love. But while I've been too damn stuck in this idea that I won't give in to Ileana's spell, that I won't be another mark on her belt, I've ignored what's been directly in front of me.

And now Monica's in my arms, dying – and I'm the only one able to bring her back. And in so doing, tie myself to her – forever.

Can I do it? Sì.

Will I, though? After everything I've stood for, and all I've stood against?

One glance down at her pale cheeks, the lashes fluttering against them, those lips I've kissed so deliciously, and I know my answer.

Certo che sì.

Without a fucking doubt.

I'll brave Hades himself if it means I get to spend more time with her.

So I raise my hand over her chest, and close my eyes. When I next open them, I can see her soul wavering above, departing – or trying to, at least. It's the size of a large snowflake, emitting a soft, blue light that pulses timidly. I gently pick it in my between my index and my thumb, treating it like the most fragile of things. And then, I push it back inside her, willing it to stay. Willing *her* to stay.

Like I wasn't able to do for Matteo, or Mamma. *Come back to me, cara.*

Monica breathes in as if she was underwater, then relaxes in my arms. Her eyes flutter open, and those icy orbs land on me once more.

"Couldn't let me go, huh?"

A dark chuckle escapes me, and I drop my forehead to hers. "I found it harder than anticipated, tesoro."

Monica

I wake up to sun streaming down my face, and a hot, heavy arm wrapped around my waist. *Lucas.* The grin spreads on my lips unashamedly, and I turn into his hold, nuzzling his throat.

I can feel his smile against my forehead as he whispers, "Awake, already?"

After he resuscitated me only hours ago, Lucas ensured his pack was fine, and brought me to his old room. Everyone split across the house, which is now empty from the craziness of before. It feels weird, in a way, being back here. And yet I feel like I belong. Truly.

It's home only because Lucas is here, hence the nuzzling and waking up.

His hand goes from my waist to my hip, slipping under the t-shirt he lent me and tracing my hip bone. "How are you feeling?"

I tilt my head back so I can look at him. "Never felt more alive."

Then I push him on his back, and straddle him. My nails trace his bare chest, and suddenly even the sweatpants he wears are too constricting. "I want more," I whisper.

"I'm all yours, tesoro."

With a grin I can't hide, I bend down and kiss him. It's soft – for about a millisecond. Then Lucas digs his hands in my hair, angling my mouth to better plunder, and my body overheats. I'm undulating over him, needing more – so much more.

Feeling it, Lucas lets one hand slide down to my hip, angling me on him, and I gasp as I come in contact with his hardness. Then his other hand releases my hair and goes under my shirt, tracing the underside of one breast, and the other.

"I've missed the softness of your skin," he murmurs and gets to a half-standing position. His mouth moves over my pert nipples, licking and biting through the shirt – and then it's gone in an impatient toss, falling somewhere on the floor.

The moment after, Lucas rolls us over and hovers above me. He freezes, and the moment remains suspended with him staring at me, me staring at him, and then his mouth curls in a self-deprecating smirk. "Merda, but that witch was right."

Then he drops his mouth to mine again, kissing me until I lose sight of who I am, and what I'm meant to do. My panties are gone in a flash, as are his sweatpants. And then he's there, nudging my thighs apart, sliding inside me, and everything clicks.

I open my eyes, not wanting to miss a single moment of this righteousness. Lucas is still staring at me, and he drops his mouth to kiss my cheeks, my chin, my forehead, and finally my lips. I hold on to him like he's my salvation, and in a way, he is.

His strokes become deeper, and I feel the wave coming, nearing... "Lucas..."

"I know," he whispers, and he moves one hand to my breast, caressing it reverently before bending his head down to sample it. "Let go," he whispers, and I do.

Lucas

I watch her come apart under me, feel her tightness around me, and I can't hold on any more. Deeper and deeper I go, waiting for that second peak – and when Monica's skin flushes more, and her eyes widen, I know she's almost there. I switch the angle of my stroke just so, and she goes off like a firework – I follow a second after.

And if before I thought the sex blew my mind, this time, I'm left speechless. I drop my head to her chest, trying to keep most of my weight off her, but Monica shifts under me. Her skin is soft under my cheek, and the smell of cherries wafts up to my nose. I inhale it deeply, more grateful than I can ever recall being.

I almost lost her, earlier. Now, having her breathing, satisfied body underneath mine feels like I'm the luckiest bastard in the world. And maybe, just maybe, I'm starting to get what all the fuss is about, and exactly why my wolves fell so fast.

A moment passes, then another. Monica's heartbeat slows down and she starts stroking my hair, her long fingers teasing the strands. It's then I finally choose to let out the words that have been running rampant in my head. "Just so you know, I love you. Despite my better instincts. Which means you're stuck with a stubborn, arrogant alpha as your mate, cara. No return policy."

Her hands have stopped stroking me, but I can hear her heart beating fast. Then she cups my cheeks, forcing my chin up so she can stare at me. "Are you for real?"

I prop myself up on my elbows, grinning down at her. "Never been more real, tesoro."

A lone tear escapes, and she sniffles. "I love you, too." I nuzzle her neck, and she adds, "But that return policy needs negotiating."

Later, we head down and the smell of food drags us into the kitchen. Everyone's there – Dani and Tristan by the oven, Luz and Dom fighting over drinks, and Elle and Finn setting the table. I should feel sad, perhaps melancholic over other

dinners that have taken place here. Over Matteo, and
Mamma... But the truth is, no scene in this mansion has ever
felt more like family than this.

When Monica and I walk in hand in hand, they all stop
– then Tristan breaks the silence with a massive "Hurrah!"
that's soon echoed by everyone else.

Monica blushes deeply, and I pull her into my side and wave
my hand. "All right, all right, settle down, amici. Let's not
scare her off, hmm?"

Once the food is cooked, we all take a seat and they let me
have the head of the table. It takes me a few more minutes
into eating and easy banter before I address the elephant in
the room. "Dominic, I owe you an apology."

"Again," he says, sipping my father's best cognac.

"Scusi?"

"You owe me an apology, *again*," he grins, raising his glass my
way. "But who's counting?"

Luz elbows him hard enough to make him wince, and I
snort. "You are, apparently. But you are correct. I owe you
an apology, again. Kicking you out of the pack... It wasn't
deserved. Mi dispiace."

Dominic stares into his drink, and for a moment I think
he's playing it to lengthen my apology. But then he looks up
and smiles my way, though in a sadder way. "It *was* deserved,
though. You're right, you and I never settled old accounts,

and it was bound to come to a boil. But... Luz helped me understand, you know? And I think, for what it's worth, that it was the right call to kick me out."

Finn and Tristan don't seem surprised. Neither do their girls. Everyone's listening, as though waiting for something they've already known. "I've tried since the vrykolakas have showed up to split myself between them and this, but the truth is, they need a leader. A proper one. And... Ileana is right."

"She generally is," I mutter. "But what about, in particular? And when did you see her?"

"After you guys went to sleep," he says. "She came to say bye. Said she's returning to Romania, and that my wolves should, too." He takes another sip, and reaches for Luz's hand. "And we've decided we want to go with them."

I stare between him, and Lucrezia, and then Monica takes my hand, squeezing it. I hadn't expected it, not this soon. But, was there any other way for this to end?

"I respect your choice," I nod at him. "Just know you're always welcome to return."

Dominic grins then, his usual mischievous self. "You'll regret saying that."

∞ ♦ ∞

Later, when the food is almost done and the wine completely drank, I head onto the patio for a breath of fresh air. A few moments pass by, then Lucrezia joins me.

"You're really okay with this?" I ask her. "Going to Romania, leaving all of this behind?"

"Yeah. Dominic would've stayed, trying to split himself and make everyone happy, but I didn't want him to. He has so much to offer, and I really believe he'll help those poor souls."

I nod, reaching out to hug her. Showing emotions seems to get easier...same as letting people go. For the right reasons. "If you ever need me, or any of us, you know where to find us."

Lucrezia pulls back then. "What, here? You're okay with staying?"

"Sì. We need a new home and... These walls have seen much, but we can make new memories here. Plus, it's easier than showing up in some other town, or separating the pack."

"What of Alessandro's wolves?"

I shrug. "I'll go talk to the ones lingering behind. If they're serious, and want to stay, they'll be following a new rule of law from now on."

Lucrezia smiles. "I'm happy for you. And for Monica."

We head back inside, to the raucous laughter and food tossing started by Tristan. Lucrezia heads by Dominic's side and leans over for a kiss. And when I reach Monica, she holds out her hand. I pull her into my arms and kiss her deeply, amid hollering and cat-calling – and a new kind of happiness blossoms in my chest, chasing out the darkness.

This is family. *This* is love.

And this...is our new beginning.

∞ ∞ ∞

EPILOGUE

Far away from the laughter of the wolf party, Ileana walked the woods alone. The moon would soon rise, but she enjoyed these moments between the sun going down, and moon rising. They helped calm her down.

And calm she would need, to deal with her next tasks.

Footsteps joined hers, and she didn't have to look up to find Făt Frumos, her consort. His profile was etched in her mind, as beautiful as if he was carved from stone. "What bothers you, draga mea?" he asked.

Ileana sighed, then turned to face him. "I saw Hades, the other day."

His normally open expression shuttered, and she reached out to cup his cheek. "I know you have your differences, but I had to go down there. Lucas needed a little nudge in the right direction."

Făt Frumos toyed with the collar of his shirt, then his cufflinks, his agitation clear. Ileana did not understand his love of these garments modern men called suits, but men would be men.

"Did he say anything?" he asked.

"Only pleasantries. However, the Underworld doesn't feel as...safe as before."

"What makes you say that?"

"For one, Cerberus is running wherever he pleases. And for another, Charon and his machinations."

"Are you sure you're not just focused on them because of these wolves you love so dearly?"

Ileana's hold on his jacket tightened. "No. Hades does not realize it, otherwise he would have done something about it."

Făt Frumos sighed, annoyance etched on his features, but finally he nodded. "Very well. Do you know what causes this disturbance?"

"I believe our rather powerful prisoner, Declan, started something, when he was at his old home. Tytus is on his way there to fix it, but we need to do damage control."

"You speak of becoming involved, *really* involved, Ileana."

"Da," she nodded. "I do."

His love for her shone in his eyes, as did his exasperation. "And what is your reasoning this time?"

Ileana looked away, knowing he would be angry. "Constanza is."

"Constanza? What does our daughter have to do with any of this mess?"

Ileana met his gaze then, silently pleading. "She wanted to spend some time with Persephone, and I allowed it. Only...."

"Now you're afraid the Underworld is too dangerous for her, too."

"Yes."

"And we cannot force her to come back, nor is it safe for us to return."

Ileana bowed her head then, fighting back a tear. These emotions were unusual for her, but her daughter was so beautiful, so innocent... "Exactly."

"And what do you propose we do about it? Hades himself banned me from the Underworld, and I will not let you fight this battle alone."

A small smile formed on her lips. "I would not have to. We have someone we can use, someone who will be eager to serve in return for a prize."

Făt Frumos frowned. "Who?"

"Declan."

The name sounded like a gunshot in the otherwise quiet woods. After a beat, Făt Frumos nodded, and his expression finally eased. "Yes, that could work, draga mea." He offered his arm out to Ileana. "Shall we go pay him a visit, then?"

The immortal glanced over her shoulder one more time. In the distance, she could almost hear Dominic's laughter, and Lucas'. The rest of the pack was at ease, their mates content. In her heart of hearts, she knew they would be safe, now. And though she would miss them, another story required her focus... And another challenge awaited.

For an immortal, eternity never did get boring.

Keep your eyes peeled for more of Ileana and Făt Frumos, as well as Tytus and Declan, in the *Moonlight Rogues* spinoff duology, *Flaming Rogues*! Spring 2020 ☺

Or better yet, <u>sign up for my newsletter</u>[1] and I'll keep you up to date on any new releases, bonus content, and more ☺

---

1. http://www.alexawhitewolf.com/contact

Preview of Tytus' story, Fanning the Flames (Flaming Rogues, #1)
A Moonlight Rogues Spinoff

Tytus

Millenia I've lived, and for the first time I feel like I'm connected to something. To more than something, to someone. And I've just left them behind in a small town filled with secrets, because I have something more important to do.

I lied when I said I needed to heal. It's what I do – because the truth would be too much to explain. In the mountains of my youth lies a dark, dark secret. One my brother rediscovered, and one I must hide from humans at all cost.

Because if it's let loose, it'll fracture the supernatural world in a way no one has foreseen.

Deep in my thoughts, I've made it so far as the meadow. I dig inside, accessing that raw, primal energy, ready to let my zmeu loose. And then I catch the sound of footsteps – slow, timid. I turn around and find the witch emerging from the trees.

"Looking for something?"

"Yeah. You, as a matter of fact. I want to come with."

That... I didn't see it coming.

Fiona

I'm probably crazy, signing up for something I'm nowhere prepared for. But I've lived the last of these years in captivity. And despite his hard exterior, Tytus is a good man. Or, at the very least, he's not like the ones I've known.

Given the havoc I helped cause, and everything else that happened as a result, I need to do some good. Maybe I'll fail. Maybe I'll lose my life. But... I have to try.

Drawing in a deep breath, I meet those grey eyes of his and say, "You're wounded. Having a witch on hand wouldn't hurt, right?"

He frowns at me, as though he sees right through my bullshit. He probably does. "And what's in it for you?"

"I only ask...that after I help you, you drop me somewhere with as few people as possible." The frowns deepens, causing me to blab. "I'm done with this world, with being used. I just want to be left alone, to live in peace."

More moments pass, and then he nods, those stormy grey eyes filled with understanding. "Alright."

Preview of Declan's story, Igniting the Ice (Flaming Rogues, #2)
A Moonlight Rogues Spinoff

Declan

Something changed in the air. Unsure, yet intrigued, I lift my black muzzle off the ground and sniff. Nothing.

Perhaps I was mistaken.

Incredibly bored out of my mind, I drop my head back on the cave's cool ground and rest it on my front paws. One would think living permanently in my zmeu form would be comfortable, and offer heat, at least. And one would be correct.

Yet I also miss the human. See, as a Romanian dragon, I'm a shifter. Among many, *many* qualities, I can use elemental magic to the point of becoming a storm myself. And yet I have once more become imprisoned by a witch's hand, all thanks to my dear, fucking brother.

Tytus.

A growl escapes me, reverberating in the cavern. *Patience. Soon enough, they will figure out this prison will not last.* When I shift to a more comfortable position, the massive gold cuffs around my paws catch the dim light.

And then... It happens again. The air changes, and the scent of cinnamon permeates it fully. My eyes open once more, landing on my hated jailor.

What now?

Constanza

"Constanza!"

I cringe at the loud booming voice. Part of me wants to cower away, and the other part, well... I share a mischievous glance with my best friend, Persephone. "Oops."

She rolls her violet eyes and stands from the grass. We'd been fooling around in the gardens near Lethe – again. It was my idea, even knowing Hades hates it when we linger here, on account of the dangers of the river.

And, given I'm his long-standing guest, I really should pay more attention to his instructions. It's not like he's a control freak – much. Still, something about the silver river calls to me, and not in order to drink from it. It's just...pretty.

"Constanza!" He calls again, this time closer.

Persephone flicks a lock of her dark brown hair and winks at me. "I'll take care of this. But, umm, maybe go for a long walk, yeah?"

With a grin and an air-blown kiss, I take off under some bushes. Hades' voice echoes behind me, followed by Persephone's softer murmur as she calms him down. She knows he's afraid of losing her to the depths of the Underworld, that is all. Which, in a way, is super romantic – the fact he loves her enough not to let go, not the other part.

I wish I had someone like that.

The thought lingers, not unlike previous times. It's becoming more frequent lately. Mom and Dad leave me be, I mean after all I'm immortal and have the rest of eternity ahead of me to find someone.

But a girl has needs... And it's getting bad enough that I'm starting to have dreams. Sexy, sexy dreams of a dark blond god with eyes of molten gold. I lick my lips at the reminder, and suddenly, I'm feeling like it's time for a nap.

Maybe I'll see him again. There's no harm in dreaming, right?

Love my books?

Want to get your hands on them first, before anyone else?

Sign up for my[1] ARC team now

And you'll get to read everything first....

Including my next short story collection, *Tales of the Moonlight Rogues*, following your favorite four Rogues on individual adventures with their mates ☺

Email me at info.author@alexawhitewolf.com

And sign up now!

Moonlight Rogues Merch!

Did you love the *Moonlight Rogues* series?

Grab a mug – or sweater memorabilia – to remember themby!

 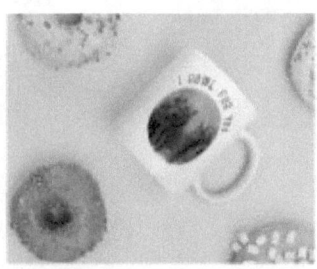

WhitewolfByAlexa[1] caters to fans of Alexa's work. Not only will you find cool gifts for book lovers, but you can also find this awesome magic mug featuring the four hunks from Rockland Creek!

---

1. https://www.etsy.com/ca/shop/WhitewolfByAlexa

Get a 10% off discount with coupon code

ROGUES2020

Shop now!

Sign up for my readers' group **at www.alexawhitewolf.com/contact** and receive a copy of *Unconditional Love* for **FREE**, as well as first dibs on cover reveals, discounts, giveaways, prizes **and more!**

Did you love *Last to Love*? Then you should read *Blood Ties Love Binds* by Alexa Whitewolf!

Cassandra DiCavalier thinks she has her life sorted out, when Damon Voight storms back in. Sexy and overprotective, yet with a soft side, this ex-military guy is every girl's fantasy. And he's not back in town just for kicks...but to protect her. From what? Only he knows, because those tempting lips sure as hell aren't talking. Enemies on their heels, these two have a second chance at love - but will they take it? And more importantly, will they live long enough to enjoy it?

Read more at https://www.alexawhitewolf.com.

About the Author

Alexa Whitewolf is a dog-loving, caffeine-addicted, all-around traveling enthusiast. Author of three series of fantasy, paranormal and young adult, she spends her nights dreaming up new stories and her days fighting reality. She lives in Ottawa, Canada, with her husband and two mischievous furballs- Zeus and Achilles. Check out her website at www.alexawhitewolf.com !

Read more at https://www.alexawhitewolf.com.

Also by Alexa Whitewolf

Moonlight Rogues
Moonlight Rogues: Origins
First to Fall
Second to Surrender
Third to Tumble

The Avalon Chronicles
Avalon Dreams
Avalon Wishes
Avalon Nightmares
The Avalon Chronicles - Complete Series

The Sage's Legacy
The Dragon Medallion
The Dragon Manuscript
Relics of the Underworld
The Sage's Legacy - Complete Series

Standalone Novels
Unconditional Love
Blood Ties, Love Binds
Blazing in a Storm of Ashes (Coming Soon)

Watch for more at
www.alexawhitewolf.com.

www.ingramcontent.com/pod-product-compliance
Lightning Source LLC
Chambersburg PA
CBHW021439240626
47153CB00001B/210

* 9 7 8 1 9 8 9 3 8 4 0 6 0 *